WAKENED

The Silvervane Chronicles
Book I

Rachel Berlynn

WAKENED

Library of Congress Cataloging-in-Publication Dara
Berlynn, Rachel
Wakened /Rachel Berlynn-2nd ed.
p. cm.

I want to dedicate this book to everyone who has contributed to this storyline throughout the years. A special thanks to my sister Noriah, who stayed up late into the night brainstorming with me about this fictional world in the beginning. To my mom, for championing me throughout this eight-year process and reading several revisions along the way. To my friend A.C., for reading, editing, and giving me valuable feedback on this book. I couldn't have done it without all of you! And finally, to my dog Alister, who stayed by my side as every word was written.

CHAPTER ONE

Ryder Payne stood in the pouring rain with his black umbrella still folded and clenched in his left hand, as a steady stream of water trickled from its tip down the side of his leg. His messy brown hair was dripping across his forehead and high cheekbones. His chocolate brown eyes were narrowed in unnerving concentration. His father's memorial service had ended forty-five minutes ago, and he had been the only one there to witness it. The angry gray clouds overhead were no match for his mood, nor did the frigid gusts of wind chill him. Water was splashing from the headstones of nearby graves, as the grounds men struggled to fill in the newest burial plot before the wind tore the portable canvas covering away, exposing everything to the elements.

Ryder didn't care about the rain. He didn't really care about anything at the moment. He couldn't take his eyes from the spot where he'd seen his father's casket disappear into the earth. He felt dead inside, like his heart had stopped beating. His feet were numb from standing outside in the cold mountain air so long. His right hand was shoved deep into the pocket of his long black trench coat; clasping the letter his father had given him in his dying moments.

He hadn't read it yet. He refused to accept his father's death until he'd seen the last shovel full of dirt tossed onto the grave, concealing the casket forever. He watched in reverential silence as the grounds men sealed the gravesite with patchy clumps of grass and sod. He remained rooted to the semi-frozen earth beneath him, as the canvas was taken down. The burial crew threw their shovels and tools into the back of an old rusty pickup truck and climbed in, giving him a solemn nod before driving off.

Now he was alone—in every sense of the word.

Ryder walked slowly back to his car. He paused with his fingers on the handle of his silver Camaro, remembering how excited his father had been to give it to him for his eighteenth birthday.

That had been only two weeks ago.

He drove home in vacant, emotionless, silence. Nothing would ever be right again. His family was gone. Every person he loved on earth had been taken from him, and his father's death had been far worse than all the rest. His father had been his anchor. His stability. His compass. Without him, Ryder didn't know who he would become.

He pulled up in front of Payne Mansion, the castle-like home that had belonged to his family for centuries and now belonged to him. He put his car in park and slid out of the shiny Camaro, entering the mansion through a side entrance, the quickest way to his father's study on the second floor. After climbing two very steep, winding staircases, Ryder found himself standing in the middle of the room, pulling the letter from the damp pocket of his coat. He was still dripping from head-to-toe, but he didn't even notice. He carefully opened the melted, wax seal bearing his father's initials and extracted the letter from its envelope, unfolding it slowly. He forced himself to take his time, knowing that these were the last words he would ever read from his father.

Dear Ryder,

If you are reading this letter it means something terrible has happened to me. I cannot tell you how sorry I am to have left you with the secrets the journal contains. Now you are in great danger. I had hoped to spare you from the pain and suffering that undoubtedly lie ahead and I am grieved that you must face Edryd's Order alone. I hope that someday you will understand why I couldn't join them. I know how angry you must be but you cannot join them, Ryder. Finish what I started. Find the Prince. Find freedom at any cost. I will be watching over you—even from beyond the grave.

Love Always,

Your Father

Ryder crumpled the damp piece of paper in his hand and threw it angrily across the room. He didn't care about the worthless, old manuscript his father had left him. He was dead now…along with everyone else Ryder had ever loved.

And it was all because of an old journal.

He glared at the brown, tattered cover with disdain. His great-grandfather had copied legends from a forbidden, ancient manuscript that had been passed down in his family from father-to-son for centuries. His father had now passed it on to him and expected him to continue the quest for the Lost Prince, but he wanted nothing to do with it. Everyone who had ever laid eyes on the journal wound up dead…and that was no exaggeration.

He stormed over to his father's mahogany desk and brushed the old manuscript off angrily, scattering loose pages all over the floor. He stomped out of the library, slamming the heavy door behind him. Barreling through one dark passageway after another, he found his way out to the Mansion's center tower balcony. From this high up, he could see the crumbling, concrete bridge that crossed over a wide stream, connecting the Payne Estate state to Silvervane forest. His nearest neighbor was more than five miles away.

Ryder sighed heavily. He needed to clear his head. He had inherited the Mansion and the entire estate, of course, so he didn't have to worry about where to live now that he was on his own. Having turned eighteen two weeks ago, there were no concerns regarding legal guardianship, but he would need to speak with his father's attorney right away to get everything settled. In addition to the wealth wrapped up in the Payne Estate, his father had more money invested than a person could spend in three lifetimes, but he would gladly give it all away just to be free of the place and the memories that haunted it.

The only thing keeping him from leaving the haunted Mansion and the small town of Silvervane this very moment was the fact that he hadn't graduated from high school yet. He knew it didn't actually matter since he didn't have to get a job to support himself, but his father had instilled in him a strong value for education and the importance of developing a good mind. And besides, the secondary school he attended was the best in the northern hemisphere. He'd gotten a little behind in his studies over the years because of all the traveling he'd done with his father, but he didn't let it bother him. He was so close to finishing now that quitting would be unthinkable.

All those worthless expeditions, Ryder thought vehemently, remembering the trips he'd taken with his father. Like chasing an imaginary pot of gold at the end of a fictitious, magical rainbow. His father had been unbelievably stubborn and naïve. He'd spent his entire life chasing fairy tales about a lost kingdom and an immortal prince who was meant to restore true freedom and justice to the world. It was all so absurd. The world was a screwed up place—that's just the way it was. No magical prince could solve its problems and trying to find him only led to an early grave.

Ryder was so angry he could hardly think straight. Why couldn't his father have taken up a hobby or pursued a gentlemen's profession like other men of his societal rank? Why had searching for a mythical prince been more important than protecting his family's honor and blending in with the local people of Silvervane? And if he'd known Edryd's Order was trying to hunt them all down, why hadn't he insisted on moving away from this place before the entire family was murdered?

He turned to stare at the cold, limestone face of the castle-like mansion he called home. His European ancestors had built it in the 1600s, which was obvious from the French Renaissance style architecture, the asymmetrical and elaborate towers, spires, steeply slanted roofs, and concrete statues fashioned after mythical creatures. The Paynes had occupied it for more than two hundred years and the bones of their deceased members were buried in the crypt below it. Ryder understood why people thought it was haunted and he didn't blame them for believing it—especially with all of the mysterious deaths in the last five years.

The rest of the Payne Estate was so vast that four towns the size of Silvervane could fit inside of its 25,000 acres, with room to spare. The Mansion was nestled in the center of a large clearing, where streams, well-maintained gardens, orchards, and grassy fields dotted the landscape in every direction. Beyond the clearing, it was strategically hidden, surrounded by a massive concrete wall within the outlying boundaries of the vast Silvervane Forest. Completely cut off from the outside world, the mansion was almost entirely devoid of the modern conveniences of the 20th century. It was so large that hundreds of farmers, tenants, and housekeeping staff lived within its borders. The men typically took care of the land and stables, while their wives and daughters rarely went to high school, preferring to secure jobs as maids, housekeepers, or cooks. It was good job security and it was all they had ever known.

Life at the Payne Estate had never evolved farther than the conventions of Victorian Era England. No one seemed to notice or care how outdated and impractical the social system and its traditions were. The older staff and its tenants rarely left the Estate and had no idea what it was like to live outside of its walls. Very few of the children were educated or accomplished enough to be admitted to the elite preparatory school in town, so most of them received less than an eighth-grade education before beginning employment at the Mansion. With 25,000 acres of land and the estate's merchant economy to cultivate, along with the vast responsibilities of the mansion's upkeep, they had enough work to keep them slaving away from dawn till dusk.

Ryder, on the other hand, had never been content isolated within its walls. More than ever he wanted to be free from its restrictive, outdated customs and the acres of lonely, rugged landscape that stretched out in every direction as far as the eye could see. He gritted his teeth. A solitary tear trickled down his cheek, unbidden. Despite his resolve to be tough, he couldn't completely conceal his grief. He hastily wiped the tear away. He didn't have time to mourn.

Edryd's Order would be coming for him now.

Ryder had known about The Order for as long as he could remember. His father had told him all the legends about his murderous ancestors—an ancient order of corrupt druid priests with dark powers who still practiced in secret, meeting in underground tunnels and hollows. They often hid their sordid agendas and pagan practices behind the guise of an exclusive group or organization, concealing their clandestine meetings and rituals from the public eye. For centuries, they had been quietly plotting to overtake the major political systems of the world and overthrow democracy to establish a One World Order with a centralized, global Monarchy. They had already succeeded in infiltrating several prominent governmental and political structures and their ultimate goal, of course, was to bring their beloved founder, Edryd, back from a dark, enchanted sleep to make him the supreme ruler of this new world order.

The whole concept was absurd, of course. Strong, democratic governments would never allow such an uprising to take place, not to mention the fact that these primitive druids would have to get past each country's vast army and all of their allies before such a takeover would ever be possible. No one would give up their freedoms to a renegade group of sociopathic sorcerers—no matter how powerful they might be.

Still, Ryder was forced to acknowledge that there was some truth to the legends. Anyone who deserted The Order, for example, or acted to help its enemies, was said to be under a curse—subjecting their entire bloodline to brutal and savage deaths. Now that every person in his family was dead, there was no denying that the curse was real. His grandfather had been the first to renounce Edryd's Order and the first to refuse to take his rightful place among them. One by one, the rest of his family had been eliminated. Defecting was considered the worst form of betrayal among Edryd's loyal followers and nothing would stop the curse but re-joining their ranks.

The whole situation felt hopeless. It wasn't like Ryder could just storm into the police station and explain that he was descended from an ancient line of sociopathic druids who had power to kill people without leaving a trace. The people of Silvervane would think he was crazy if he attempted to explain any of it, he was sure of that. They were already blaming him for his own father's murder, declaring that his unusual upbringing had rendered him deeply disturbed and mentally unstable.

He stood on the balcony looking out over the gloomy landscape for what seemed like hours. When the light finally began to fade from the troubled sky, he had resigned to finish out the school year and leave Silvervane forever. He went back into the mansion and wearily changed out of his soaked clothes, draping them haphazardly across a winged-back armchair to dry in front of the fireplace in his bedroom.

There were fifty fireplaces in the Mansion, providing its only source of heat and warmth. They were lit day and night from early October through the end of May. Installing a modern heating system in a stone castle was apparently not a viable option, and Ryder had long since grown accustomed to its outdated quirks. He crawled into bed feeling nothing but emptiness as he drifted off to sleep, falling into a black hole of oblivion.

The next morning, Ryder awoke to the sound of someone knocking on his bedroom door.

"Mr. Payne," the old butler called from the other side of his bedroom door. "The police Chief is here to see you. He's waiting for you downstairs in one of the sitting rooms."

Ryder rubbed his eyes tiredly and forced himself to get out of his king-sized, four-post bed, dragging his feet as he made his way to the bathroom to brush his teeth. He tried to run his fingers through the tangled mass of brown hair that had clumped together from being wet for so many hours the day before, but it didn't help much. He was in desperate need of a shower, but he didn't want to keep the police Chief waiting.

No doubt the Chief had more questions about his father's murder. There was no end to them. It had been the same exact way with everyone else in his family. Now, he alone would be harassed for details and answers he didn't have.

He took a deep breath, and went downstairs to meet the Chief.

When he entered the sitting room, Chief Blair was studying a family portrait on the large, marble fireplace mantel on the east side of the room. He turned when he heard Ryder come in.

Chief Blair actually looked very similar to his father in some ways. Dark hair, dark eyes, confident expression. But this man's confidence was more like arrogance, and his demeanor was cold and abrupt. He didn't show an ounce of real sympathy or respect for Ryder or the death of his family members.

"I have a few questions," the Chief began, furrowing his greying, bushy eyebrows.

"Of course you do," muttered Ryder, allowing a lazy yawn to escape. "But couldn't they have waited until later?"

"You have school," the Chief stated, callously. "I wouldn't want to be responsible for making you late."

Ryder rolled his eyes. "I hardly think I'll be expected to attend classes today," he said, looking bored. "I buried my father yesterday. I doubt the Principal would hold an absence against me." He had every intention of going to school today, but Chief Blair didn't need to know that.

The Chief ignored his reply. "Tell me again exactly where you were when your father was stabbed," he said, taking out a familiar pad of paper and a pen. There were already several pages of statements about the incident in the notebook he held, and Ryder was annoyed that this man seemed bent on wasting his time.

"I've already told you everything I know," Ryder said, clenching his jaw.

"I have to be thorough, Mr. Payne," The chief said patronizingly. "Please don't allow your emotions to interfere with the integrity of this investigation."

Ryder rolled his eyes. "I was asleep in my bed," he said each word slowly, emphasizing the last word.

"That's right," the Chief muttered condescendingly. "And how exactly did you hear your father gasping for breath all the way from the third floor?"

Ryder was seized with the sudden urge to hit the Chief square in the jaw. Or at the very least, leave him with a black eye. This man had all the tact and sensitivity of a ton of bricks, and he needed to be taught a lesson.

"As I've already said at least a half-dozen times, the butler heard him moaning and sent one of the maids upstairs to wake me," Ryder said through clenched teeth.

"Right," the Chief nodded. "Then what did you do?"

"I ran downstairs as fast as I could."

"And when you got there, he was lying on the floor with a knife sticking out of his chest?"

Ryder nodded mechanically.

"The knife was sticking out of his heart?" The Chief specified, rather than asked, as he scribbled more notes.

"Yes."

"And you didn't see anyone lurking around? You didn't bother to search the grounds to see if you could find his attacker?"

Ryder took a deep breath, trying to calm himself. He could feel the blood in his veins beginning to boil. If he lost his temper it wouldn't be good for him or the Police Chief.

"No, I didn't. I was a little preoccupied with the blood spurting out of my father's chest and the fact that the floorboards were soaked in it," he retorted with a glare.

"You said your father died only minutes later. Why didn't you look for the killer then?" The Chief probed, with infuriating coolness.

"I don't know, maybe it was because my father's incident was the fifth murder I've witnessed in my own family in the last five years. Perhaps I was in shock, like any normal human being in that situation would be," Ryder spat. "Or maybe I did it myself. Is that what you're waiting to hear? Because I don't have time for this."

Chief Blair raised a critical eyebrow, "Is that an official statement?" He stared accusingly into Ryder's eyes, trying to provoke a confession.

"Think whatever you want," Ryder said, keeping his tone even and civil. "I'm done answering your questions. If you need anything else, you can go through my attorney. Now if you'll excuse me, I have to get to classes."

He spun on his heal and strode from the room, leaving the Police Chief to find his own way out.

Ryder took his time getting to school. He wasn't worried about the consequences of being late—surely everyone had heard about his father's death by now. He would be excused from classes for at least a week. No one would expect him to show up today, and no one would care if he didn't. He knew the drill...he'd been through it four times already in the past five years.

He scowled as the centuries old campus came into view. How he longed for the day when he would never have to return to it! Four years in the prestigious academy was about all he could take, with its strict rules and superior, elitist faculty. Silvervane Preparatory Academy was the most elite secondary school and post-graduate program in the Northern Hemisphere. Most of the student body was composed of International student boarders, but there were a small percentage of students who lived locally and commuted to the school each day. All students were forced to adhere to a very strict code of conduct, which included the wearing of school uniforms and participation in all campus-wide activities and school-sponsored events.

The school was split into two large, scenic campuses—one for secondary students and one for students attending post-graduate school. The secondary school provided gender specific dormitories for their student borders, while post-graduate boarders were housed in co-ed dormitories, with the exception of the housing options that existed for the many fraternities and sororities represented on campus. Both campuses were located on the outskirts of Silvervane, a small historical town with a mysterious and sordid history. Still, the rich legacy and academic excellence of the school was so well known around the world that its reputation remained unchallenged, in spite of its remote location.

The town of Silvervane was nearly off the grid to the rest of the continent and, making it an ideal location for students seeking a focused learning environment. Student life on campus was enriched by the many activities, clubs, and opportunities provided by the school and there was very little for students to do outside of these campus-initiated activities, which kept them out of trouble and under constant supervision.

Ryder silently braced himself to face the same predictable, teenage clichés of self-centeredness and shallow concern he had encountered every day for the past four years. No one would care enough to inconvenience him with condolences or concerns for his wellbeing. This was just fine with him, because Ryder despised pity with all of his being. His secret desire was to make it through the day without having to talk to anyone at all.

Chapter Two

Aylie Bryant slid into her desk just as Mrs. Fletcher began taking attendance. She'd been sick with the flu and had missed almost an entire week of classes. The timing of her absence couldn't have been worse, with first semester finals looming so close on the horizon. She leaned over to nudge her best friend with her elbow; her long, blonde hair partially covered her face as she spoke.

"What did I miss?" She asked.

"A lot," Lacey whispered dramatically, the excitement of juicy gossip glinting in her light green eyes. Their sparkle was a stark contrast to her dark, ebony skin. "Did you hear about Ryder's father?" She pushed her long, straightened black hair behind her right ear.

Aylie shook her head. "No. What about him?"

As if on cue, Ryder Payne strode into the classroom, passing right in front of Mrs. Fletcher without so much as a glance. He kept his eyes forward and avoided eye contact with everyone as he took his seat.

Lacey leaned in closer. "His father died last weekend."

"His dad, too?" Aylie glanced over at Ryder. "I don't understand why everyone in his family keeps dying."

Lacey huffed. "I don't feel that bad for him, he probably just became the richest person on the planet."

Aylie frowned, her ocean-blue eyes filled with sympathy. "But he's all alone now, Lacey, money can't fix that."

"Well, you know what they're saying...."

Aylie raised a questioning brow.

"The police think Ryder might have something to do with it...with all of the murders."

"That's ridiculous," Aylie hissed. "He's only a teenager."

"Well, he's the only one still alive so that's got to mean something. Think about it—first his mom, then his brothers, followed by his grandfather, and now his dad? They were all murdered in that Mansion, but somehow he survived?" She theorized dramatically. "Besides, everyone knows he's mental so it makes perfect sense, in a twisted, sadistic sort of way." Lacey shrugged and turned her attention to the front of the classroom.

Aylie blocked out the droning sound of Mrs. Fletcher's gravely, voice and studied Ryder's expression. He looked solemn, but not exactly sad. He held his head high, as if to convey a sense of self-confidence. His demeanor definitely didn't scream serial killer.

Most girls considered him a forbidden sort of eye-candy, the epitome of the 'bad boy' stereotype. His messy, brown hair fell across his left eyebrow, partially concealing his high, perfectly sculpted check-bone. His brown eyes were deep and guarded. He was also one of less than eighty students who commuted to the school each day, rather than attending as a boarder. He hardly talked to any of his classmates and rarely participated in school activities, which made him even more mysterious.

Aylie tried to imagine what he must be feeling. She had an

uncanny ability to sense the emotions of people around her, sometimes even before they were aware of what they were feeling themselves. She liked to understand people—to figure out what made them act the way they did. This secret talent usually gave her a distinct advantage in that department.

She studied his rigid profile and the tired, weary look on his face. He wore a white, uniform oxford shirt unbuttoned at the top, which would normally be a demerit, but the rules didn't seem to apply to the Paynes. They were considered royal blood and the wealthiest family on the continent. They didn't socialize much with the outside world, and their interactions at the academy were very limited, in spite of its superior social status.

I don't believe you had anything to do with your dad's murder, she thought decidedly.

Suddenly Ryder's head jerked in her direction.

Aylie's eyes widened and she blushed, lowering her gaze to the wooden surface of her desk. She could feel him looking at the side of her face and found herself silently wishing to disappear. Not that staring at Ryder Payne was something out of the ordinary. All of the girls ogled him from time to time—some were more obvious about it than others. He was, without question, the most attractive boy in Silvervane, but Aylie had never really paid much attention to him because he wasn't in her circle of friends. He was an unsolved mystery. A loner, dark and brooding. Definitely off-limits to any girl with a sense of self-preservation.

Besides, he wasn't her type at all. She hadn't dated very many guys, but the ones she had gone out with were charming and friendly; well-mannered boys her parents would approve of. She couldn't help feeling mortified that Ryder had caught her staring, the one and only time she'd ever glanced in his direction. When he finally looked away, she let out a deep breath—she hadn't even realized she'd been holding it. For the rest of class, she forced herself to focus on what Mrs. Fletcher was doing at the front of the room and went back to the version of reality where Ryder Payne didn't exist.

At lunch, however, he was the topic of conversation at every table. Aylie wondered how he'd feel about it when he came into the dining hall, but he never showed. She felt secretly relieved, for his sake, and silently listened to the wild theories spreading all over campus.

"How did his dad die, again?" Asked Marcus, a tall, blond boy who happened to be Aylie's ex-boyfriend and captain of the hockey team. He was one of the players who made up her close circle of friends.

Kyle, a rather self-absorbed hockey player with spiked brown hair and hazel eyes snorted mockingly. "Probably the same way as his grandfather." He drew a circle around his neck with his index finger tracing an imaginary noose, and pretended to choke as if he were hanging. He nudged his buddy, Chance, in the ribs.

"The police are calling it another murder," Lacey chimed in. "I think there's definitely something wrong with that place. Have you ever noticed that every person that's ever lived in that Mansion ends up dead?"

"Technically, it's a castle," said Rene, rolling her dark eyes. "Obviously you think Ryder did it." She was a petite, dark-haired girl from the Philippines and everyone called her Ren. She lived in the dorms at Silvervane Prep and her older brother Derek lived on the post-graduate campus.

Lacey frowned. "I'm not the only one who thinks so," she retorted. "My mom is the principal, after all. She's been talking to the police chief and the detectives on the case for years. And anyways—It's not like they're dying of old age, Ren—they're dying of unnatural causes. Their bodies are ripped apart, or mangled, or...hanging from things." Lacey shuddered and went silent, staring blankly at her salad.

Aylie couldn't help feeling sorry for Ryder in the face of all the accusations. "Do you think anyone is checking in on him?"

"What for?" Marcus laughed. "He's eighteen. He's practically a man now, I'm sure he can take care of himself."

"I wonder if they have servants or something up in that castle of theirs," Kyle mused.

"Of course they do," Lacey said, condescendingly. "Have you

ever seen pictures of it? It's enormous."

"He's lucky he doesn't have to live in the dormitories," Chance said wistfully. His real name was Chancellor and he was from Wales. He was easy going and by far the friendliest guy on the hockey team—everyone loved Chance.

"It's not that bad," Ren murmured. "There's always something fun to do on campus."

"Don't you ever miss your family, though?" asked Madison, as she took another bite of her salad. She was a tall and confident volleyball player with highlighted light brown hair and she was Kyle's girlfriend.

"Of course," Ren replied, "But at least I get to see them during the summer months—it's better than what Ryder has to deal with."

The bell rang just then, signaling the end of break. Everyone hurried to dispose of their lunch trays and get to class before the tardy bell, to avoid a demerit. Too many of those made for a very unpleasant weekend at Silvervane Prep.

The rest of the day seemed to drag and Aylie had listened to all the gossip she could take. She loved her friends, but sometimes their chatter made her head want to explode. She felt relieved when it was finally over and she could walk home from school in silence. She enjoyed the natural quiet of the outdoors and reveled in the long walk immensely. She felt extremely lucky to be one of the few who had the privilege of attending such a prestigious school while being able to live at home with her family.

It was early November, and the temperatures were quickly dropping by mid-day. Silvervane would soon be overtaken by frigid winds and heavy snowfalls. The trees would be covered in icicles and the walk to school would be treacherous. Her father would have to drive her and her little brother Sam to school everyday, just like he did every year around that time. Sometimes she opted to stay with friends on campus, rather than taking the mountain roads home in extreme inclement weather.

Aylie didn't mind the winter. She looked forward to the sound of crackling fireplaces and the woody scent of burning cedar at the Bryant Ranch. She didn't even mind stacking and carrying armloads of firewood. The only thing she really detested was cleaning out the ashes, and that was her little brother Sam's job, anyway.

She reached the edge of town and took the unpaved road that led to her family's ranch. She paused to look out over the rugged mountains that stretched along the horizon line in every direction. To the right of the ranch, lay the opening of the Silvervane Forest. The Payne Estate was tucked away about five miles into the forest. She couldn't help thinking of Ryder now as she gazed down the deserted mountain road. Far off in the distance, high above the treetops, she could see wisps of billowing smoke rising from the castle chimneys. What would it be like to live alone at such a young age? To lose everyone you loved and cared about... to be stuck in a haunted, gloomy Mansion all by yourself?

Aylie shuddered. Just the thought of it filled her with a sense of isolation. She wished there was something she could do. She didn't know Ryder at all, so it's not like she could just check up on him to make sure he was okay, but she felt that someone should. Maybe she could talk her dad into driving out there one day next week....

Suddenly she heard something behind her, like the sound of a thick tree branch snapping in two. She spun on here heel. There was nothing there but tall prairie grass and a few trees. Her heart started to beat erratically, filling her with a sense of alarm. She strained her eyes but couldn't see anything in the distance.

But she was certain she could feel something...or someone. The hair on the back of her neck stood up. Out of the corner of her eye, she saw a dark shape moving through the tall grass. She took a few calculated steps forward, trying to identify it. She stood completely still and held her breath, but the animal must have sensed her presence. It turned its head in her direction and quickly darted into the forest before she got a chance to see what it was.

Disappointed, Aylie slowly turned back toward the Ranch. There were bears and mountain lions in the area, but they usually didn't stray this far from the forest in broad daylight. She couldn't imagine what else could be out there, but the thought of not knowing made her quicken her pace. A breeze was beginning to blow, and the trees along the roadside were swaying forcefully. Maybe the sound she'd heard had merely been the wind picking up speed.

She was considering the probability of this explanation when she heard the unmistakable sound of footsteps crunching on the gravel behind her. She turned again in surprise—no one ever ventured this far outside of town, except for an occasional relative or close family friend, and they never visited on foot. Who else would have a reason to come this way?

Aylie did a double take.

Ryder Payne was walking toward her.

She stared at him, bewildered. She had never talked to him before and she wasn't sure what to say. How do you greet someone who has just lost his entire family? What is the protocol for consoling a teenage boy who suddenly wakes up and finds himself an orphan? She stood frozen, debating what to do.

Ryder slowed to a stop a few feet away from her and cocked his head to one side, narrowing his chocolate-brown eyes. "Are you lost?" He asked.

She opened her mouth to reply, but no words came out. His voice was strong and resonate, with the slightest hint of a European accent. She was surprised that he sounded like a foreigner even though he'd lived in the area for most of his life.

Ryder waited for her reply expectantly. "Are you afraid of me?" He asked after an awkward pause.

Aylie blushed, shaking her head. "No, of course not. My house is just down the road about a mile or so. I was walking home from school...."

Ryder nodded.

"What are you doing out here?" She asked, finding her voice and a little more nerve. She was anxious to turn the conversation away from her awkward behavior.

"My house is this way," he said, with a look that implied it should be obvious. "How else would I get home?"

"You walk all the way home from school?"

Ryder looked slightly amused. "Well, so do you...."

"Yes, but I just live over there," she said pointing toward the Ranch. "The Mansion...I mean, your house, isn't it miles from here?"

Ryder shrugged, "Something like that."

"Why do you walk so far? Don't you have a car?"

He nodded, his face expressionless. "I have three cars, but sometimes I like to walk—a preference it appears we both share."

Aylie didn't know what to say. Walking almost ten miles to school and back seemed a little crazy. She was shocked and impressed all at the same time.

"It must take you hours," she murmured, "Doesn't it get too dark to see?"

Ryder almost smirked. "I think I'm old enough to handle the dark. It's pretty hard to get lost walking down a road that only has one destination."

"Oh...I guess that's true." Aylie fell silent. She was starting to feel like conversation with him was pointless. Every comment she made was greeted with a short, sarcastic reply. Maybe there was a reason no one ever talked to him. She stared at her feet, unsure of how to end the conversation without making things more uncomfortable than they already were.

Ryder's voice interrupted her thoughts. "I apologize if my answers seem a bit abrupt. I'm not used to people caring what I do or where I go."

Aylie glanced up at him through her lashes. He was wearing a long, dark coat over his oxford shirt. His uniform pants looked brand new, though she doubted he'd bought them himself. No one had ever seen him in town and there were a limited number of places to shop. Perhaps he had a servant of some kind who tailored his clothes for him?

She considered his apology. "I wasn't implying that you should be careful of the dark, itself," Aylie replied defensively, "but everyone knows there are bears and mountain lions around here—especially so near the forest."

He smiled, a little condescendingly. "I appreciate the concern, but I know how to handle them if they cross my path."

Aylie felt a little annoyed. He seemed determined to ignore whatever she said so there was no use saying anything more.

"You, on the other hand, probably shouldn't be wandering around out here by yourself." Ryder looked at her appraisingly. "I highly doubt you know much about how to defend yourself against predatory animals."

The amused look on his face was insulting.

"You're assuming I don't know how to handle myself because I'm a girl?" She could feel the heat in her cheeks.

"Am I wrong?"

"For your information, I have a dad and two brothers who love to hunt and I go with them sometimes. I know how to shoot a gun and I'm a decent shot with a crossbow."

Ryder arched an eyebrow. He raised his hands, palms out. "I stand corrected."

Aylie shook her head in frustration. No wonder you don't have any friends, she thought. You're incapable of having a pleasant conversation.

Ryder's expression suddenly sobered. "I think you should be getting home," he said, gazing off into the distance. His eyes were fixed on something, but Aylie couldn't tell what it was.

"I think you're right," she said, feeling ready to be out of his sight. "I was just trying to be a friend—it seemed like you could've used one today."

"I don't need any friends," he replied, shrugging. "I've done just fine without them for eighteen years."

Aylie bit her lower lip, choosing her words carefully. "But you don't have a family anymore, Ryder. You can't live isolated and hidden away in that place."

"Oh I see," Ryder snapped. "And you think you're the person who can magically make everything better?"

The sudden harshness in his words both shocked and stung her. She wanted to lash out at him, but his face was filled with so much pain and repressed anger that she couldn't. He looked injured. Exposed. Vulnerable. He was like a wounded little boy inside, and it melted her defensiveness.

The silence in the air around them was deafening. She imagined she could hear his heartbeat thundering against his rib cage. He was heaving breaths like he had just run a marathon. His dark eyes were flashing. He was trying to maintain control of his emotions.

"I'm sorry," she said. "I didn't mean to make things worse."

He swallowed hard, but didn't speak. He was staring at the ground like he wanted to burn a hole through it.

"You may not want a friend right now, Ryder, but I think you need one." She said matter-of-factly.

He refused to look at her.

"It doesn't have to be me," she continued cautiously, "but you need someone."

Ryder nodded dismissively. He was like a wild, hurting animal. He would have to realize his need for a friend on his own terms. Aylie recognized this behavior from having watched her father release injured animals back into the wild, after being caught in a fox or bear trap by accident. They had to be tricked into feeling like they were in control, or they would fight the very person trying to free them.

Suddenly he broke the silence. "What makes you so sure I didn't do it?"

Aylie blinked, a little confused. "What?"

"I know what they're saying—I've already heard the rumors. They think I'm the murderer."

Aylie shook her head in disgust. "I don't believe that for a second. There's nothing malicious about you."

Ryder almost chuckled in response.

The strange look in his eyes raised a silent alarm in the back of Aylie's mind, but she ignored it. "You couldn't have done something like that to the people in your own family. I know what they think, but they're wrong."

"You can't possibly know that."

"I can sense things about people. Call it a gift." Aylie smiled confidently.

Ryder cracked an unwilling smile in return, shaking his head. "You're the most interesting girl I've ever talked to," he mused.

"I'm probably the only girl you've ever really talked to."

Ryder was thoughtful. "Perhaps, but I've observed enough to know that you're a little out of the ordinary."

"I'll take that as a compliment." She looked out over the vast, grassy field separating her from her family's ranch. "I should get going." She gave him an awkward, half-smile. "My mom will start to wonder what happened to me; she hates it when I walk home alone."

"That's understandable," he replied. "Not that I'm saying you can't handle yourself," he qualified with a smirk.

Aylie turned to cut through the grass and was surprised to hear his voice trail after her, "See you later, Aylie."

She looked over her shoulder to reply, but he was already gone. She glanced down the gravel road, but he was nowhere to be found. Puzzled, she made her way home, wondering how he could've disappeared so quickly.

Chapter Three

When Ryder reached the mansion, it was nearly five O'clock and the sun was just beginning to set. The sky was bursting into effervescent colors of orange, yellow, red, and pink. He paused to appreciate the display, despite his gloomy mood. In all honesty, his feet had begun to ache from the long walk in less-than-ideal shoes, but his soul felt more at peace and he wasn't sorry he'd done it. The exercise helped him burn off steam and it had given him time to formulate a plan.

In six months he would graduate from Silvervane Preparatory Academy. After that, he planned to travel Europe and spend some time with the only relatives he had left. His estranged uncle Alexander and his cousins, Roman and Blake. They lived somewhere in Europe—though he didn't know exactly where. He'd spent his summers with them as a boy and had even grown close to them at one point. He hadn't seen them in years, but he was sure they would welcome him back, especially since the rest of his family was gone now. He'd always resented the way his father had suddenly cut off all contact with them just after his fourteenth birthday. It was about time he patched things up.

There was nothing left for him in Silvervane anymore anyway. No friends to tempt him to stay. He didn't have any sentiments about the Estate or what happened to it…the Mansion could burn to the ground, for all he cared. The town might even thank him for it. It was bad for the economy to have a haunted castle within its borders.

As he neared the large, iron gate surrounding the Mansion, a picture of Aylie Bryant flashed through his mind. She had been an unexpected part of his day. There had been something unsettling about seeing her alone on that forsaken, mountain road—completely unaware and defenseless against the evil that lurked in Silvervane Forest. He wasn't sure why, but it made him feel an inexplicable sense of responsibility to make sure she got home safely.

He hadn't told her that, of course. Judging from the way she'd reacted when he'd pointed out her lack of skill in self-defense, he felt like his decision to keep that information to himself had been a good idea. Just thinking about their conversation filled him with a strange emotion he'd never really experienced before. He'd lived such an isolated life up until now, with only his family to socialize with. He didn't have much experience when it came to talking to girls and he had never really felt like he was missing out on anything.

He tried to pinpoint what it was about Aylie that had made such an impression on him. She was beautiful, of course. Her dirty, blonde hair fell perfectly straight, well past her shoulders. The sun had bleached several strands, making it look highlighted that way on purpose. Her eyes were the bluest he'd ever seen before, deep like an ocean and full of feeling. Her body was thin and willowy; she was the type of girl every guy noticed.

But it was more than that.

Perhaps it was the genuine care and concern she'd shown him, in the face of all the ugly rumors and accusations. Maybe it was because she didn't fear him or gossip about him behind his back like everyone else did. For in spite of her obvious annoyance with him in their brief interaction, she hadn't drawn conclusions about his character based on his rude behavior. She chose to believe the best—even though she knew nothing about him and she thought she could sense a goodness in him that rendered him incapable of the evil people were accusing him of.

She was wrong about that, of course, but he wasn't in a hurry to show her what she didn't want to see. He was content with the fact that she was innocent enough to imagine the good in him and hoped deep down that she might be right.

Ryder smiled to himself, as he made his way past the gate and through the courtyard. He wouldn't mind running into Aylie again sometime. He wouldn't go looking for her, but he wouldn't try to scare her off, either. If she was crazy enough to enter his world without knowing what she was getting herself into—that was her choice.

When he reached the carriage house, his mood suddenly turned dark again. He quickly darted through the large, stone-carved structure that extended from the front entrance. It was an old fashioned sort of parking structure that provided a place for guests to draw up their carriages or park their automobiles in order to enter the mansion without being exposed to the harsh elements of snow and rain.

Two years ago his grandfather's body had been found hanging from it's roof, suspended by a rope around his neck. The police had declared it a suicide at first, but later concluded that he couldn't have hung himself from that exact angle and altitude on his own. In the end, it was determined to be foul play—the fourth unsolved Payne family murder in four consecutive years.

Ryder shook his head, trying to dismiss the images from his mind. He usually entered the Mansion from a different entrance to avoid re-living the memory of that horrific incident, but he'd been distracted by thoughts of Aylie and had taken this way out of old habit. He couldn't help shuddering inwardly as he pushed open the heavy front door. He entered and slammed it again forcefully, shutting out the world behind him. The memories of all he had lost followed him wherever he went—there was no escaping them. Even when he managed to fall asleep at night, he often found himself dreaming of his father as if he were still alive, only to discover upon waking that he was really gone. And then it was like reliving his death all over again.

Ryder paused in the dark entry room, or Great Hall, as it was usually called. He looked up past the spiraling staircases and balconies that wrapped around the interior of the Mansion. Hundreds of feet above him, was a domed skylight—the highest point of the mansion. He could see the sunlight, sinking behind the clouds as the evening sky fought to overtake it.

The solemn stillness of the great empty room enveloped him. It was hard to believe that only a week ago his father had been alive and well, pouring over that cursed book in his study night and day. Damn that journal, Ryder seethed inwardly. I should burn it to ashes.

He actually considered it for a few minutes, stalking angrily through the Mansion and up the two, familiar flights of stone stairs to his father's study. The pages were still scattered all over the floor where he'd left them the night before. He bent down to retrieve them and his resolve quickly dissipated. This journal had been his father's most prized possession. As much as Ryder hated it, he couldn't bring himself to destroy the old book. It was all he had left of his father's legacy. There would never be another philosophical debate about it, or spur-of-the-moment expedition to a remote and distant country that dead-ended into an argument.

Ryder had grown up listening to his father read stories from it for as long as he could remember. It contained all of the history known about his ancestors, among whom was a powerful ancient Celtic king named Ruardian. This king was believed to have been Immortal, and the creator of what is known in the modern world as "magic." These legends were first recorded long before Greek or Norse mythology ever existed, and before the Romans had named their gods.

Ryder knew the king's legend like the back of his hand. His

father had actually taught him how to read using these very pages and he had devoured the stories as a four-year-old boy. He flipped through them now almost lovingly as the memories came flooding back. As the legend went, Ruardian had once ruled a kingdom called Zohar, a place unmarred by pain, death, or tragedy. (Ryder and his father had searched the region where it supposedly existed several times but there was no sign of a place like what the legend described.) The great King had two sons—Rhydian and Edryd, who were both immortal just as he was, but possessed only the power of demigods. Born from different mothers, they had each inherited half of their father's abilities, along with a piece of humanity to keep them in check—this was Ruardian's way of ensuring a balance of power.

After ruling for only a few centuries, however, it became apparent to the king that some of the immortals in his kingdom were becoming more and more selfish and destructive. He created a magical dagger with the power to destroy an immortal being, and, as a safeguard, only the true heir to his throne could wield it. He knew this measure alone, however, was not enough to keep his kingdom safe. Secretly, Ruardian enchanted the dagger, cursing anyone who used it unjustly to lose their immortality.

As time went on, Ruardian noticed that his younger son, Edryd, was becoming extremely jealous of his older brother's magical abilities. Having the power to see the future, King Ruardian knew that one day Edryd would seek to overthrow him and murder his brother to take control of the kingdom. When the time drew near, Ruardian summoned his eldest son to his chambers and warned him of his brother's evil plans. He commanded Rhydian to flee for his life in the night.

The very next morning, king Ruardian was found dead in his bedchamber, with the sacred dagger plunged through his heart. Since Rhydian had fled, Edryd became the next king of Zohar. No longer concerned about his brother's claim to the throne, Edryd began to hunt down and annihilate the rest of the immortal, royal bloodline so that no other heir to the throne remained alive to challenge him. He thought this would guarantee his eternal rule and carried out his plan with ruthless fervor. He had no knowledge of the curse his father had placed on the dagger.

Fifty years later, Edryd noticed that he was beginning to age and realized what his father had done. Knowing that his days were now numbered, he invented a new, distorted kind of magic—more commonly known as Dark Magic. He invented evil curses and incantations to use against his enemies and prolong his life. He destroyed the rest of the immortal race and created an army of flawed mortals to do his bidding and carry on his plot to conquer the surrounding nations.

Finally, unable to find a cure for his mortality, Edryd appointed a priest to take over command of his Order until his return. Then he put himself into an enchanted sleep, with instructions for his followers to awaken him when they had discovered a cure. He made them swear an oath of absolute allegiance—binding themselves and their bloodlines to his service forever. He charged them to hunt down Rhydian and kill him, thereby ending any possible threat to his future reign.

Ryder forced himself to stop reading. Most of the legends were nothing but an elaborate hoax, in his opinion. His ancestors had been powerful druids, and as such, they had possessed certain abilities that other human beings did not. But the concept of a kingdom ruled by immortal gods and demigods seemed seriously far-fetched. If such beings existed, someone would have discovered them by now.

He dropped the manuscript back on the desk with malcontent. Suddenly he couldn't stand the thought of being in that room another minute, with nothing but the empty memories and fairytales for comfort. He looked out the castle-like window beside him. There was a full moon rising and not a cloud in the sky. It would be the perfect night to go hunting—something he and his father had always enjoyed doing together on nights like this. It would be his first hunt alone, but he had been well trained, and he didn't fear anything.

He didn't fear anything at all.

Chapter Four

Aylie woke up early Saturday morning and rubbed her eyes. The sun wasn't quite up yet, but she knew it was time to get up and do her barn chores. The horses would need to be fed and put out to pasture so she could muck out their stalls, and the goats of course, would need to be milked. The chickens were Sam's responsibility, so at least she got to dodge that bullet. There was nothing worse to Aylie than the sharp, pungent odor of a chicken coup.

Her gray kitten, Millie, was pawing at the corners of her queen-sized quilt with sharp, little claws. She meowed and stretched and purred, as Aylie slid out from under the warm blankets and stepped onto the cold, wooden floor with her bare feet.

"Burrrrr," she chattered to Millie, scooping the cat into her arms. "Why is it so cold, girl?" Millie meowed, and Aylie set her down by her food bowl to feed her.

After taking care of Millie, Aylie got dressed to face the cold morning air, layering thermals with a sweatshirt, leggings, coat, hat, gloves, and rubber boots. Eventually she'd get too hot cleaning out the horse stalls, but for now she needed all the warmth she could get. She checked the thermometer on her way to the barn and saw that it was a mere eighteen degrees Fahrenheit.

She milked the goats first, filling up several pails, and then set them aside. It was cold enough in the barn that she didn't need to worry about refrigerating them until after she'd finished the rest of her chores. Next, she turned her attention to the horses, who seemed to be enjoying the quiet solitude of their stalls. They weren't the slightest bit interested in seeing her and paid her no attention, until she pulled out handfuls of fresh hay to stuff their wire feeding baskets.

Prince was the first horse to greet her with her handful of hay. He was a feisty, gray Appaloosa, with a stubborn disposition that had been reluctantly tamed over the years. At seven and a half years old, he was a pretty even mixture of sweetness and free spirit, and Aylie adored him. It was a mutual relationship of respect and trust—but he was her mom's horse.

Bailey was a sleek, brown quarter horse, with a shiny chocolate coat and a black silky main and tail. He was their racing horse, and Aylie's dad took him to the track several times a year so that her older brother, Lucas, could race him. He'd won a far share of awards and was one of the best jockey's in the county. He wasn't focused as much on racing now that he was away at college, but he came home sometimes on the weekends just to visit Bailey and take him for a run.

Lilly was a sweet-tempered Palomino, with a beige coat and a white-blond main and tail. She was Sam's horse, for all sakes and purposes. She was nearly ten years old, but had yet to show any signs of old age. She was gentle and trusting, and even an inexperienced child could ride her without fear of harm.

That left only Knight's stall to clean. He belonged to Aylie and would tolerate only her. No one else in the family had ever been able to mount him without being thrown off. He was a large, black draught horse her father had won on a bet the day she was born. In fact, her father had received the unexpected news of her birth while riding the horse home and had determined back then that the horse would be hers when she was old enough to ride him. His coat was a solid, satin black, with the exception of a tiny streak of white on his forehead and thin white bands around his hooves. He was nearly a foot taller than the other horses, and his back was twice as thick. He towered over the others and they left him alone.

It was his stall she cleaned out last. He was the largest horse and seemed to leave the biggest messes. Aylie wiped sweat from her forehead as she put her back into heaving yet another shovel-full of manure into the wheelbarrow. Somewhere in the distance she heard a strange sound, like a high-pitched growl or a shriek. Aylie paused, with her shovel in mid-air. There it was again. This time the horses, too, stood eerily still, with their ears perked up, listening to the mournful cries of the unfortunate animal in the distance.

Aylie couldn't quite place the sound of the animal...maybe a coyote or a wolf? But if one of those were the animal growling in pain, what predator could be large enough to take them down? There were plenty of black bears in the area, but they didn't hunt coyotes or wolves. Perhaps the predator was a desperate mountain lion. It was unlikely, but not impossible.

She listened as the animal gave one last morbid cry and the sound ceased. The deathly stillness that followed made Aylie shudder, and she finished mucking out Knight's stall as quickly as she could. She dumped the wheelbarrow loaded with horse manure onto the burn heap behind the barn, and then carried the pails of milk into the house. She had to pour the contents of the pails into storage containers because there was too much milk to use up in only a day or two. She then put the containers of milk into the pantry refrigerator in the basement and shed the extra layers of clothing that were now beginning to suffocate her, before carrying in a few armloads of firewood.

Mrs. Bryant was already making breakfast in the kitchen. Eggs, bacon, toast, and fresh-squeezed orange juice. Saturday breakfast was the best meal of the week at the Bryant house, and Aylie always looked forward to it after a long morning of barn chores.

She went to the bathroom and scrubbed her hands to get rid of any trace of animal manure or dirt. She glanced at her face in the mirror, pushing her long, silky blond hair out of her face and tucking it behind her ears. Her blue eyes were full of determination—they were her favorite facial feature. She had a long, slender nose and an oval face, with a fair complexion. Her skin wasn't flawless, but pretty decent for someone passing through the treacherous phases of adolescence. She rinsed her hands in the warm water gushing from the faucet and dried them on the plush, ivory towel hanging on the rack by the door.

When she re-entered the kitchen, her mom was scooping two more fried eggs onto a plate to keep them warm in the oven until all of the food was done, and the rest of the family was ready to eat. Her mom looked just like her...same dirty blond hair and sparkling blue eyes. She even had the same smile, except for the laugh lines around her mouth and a few wrinkles near the corners of her eyes. She still looked young and bore her age well, in spite of the hard work it took to raise three kids and keep up such a large ranch.

"Can I help, mom?" Aylie asked, looking around to see what still needed to be done.

"You can set the table," Mrs. Bryant, said, handing her four brown, stoneware plates.

Aylie put the plates in their proper places on the table, and then proceeded to dole out napkins and silverware for each place setting.

"Mom...did you hear about Mr. Payne?" she asked hesitantly.

Mrs. Bryant answered from the kitchen. "Yes, what a tragedy!" She popped her head into the dining room where Aylie was finishing the table. "Mr. Payne still has a son living, right? Do you know him?"

Aylie nodded. "His name is Ryder. He's graduating with me this year."

Mrs. Bryant looked at her daughter thoughtfully. "You must have classes with him, then."

Aylie nodded again, lowering her eyes. She didn't know why she did it, but the question made her feel uncomfortable for some reason.

"Does he have any other family around here?" Mrs. Bryant asked, walking back into the kitchen.

"No," Aylie said quietly. "I think he's all alone now."

"That can't be good for a boy his age...growing up in a place like that."

"That's what I was thinking." Aylie murmured.

Mrs. Bryant came back into the dining room carrying a plate piled high with bacon in one hand and another plate filled with fried eggs in the other. "I wish there was something we could do."

Aylie paused for a moment, studying the concerned look on her mom's face. "Do you think we should...maybe...check on him? Bring him dinner or something, since we're his only neighbors?"

"I suppose we should." Mrs. Bryant said thoughtfully. "We can check on him this evening, if you want." She smiled and disappeared back into the kitchen.

Several moments later, her dad and little brother came in from the barn and washed up for breakfast. She always sat across the table from her little brother, Sam. He had blond hair like Aylie, but brown eyes like her dad. Her older brother Lucas, on the other hand, was the spitting image of her dad—dark brown hair, brown eyes, thin lips and a very dry sense of humor.

After breakfast, Aylie spent most of the morning working on an English paper. She was particularly good at writing and always felt accomplished when she was finished. This one, however, counted as a mid-term exam grade, so she spent a bit more time on it than she normally would have. When she was satisfied, she printed a copy and stuffed it into her book bag so that she wouldn't forget it Monday.

Then she went into the kitchen for a glass of water and found her mom busy making casseroles to take over to the Mansion. Feeling guilty that her mom was doing all of the work, she tried to think of what she could contribute. Her favorite dessert was Dutch Apple Pie, and she thought there was a pretty good chance Ryder would eat it—most people liked apples, so it seemed like a safe bet. She didn't want to bother her mom for a trip to the store, so she decided to bake it from scratch. Surely it couldn't be too hard, right?

She'd never actually baked a pie from scratch before and found the process of peeling and coring the apples extremely boring and monotonous. The homemade crust wasn't quite as time-consuming, but she vowed she'd never do it again, if given the choice. She understood now why most people bought frozen pies that only had to be warmed in the oven.

Around five O'clock, Aylie and her mom started the five-mile drive down the winding, gravel road that lead through the Silvervane forest and into the Payne Estate. It took almost thirty minutes to get there by car because of the sharp turns, steep inclines, and gravel washouts along the way. Aylie could only imagine how long it would take to walk all the way there.

They pulled up in front of the massive, iron gate guarding the entrance to the Estate. Aylie's heart sank a bit…she hadn't thought about a gate. She'd never been to a place like this before. It looked like every version of Dracula's castle she'd ever seen. There was a massive parapet with a steeple in the center, and four shorter, parapets, one on each corner. The walls were made of white limestone and crowned brick. The exterior of the Mansion was adorned with exquisite etchings, gothic architecture, and statues. The tiling on the roof was a deep, royal blue, and the main body of the mansion had at least four stories, each with its own separate balcony. The spire of the central tower had to be at least five stories high. Some of the oldest, largest fur trees in the forest couldn't reach its tip.

Dumbfounded, Aylie looked at her mom nervously. "What should we do about the gate?" she asked.

"Try the call button, sweetie," Mrs. Bryant suggested. "I don't know how young Mr. Payne would feel about trespassers right now if we attempted to climb it." She winked.

"Right." Aylie slid out of the suburban and walked slowly over to the little black box mounted to the large, concrete column on the left side of the gate. She hesitated for a moment, looking up at the ominous, old Mansion, and swallowed hard.

I never imagined how spooky this place would be, she thought to herself.

"Is everything okay, dear?" Mrs. Bryant called from the car window a minute later.

"I'm trying the button now." Aylie shouted back.

She pressed the button, unsure of whether to wait for acknowledgement or to start talking. When she didn't hear anything on the other end, she whispered into the speaker hesitantly. "Ryder? It's Aylie...Bryant. My mom is here with me—we brought you some food." At first there was no response, but then she heard the sound of a buzzer as the gate began to slide open. She quickly climbed back into the suburban and they drove through the gate, parking beneath what looked like a sculpted awning or carport of some kind. Aylie remembered seeing this part of the Mansion in news reports when Ryder's grandfather had been murdered a couple of years ago. Seeing it up close definitely gave her the creeps.

Once they'd parked, she stepped out and took a deep breath. If Ryder didn't want visitors, they could be walking into a very awkward situation. Suddenly she wasn't so sure this whole thing was a good idea. If her mom hadn't spent the entire afternoon making those casseroles, she would've insisted on leaving immediately. Get ahold of yourself, Aylie thought inwardly. You're being a coward.

Mrs. Bryant led the way and she followed a few steps behind, looking around at everything as they made their way up the concrete steps to the daunting front entrance of the Mansion.

"Have you ever been inside this place before?" Aylie almost whispered.

"No, I haven't," Mrs. Bryant smiled playfully, "but I've always wanted to see it."

Suddenly the door opened. Aylie jumped, looking startled. Mrs. Bryant glanced sideways at her daughter and stepped forward.

"Hello. I'm Mrs. Bryant—Aylie's mom," she introduced herself, holding out her hand.

Ryder stepped into the doorway. He was wearing blue jeans and a light gray sweater, just tight enough to reveal his muscular torso. His hair looked a little disheveled, giving him an effortlessly, wind-blown look.

Aylie stared at his feet.

Mrs. Bryant continued without missing a beat. "Aylie said you were living here by yourself now. We wanted to bring you something to show our sympathy for your loss—we were so sorry to hear about your father. I can't imagine how hard this must be for you."

Aylie was afraid that Ryder was going to bark out a sarcastic reply, but instead he held his composure and reached out to take her mother's hand, shaking it firmly. "It's nice to meet you, Mrs. Bryant," he said pleasantly. "Were you waiting at the gate long?"

"Only as long as it took for Aylie to figure out how to use the call button," Mrs. Bryant replied good-naturedly, making Aylie blush.

Ryder smiled. "Would you like to come in?"

Aylie was about to protest, but Mrs. Bryant quickly replied, "That would be nice, thank you."

Aylie followed her mom into the mansion apprehensively. She couldn't help thinking of all the stories she'd heard about vampires and werewolves who lived in dark forests and haunted creepy castles like the one she was now walking into. There were no modern lights hanging from the ceilings and the windows were cut straight out of the stone in the walls. They were positioned much higher than normal windows and very little natural light was able to shine through. Ornate candelabras were the main source of lighting, with an occasional chandelier here or there in the more elaborately furnished rooms.

It was quite cold outside, and it was obvious from the moment they entered the Mansion that central heating was certainly not one of its many features. There were fireplaces in every room, but the natural darkness of the stone-enclosed living spaces was a little overwhelming. The shadows on the walls were beginning to play tricks with Aylie's imagination. What if there really were strange things that roamed this castle at night? What if the Payne murders had been committed by supernatural beings from some bizarre, alternate reality? What if Ryder was one of them? She knew vampires didn't really exist, but if they did—Ryder could easily pass for one. She tried not to picture coffins in the basement as she followed him further into the house.

Just then, a young girl about Aylie's age entered the room, wearing a very plain, navy blue dress. Her brown hair was pulled up into a bun on top of her head and she wore a white apron—clearly a maid. She took the casserole dishes and the pie plate carefully from their hands, as Ryder murmured something to her in a low voice. She glanced at Aylie shyly and smiled, then left the room hastily without a word.

Aylie stared after her for a moment. The girl looked vaguely familiar, but she couldn't remember where she'd seen her before. The maid didn't seem old enough to be out of school yet, but things here at the mansion didn't exactly conform to the norms of Silvervane society on any level. Perhaps the girl had graduated early, or had been schooled at home. Either way, she looked lonely and Aylie couldn't help feeling sorry for her.

She forced her attention to the back of Ryder's head as he led them into a massive room with a high-domed ceiling. This, he announced, was the Great Hall. Aylie looked around in awe. There were winding staircases and balconies revealing four stories, swirling up into a gradual spiral, which dissolved into a domed skylight. She could see the clouds slowly passing overhead as she stood several hundred feet beneath it. This was only the center of the castle, he informed them. There were two other wings that were too boring to mention—one on the east and one stretching toward the west.

"I've never seen anything like this before," Mrs. Bryant said in a tone that betrayed her amazement and admiration.

"If you think this is impressive, wait until you see the vault," Ryder chuckled.

"Really?" The curiosity in Mrs. Bryant's voice was unmistakable.

"Certainly, if you think you're up for it. I know it's probably a lot to take in at first."

Aylie turned her wondering gaze to Ryder, who was behaving like an absolute gentleman. He was nothing like the rude, unsocialized boy from the day before. She couldn't understand how they could even be the same person. Something about him reminded her of a book they had been required to read for Literature—a disturbing story about a doctor named Jekyll and his alter ego, Mr. Hyde. She swallowed her trepidation and followed him through several more impressively furnished rooms, into a very long, very dark tunnel. She stayed close to her mom even though she knew it was childish. There was something extremely eerie about this place and she couldn't quite put her finger on it. There was a strong musty odor permeating the stale air around her and it was making her feel a little queasy.

"How much longer do you think we'll be in this tunnel?" Aylie whispered to her mom after a few minutes, hoping that Ryder wouldn't overhear. She was beginning to feel a little claustrophobic and her breaths were becoming shallow. Just when she thought she couldn't stand it anymore, a small light up ahead made her breathe a sigh of relief.

"I apologize for leading you both into total darkness," Ryder said good-naturedly, as the end of the tunnel gave way to a large, octagon-shaped room with several doors. "If I had known I was going to have visitors I would have taken the time to light the torches before you arrived."

"That was our own fault," Mrs. Bryant said apologetically. "I hope we're not being too intrusive."

Ryder smiled genially and took an old-fashioned skeleton key from the pocket of his jeans. "It's this way," he said, approaching one of the large, mahogany doors. He inserted the iron key and turned it slowly until there was a loud click. He pushed the heavy door open and ushered them through.

Aylie's jaw dropped. The door opened into a long, white hall with marble floors and a red, velvet carpet stretching from one end to the other. Suits of armor dating back to the Middle Ages lined both sides. There were plaques hanging on the wall to indicate who had worn them and which battles and eras they had fought in.

"Did these belong to your relatives or are they collectibles?" Mrs. Bryant asked, taking the time to read each plaque as she made her way down the long, marble hall.

"These have been in my family for hundreds of years," Ryder replied. "Along with all of the weapons you're about to see."

He led them into an enormous chamber of rooms at the other end of the hall. In each part of the chamber, there were swords, shields, maces, muskets, bayonets, and every other kind of weapon imaginable mounted on the walls and displayed in elaborate, glass cases. There were also artifacts, gems and other strange objects filling shelves in every corner. These rooms alone could put some of the largest museums in the world to shame.

Aylie walked from room to room, looking at everything in amazement. This treasury had to be worth millions of dollars. She was astonished that he was allowed to keep all of this to himself. Then again...it was unlikely that anyone outside of his family had ever seen these things before. She could hardly take it all in.

After exploring the vault for what seemed like hours, the dimly lit room began to give Aylie a headache. She noticed that the air around her seemed to be getting thicker as well, making it harder to breath. She glanced over at her mom to see if she was feeling it too, and noticed that her face was unusually pale, the worry lines on her forehead more pronounced than usual. Aylie went to her side at once to see what was wrong.

Mrs. Bryant was staring through a glass case at a long, slightly curved sword. There were etchings on the blade in a language that Aylie didn't understand and an emblem of some kind engraved on its handle. She looked from the sword to her mother and back again.

"What's wrong?" She whispered.

Suddenly Ryder was standing beside them. The unexpected sound of his voice made them both jump. "That sword belonged to my great grandfather." He said, looking at the object indifferently.

"What do those marks mean?" Aylie asked, pointing to the etchings on the silver blade.

"Beats me," Ryder said casually. "I never knew my great grandfather—he died before I was born."

Mrs. Bryant seemed to recover a little. "That's an interesting symbol on the handle. Is it a family crest of some kind?"

"It wouldn't surprise me," Ryder shrugged. "I don't know as much about my family history as I would like to."

"That's a shame," Mrs. Bryant said with a smile.

Aylie examined her mom's face. Her blue eyes were definitely more guarded and it was obvious that the smile had been strained. Something about that sword was bothering her, but she was trying to put up a good front.

"Thank you so much for inviting us into your home and allowing us to see all of this," Mrs. Bryant said, turning away from the case. "Sadly, I think we should probably be going. It's nearly dinnertime and my husband and son are waiting at home for us."

"Of course," Ryder said, leading them out of the room.

Aylie glanced sideways at him as they made their way back through the dark, musty tunnel. She couldn't help feeling that he knew more about that sword than he was letting on, but his countenance had been so controlled and his answer so effortless...it was almost like he had rehearsed it. A chill ran down her spine as they pressed through the narrow passage and into the thick veil of blackness enshrouding them. She was extremely relieved when they were finally through it and standing once again at the front door. She felt like they had been inside the Mansion for days, but in reality, it had been less than two hours.

"Thank you again for the impromptu tour," Mrs. Bryant said, as they stepped out into the carriage house where the suburban was parked. "It was very nice to meet you, Ryder," she looked into his eyes warmly. "If you need anything, please don't hesitate to let us know. We're your nearest neighbors, after all."

Ryder nodded. "Thank you for the food. It was very kind of you to think of me," he replied with an easy smile.

Mrs. Bryant nodded and glanced quickly at Aylie, signaling that it was time to say goodbye. She walked quickly over to the suburban, disappearing inside as the engine roared to life. Aylie turned around awkwardly, unsure of what to say. She looked into Ryder's face, which suddenly seemed very close to hers, and completely lost her train of thought. His deep, brown eyes were strangely intense and piercing. Somehow he was suddenly more attractive than she remembered. "Um...see you later," she managed, turning quickly to avoid embarrassment.

She felt his hand on her shoulder. "Don't be a stranger," he said. She felt a shockwave of sensation course through her body when he touched her and it made her even more anxious to be out of his sight. He seemed to have a strange effect on her and she wasn't sure whether it was a good thing or a bad thing.

"Sure." She mumbled. She hurried to the car and climbed into the passenger side without so much as a backwards glance as they drove away.

Chapter Five

Ryder watched them disappear and went back into the Mansion. He was more than a little intrigued that Aylie had been concerned enough about him to talk her mother into bringing him food. Under any other circumstances, the gesture would have been nothing more than common hospitality. But considering the fact that everyone believed his house to be haunted and that he, himself, was the current suspect in his father's own murder, it seemed like more than just a neighborly gesture. His stomach began to growl, so he decided it was time to track down the casseroles they had brought him. One of his maids had taken them to the kitchens so he headed to the east wing in search of them. When he entered the central kitchen, his housekeeper, Mrs. Black, was looking over a long list of some kind. It appeared to be a food menu and she was combing through it looking for unnecessary items to scratch from the grocery list.

Mrs. Black was a hard-nosed, no-nonsense kind of woman, and she ran the household like a drill Sargent. She always wore a plain, black dress of the same design and her gray hair was typically pulled into a bun at the nape of her neck. She was a woman of few words, rarely speaking unless it was to offer a rebuke or correction. Ryder could count the number of times he had seen her smile on one hand and he'd known her all his life.

"I guess your workload just got lighter, Mrs. Black," he announced, with an uncharacteristic smile. "My neighbors were kind enough to bring me dinner."

Mrs. Black looked up at him with a guarded expression. "The Bryants, Sir?"

Ryder nodded. "They seem like good people."

The old woman looked skeptical. "The Bryants came here?"

"Yes. I gave the casseroles to that maid, Bridgett. I'm sure she must have brought them in here." He glanced around the room.

"I beg your pardon, Sir," said Mrs. Black, looking slightly less composed than usual. "I didn't know you were acquainted with the Bryants."

"Neither did I," he said with amusement on his typically stoic, face. "It's a fairly recent development."

A visible shadow crossed the old woman's face, but she nodded, pressing her thin lips into a firm line. "Very well, sir. I'll find out where the maid put the casseroles right away." With that, she left the room.

Ryder waited for her to return, but several minutes later the maid entered instead. She went straight to one of the large refrigerators in the storeroom and reappeared with two casserole dishes balanced on her forearms. He had never talked to the girl before and he could tell that she was nervous in his presence.

"Your name is Bridgett, right?" He asked, attempting to be friendly.

The girl nodded, carefully avoiding eye contact.

"Did you attend the school in town before you started working here last year?" He asked.

The girl nodded again.

Ryder was curious to see if Bridgett would react as Mrs. Black had to the news of Aylie's visit. "What do you know about the Bryants?" He asked.

Bridgett set the dishes down carefully on one of the long marble countertops and proceeded to uncover them, revealing their contents so that Ryder could choose which he would prefer to start with.

"They own the ranch down the road," she said quietly. "They have horses, goats and chickens, sir."

"Are they wealthy?"

Bridgett looked up at him with a strange expression on her pale face. "Compared to you, Sir—everyone else in the country would be considered impoverished."

Ryder cocked an eyebrow at the response.

Bridgett flushed. "Begging your pardon, Sir."

"I'm curious about them." Ryder pressed, leaning casually against the counter. Would you consider them poor, then?"

"Not by any means, Sir. I would say they are pretty well-off, compared to most people."

Ryder nodded thoughtfully.

"I think Aylie is finishing school this year," she added timidly. She checked the temperatures of the casseroles and decided to reheat them in the oven before serving them.

"Do you know her?"

Bridgett pretended to be too busy to look up. "She seems very nice, Sir. My mom used to buy eggs and milk from their ranch when I was little. Mrs. Bryant was always so kind and generous—she often gave us extra eggs after we'd already paid." Bridgett smiled fondly. "I only talked to Aylie a few times. I was a little shy, I guess. It was a couple of years ago, but she seemed very sweet and kind—just like her mom."

Ryder looked thoughtful "That doesn't surprise me at all."

"She was seeing Marcus Riley, last time I heard. He's on the hockey team I think."

Ryder shrugged indifferently. "I wouldn't know."

The girl looked a little uncomfortable. "I could be wrong,

though, Sir. I heard that rumor a while ago."

Ryder nodded dismissively.

She gave him a strained, half-smile and removed the casseroles from the oven, scooping a few pieces of each onto a plate. "Is there anything else I can get you?" She asked, refusing to look him in the face.

"No, that will be fine. I think I'll eat in my father's study tonight." He took the plate she offered from her hands and walked silently out of the room.

Being on the opposite side of the Mansion from his intended destination, He took the east staircases slowly, pausing to take a bite of casserole every now and then. He passed through the great hall, and then through the cold, dark passageways that connected the east wing of the Mansion to the west wing. He had to pass through two shorter corridors, which eventually brought him to the secret entrance of his father's study. He wasn't sure why the entrance existed, but it had always fascinated him. He had only entered the room from this door a handful of times, out of respect for his father's privacy. Doing so now felt somehow sacred and he had to push quite hard against the heavy, hidden bookshelf door to get it to budge.

Ryder proceeded to set down the plate Bridgett had piled high with casserole, so that he could light the oil lamps and candles scattered throughout the large, stuffy room. The smell of his father's pipe tobacco still lingered in the stale air and in the fabric of the worn leather sofa and chairs scattered throughout the room. It was really more of a library than a study, with bookshelves lining every wall from floor to ceiling. The furniture in the room alone was worth a small fortune. He found a few pieces of kindling and some old newspapers and started a fire in the stone hearth. He waited several minutes for the sparks to truly catch and then added a small pyramid of logs, carefully placing them to allow enough oxygen for the flames to spread.

Then he reached for the journal he'd dropped on his father's desk and carried it over to the leather sofa across from the fireplace. He tried to sort through the loose pages that had scattered all over the floor, doing his best to put them back into proper order. It was a little difficult, as some of the pages and markings had faded and smudged over the years. There were at least fifty discolored pieces of parchment he had to sort through, and he vowed that he would get the manuscript bound with a good cover before the week was over. Perhaps he would even pay someone to re-write some of the faded pages so they were easier to read. No one outside of his family would have any idea of the significance of what they were reading, so there could be no real harm in allowing them to see the journal's content.

He studied the pages as he sorted, remembering more of the stories his father had told him as a little boy. He'd quickly lost interest in the tales as he'd approached adolescence, but he was feeling strangely nostalgic this evening and wanted to pretend that his father was sitting in the winged-back chair across from him once again, smoking his pipe as he read aloud. Scanning page after page, the writing was difficult to decipher by firelight in most places. His eyes were strained and beginning to hurt. He wasn't sure how long he'd been reading when he came across a passage his father had practically forced him to memorize. The handwriting on this page looked very different from the others—the style more elegant and refined. Rather than line after long line of scrawled words that were barely readable, these were short and concise lines, written almost like poetry. He mumbled the familiar words aloud.

> *Two rivers of blood shall meet as one, In the chosen love of beloved sons. They, in nobleness and strength shall meet; In fiery protector and in harmony sweet. Through tumult and outcry and in loyalty bring, Fire and poetry that shall summon their King. And with the return of the true Prince comes peace—All pain and suffering and injustice shall cease.*

Ryder frowned. He could tell from the way this page was marked and faded that the poem was the key to understanding the rest of the legends, but why was it so important? What made this story any different than all the other myths and legends people had been obsessed with through the ages? What made this story worth dying for?

He continued to read, searching for clues just as his father had done. Following the poem, there were several pages containing long and detailed genealogies—lists of the names, dates, births, and marriages of everyone in his family line, dating as far back as the early 1300's. After hours had passed, he was still no closer to an answer than he had been when he started. Frustrated, he set the manuscript aside and stared absently into the fire. He thought of his uncle Alexander, who was still living somewhere in England. Perhaps he could shed some light on all of this. Surely he knew about The Order—if he was still alive.

Ryder stood to his feet and walked over to his father's desk again. He didn't have a telephone number for his uncle, but he had an old address and had always heard that people in that part of the country tended to stay in the same place. Being English royalty, his uncle couldn't be too terribly difficult to track down.

Ryder searched for a pen and some paper and sat down to write his uncle a letter. He started to write and then crumpled the paper in disgust. He took out a new sheet and began again, surprised by how difficult it was to say what he needed to say. He wanted to apologize for the way his father had acted, cutting off all communication four years ago. He also wanted to let his uncle know of his father's passing, but the two sentiments seemed inappropriately placed in the same letter.

This letter was going to take some very careful thought. Perhaps it would be best for him to finish it tomorrow. He'd been reading for hours already by dim candlelight and was feeling the need for fresh air. He stood from his father's desk chair, stretching out his long legs. He let out a big yawn and then snuffed out the candles before leaving the room.

The Estate was ideally located only five miles into Silvervane Forest, leaving thousands of undeveloped forest acres for hiking and exploration in nearly every direction. Ryder had easy access to miles of trails and scenic waterfalls, but tonight he was searching for something different. He needed a change of scenery—something that would improve his mood.

Maybe tonight he would visit the Ranch.

Chapter Six

Aylie was putting the horses away in their stalls to close up the barn for the night when she heard it—that same high-pitched, shrieking noise from the night before. She'd lived in Silvervane for seventeen years and had never heard anything that frightened her more. It wasn't the cry of a dying animal that made her skin crawl…it was the way it was dying. As if it were being torn limb from limb, savagely, and not out of hunger. She still couldn't figure out what kind of animal could make such a piercing cry, but she didn't want to stick around to find out.

She kissed Knight on the forehead and quickly slid the large, oversized barn doors closed. She had to search around on the cold, hard ground for the padlock that had somehow fallen from the coiled chain wrapped around the handles. When she found it, she quickly slipped the padlock back into place, inserting the metal prong into its slot. She tugged on it once to make sure it was securely locked. As she turned back toward the house, she heard the unmistakable sound of footsteps crunching through the snow nearby. They were close and steady, and it sounded like they were coming straight toward her.

It was too dark on this side of the barn to see the face of the person approaching. Aylie looked around frantically for something to defend herself with and found a shovel leaning against the side of the barn. She reached for it, mentally preparing herself to cripple her attacker with it, if necessary. She tried to regulate her breathing as she peaked around the corner. She could see a long shadow approaching. A silver of moonlight betrayed the trespasser, giving her a glimpse of the hooded figure coming toward her. She lifted the wooden handle of the shovel to strike.

"Put it down, Aylie—it's only me."

"Ryder?" She strained to see him, slowly lowering the shovel to the ground. "What on earth are you doing out here this late at night?"

"Taking a walk. I do that sometimes."

Aylie rolled her eyes as her heart rate began to slow. "You scared me half to death."

Ryder shrugged, stepping into a patch of moonlight so she could see him better. His eyes were so dark they were like empty, black sockets, and his hair was more than a little disheveled beneath the hood of his dark blue sweatshirt. He was practically invisible against the night sky.

Aylie studied his face. "What are you doing here, Ryder?"

He shifted his weight to one foot, leaning casually against the side of the barn. He folded his arms across his broad chest. "I just came by to thank you for the pie. Did you know apple was my favorite?"

Aylie shook her head, blushing slightly in the dark. "I've never made one before…I hope it turned out okay."

"I'm sure it's delicious," he smiled easily. "I'll let you know when I've tasted it."

Aylie narrowed her eyes. "So…you came all the way out here to thank me for a pie you haven't tasted yet?"

Ryder shrugged again. "Why not?"

"That makes perfect sense." Aylie looked back over her shoulder toward the house. She felt a little uncomfortable with his sudden appearance, but she wasn't sure why. Her mom had given him permission to stop by any time, of course, but this just seemed a little...soon. It had only been a matter of hours since she'd been inside his mansion and Ryder wasn't really the socializing type. She narrowed her eyes at him suspiciously, trying to wiggle her quickly numbing toes inside of her rubber barn boots. Her breath was coming out in frosty puffs in the chilly night air.

The house by contrast, was cozy and warm, beckoning her to come and enjoy its safety and the soothing firelight that flooded every room. Even though she was tempted to give in to her instincts and return to the house, part of her wanted to know what Ryder was up to and why he'd walked five miles just to thank her for something he hadn't even tasted. It all seemed rather strange, even for Ryder Payne.

"How did you know I'd be out here?" She asked suddenly.

Ryder let out an exaggerated breath, watching it swirl in the icy cold air. "I didn't."

Aylie felt a shiver and folded her arms across her chest to keep herself warm. "What would you have done if I hadn't been outside?"

"I don't know. I hadn't really thought that far ahead...I prefer to live on the edge," he replied with a crooked smile.

Aylie regarded him for a moment. She didn't know what to think of this odd behavior. Was he stalking her or just feeling lonely? It had to be the latter—not that he would ever admit it. Maybe something she'd said had actually gotten through to him. She scrambled for something else to say to keep the conversation going.

"Did you hear that animal shrieking a few minutes ago?" She asked. "I've heard it two nights in a row now."

"Honestly, Aylie." Ryder scoffed. "There are a lot of animals that roam the forest at night...sounds like that are a pretty ordinary occurrence."

Aylie shook her head. "Not like this. This sound was different—like an animal tearing its prey to pieces for fun instead of killing it for food." She shuddered.

Ryder shrugged it off and took a step toward her. His expression was suddenly intense. Even in the dark, his eyes were glowing with a strange light.

Aylie swallowed. She felt both a prickle of fear and a jolt of courage simultaneously. "How do you do that?" She wondered aloud, unthinkingly.

He took a step closer. "Do what?"

She felt a little silly for asking the question out loud. "I don't know. It's like…." She couldn't find words to describe it.

"Like?" Ryder probed, his face only inches from hers.

It's like I'm drawn to you for some reason and yet terrified of you at the same time, she thought. A strange look flickered in Ryder's eyes—curiosity maybe, or surprise? She couldn't decide which. Slowly and without warning, as if he was afraid of scaring her, Ryder reached for hand. Her first instinct was to yank it away…she hardly knew him. But Ryder was staring deeply into her eyes and it was a little disorienting.

He took her gloved hand in one of his large bare ones, and stared at it for a moment. Then he looked up at her again. Without breaking eye contact, Ryder removed her glove with his other hand. Now there was nothing separating his skin from hers. She felt the warmth of his thumb pressing into her palm, as he gently turned her hand over, exposing the underside of her wrist to the cold night air. A sliver of moonlight danced across her white skin, highlighting the icy blue veins. He stared at her wrist, holding her hand firmly in both of his.

There was something strangely intimate in the gesture that she couldn't understand. The moment their palms touched, she felt both unexplainably calm and intensely uneasy in the pit of her stomach. It was like her insides were at war—the two halves of her soul fighting against each other. She was beginning to feel dizzy. "Do you think hypnosis is possible?" She blurted out.

Ryder was taken aback. His eyes were curious, as he cocked his head to one side. "Are you accusing me of trying to hypnotize you?"

"No!" Aylie exclaimed, feeling mortified.

His lips twisted into a wickedly amused grin. "I must have quite the effect on you."

Aylie wanted to disappear. She silently berated herself for not keeping her mouth shut and considered bolting into the house. It would be cowardly, of course, but it was tempting all the same. She should've listened to her gut and cut the conversation short when he'd first shown up. Why did she always say such awkward things in his presence?

"Now it's my turn to ask a question," he said, gazing into her eyes.

Aylie swallowed, feeling a little nervous.

"Don't worry…I'm not going to ask you anything embarrassing."

"What is it about?"

"I'm curious about your family," he said.

"My family?" She asked, surprised.

Ryder nodded.

"There's not much to tell. What do you want to know?"

"Anything. Have you always lived in Silvervane? Were your parents born here? What about your grandparents?"

Aylie narrowed her eyes skeptically, trying to understand why he wanted to know about her family when they hardly knew anything about each other. "I grew up here in Silvervane and my parents were born and raised here, too. My grandparents originally came from Europe, I think. They never really talked about stuff like that." She tilted her head to the side, a strand of silvery-blonde hair falling across her pale face. "Why do you ask?"

"Do your grandparents still live here in Silvervane?" He asked, ignoring the question.

Aylie shook her head. "They died a few years ago."

Ryder furrowed his brows. "How did they die, if you don't mind me asking?"

Aylie swallowed the unexpected lump in the back of her throat. "A hunting accident." Her voice quivered, but she forced herself to continue. "That's what the Police Chief said, anyway. I never actually got to see the…bodies. I guess they thought it was too gruesome for a ten-year-old." She was surprised by how sad she sounded talking about her grandparents. She didn't realize how much it still hurt. She hadn't thought of them in a long time, but suddenly she missed them terribly.

She expected to meet Ryder's usual emotionless stare, but instead, she looked up to see a flicker of compassion in his dark eyes. She was seized with a sudden urge to throw her arms around his neck, but she held herself in check. Ryder Payne was not the comforting type. "I should probably get back inside," she said, withdrawing her hand suddenly. She took a step back. "My parents are probably starting to wonder what happened to me."

"I'm sorry, Aylie," Ryder murmured. "About your grandparents."

She swallowed again. "I'm sorry about your father," she answered quietly.

The two of them stood looking at one another for several minutes, neither feeling the need to speak. They understood each other's pain and there was a mutual sense of comfort in the knowledge that they had both lost people they loved too soon.

"Do you have any idea who might be doing it, Ryder?" She asked softly. Thinking of the untimely deaths of her own grandparents was stirring up all of the unresolved grief she'd tried so hard to bury. "Who hates your family enough to kill them?"

Ryder shook his head. "If I knew who was behind all of this I'd hunt them down and kill them myself."

The look of hatred on his face was so intense that Aylie knew he meant it. She shivered, wrapping her arms tightly around her body. She couldn't blame him for feeling the way he did, but there was a savageness in his eyes that alarmed her.

"If you did that, Ryder, you'd be just like them."

"I don't care." He retorted vehemently. "I'll do whatever it takes to avenge my family."

"You can't just take the law into your own hands and go around killing people," She said, refusing to shy away from the subject. "It's illegal, for one thing. There are better ways to get justice."

"Yeah....tell that to my dead brothers. They were murdered five years ago and the killer hasn't stopped yet. So much for justice." He spat on the ground, just barely missing her boot.

Aylie looked down at her feet, trying to think of how to respond. "If you find the killer and murder him, you'll spend the rest of your life in prison—your entire life would be over. Is that what your brothers would want? Is that what your father would want?"

Ryder clenched his jaw, his hands balling into fists at his sides. "You don't know anything about my brothers or my father," he said through gritted teeth. "And you have no idea what I'm dealing with." His face contorted in rage and his body started visibly shaking.

Aylie stared at him in shock, as the muscles under his clothing started to ripple and bulge like he was flexing, only he wasn't moving at all. The veins in his neck were pulsing violently and the muscles were standing out. His eyes flashed like flames of fire, first orange then red. "What is happening to you?" Her voice was trembling, but she was fighting to stay calm.

"Get away from me!" He roared, his body thrashing and contorting like something from the Exorcist.

In spite of the fear she felt, Aylie couldn't leave him like this. She had no idea what was going on, but she took a step toward him and looked him square in the face. "Calm DOWN." She said firmly, feeling courage rise up from someplace deep inside. "Get. A. Grip."

His eyes flashed and the veins in his forehead were pulsing wildly. He looked like he was about to lunge at her.

"I don't know what you are, Ryder Payne—but you are NOT a murderer." She took another step toward him and put her hands on his shoulders. She knew it was a risky thing to do but she felt instinctively that he wouldn't hurt her. Slowly, his body stopped thrashing but he was still breathing hard, fighting against her. "

You don't know what I'm capable of." He hissed through clenched teeth.

"You're NOT a murderer," she repeated calmly, looking into his eyes.

Against his will, Ryder's breathing slowed. His body relaxed and his eyes stopped flashing, slowly returning to their usual color. His muscles stopped pulsing, disappearing beneath the skin once more as he took a deep breath and unclenched his fists. He blinked and stared through her blankly. It took several minutes for coherence to fully return. As the color began to come back into his face, he looked slightly worried. "Did I hurt you?"

"No," she replied, her voice a little shaky. "You looked like you wanted to, but you didn't."

Ryder glanced around, taking in his surroundings as if to regain his bearings. "I'm sorry for that."

"I didn't know what was happening to you," Aylie said, dropping her arms to her sides. "You looked like you were possessed or something."

Ryder cocked his head to one side. "Why on earth did you stay?" He was staring at her like she was insane.

"I couldn't just leave you like that," she said, returning his gaze.

"That's exactly what you should've done!" He shook his head angrily. "You could've gotten yourself killed."

"I knew you wouldn't hurt me," she retorted. "I wasn't in any real danger."

"You don't know what I'm capable of, Aylie. It's foolish to take chances like that."

She folded her arms irritably across her chest. "So I was supposed to just let you turn into a raging freak and run away?"

"I know how to handle myself," he snapped, "I've done it for years."

The implications of what he was saying hit her like a ton of bricks. Aylie's eyes widened. "This happens to you a lot?"

Ryder glared at her. "Not to anyone else's knowledge."

Suddenly it all came together in Aylie's mind and she took a frightened step backwards as the truth began to sink in.

"You're the one tearing animals apart, aren't you? The eerie growling sound I keep hearing."

Ryder smirked. "Do you know how crazy you sound right now?"

"Not as crazy as you looked a minute ago," she retorted. "And you didn't answer my question."

The smirk disappeared from his face. "You're the one who said I wasn't capable of savage murder." His mouth twisted in a sarcastic grin. "Having second thoughts?"

"It's barbaric." She said, shaking her head in disgust. "Why would you do something like that to innocent animals?"

"Better animals than people."

Aylie took a deep breath and let it out slowly, exhaling a large puff of frosty air. "I'm too tired for this right now," she muttered. "I'm going to bed." She started to walk away and then paused, looking over her shoulder. "You owe me an explanation tomorrow."

"I don't owe you anything," he replied haughtily.

It was Aylie's turn to smirk. "Yes you do, unless you want me to go straight to Chief Blair tomorrow and tell him everything I saw."

Ryder's lips curved down into an unpleasant frown. "Whatever."

CHAPTER SEVEN

Ryder didn't appear at school for the next three days. No one seemed to notice that he was gone, and no one but Aylie seemed the slightest bit concerned. The rumors about his father's death were still circulating wildly, but Fall Break was officially about to begin and they would soon die down. People would stop caring by the time they returned to school in a week and a half.

Aylie forced herself to focus on her exams. This was semi-finals week and she had to do well or she'd be stuck in Silvervane forever; her dreams of going off to an ivy-league university would be shattered. She had her heart set on a University abroad, but she had to finish well in order to even be considered for admission. She had already turned in her Literature semi-final earlier in the week, and had survived her exams in both Humanities and Physics. Her French exam was the only one she had left and then she would be done with school for ten whole days.

She was headed for the French room, looking down at her flash cards as she walked, when she ran into someone rounding the corner. He was wearing a light blue hoodie and was standing just outside the classroom door. He turned around with a look of surprise on his face. A little jarred, Aylie looked up at him to apologize. The boy's face was familiar, but she couldn't quite place it. He was extremely attractive with ash blonde hair and bright blue eyes. Ren was standing next to him with her older brother, Derek. She stifled a giggle.

"Aylie, you remember my brother Derek, right? He was a senior when we were sophomores."

Aylie nodded, feeling a little embarrassed. She remembered Ren's brother—dark, slicked back hair and chocolate brown eyes. He looked so much like Ren they could've passed for fraternal twins.

"This is his friend, Eli—he's from Switzerland." Ren said, nodding toward the boy she'd nearly trampled.

"It's nice to meet you," Eli said with a smile.

Aylie was taken aback by the striking blueness of his eyes. There was something almost mesmerizing about them; they sparkled like blue diamonds. It took her a second to respond. "Sorry for running into you a minute ago…I wasn't looking where I was going."

"No harm done," he replied genially.

Aylie smiled back. "Are you guys here to crash finals or something?"

Derek chuckled. "We just came by to see Coach Cole."

"And of course you wanted to see me," Ren added smugly, sneaking a glance in Eli's direction.

Aylie noticed the look but said nothing.

"You guys go have fun," Ren said, dismissing the boys with a wave of her hand. "Aylie and I have more important things to do right now—like passing our French examination."

Eli smiled at them both politely, before turning to follow Derek away down the hall.

Aylie watched them disappear and hurried into the classroom just as the bell rang, reminding her once again that her future was hanging in the balance.

When she had finished her exam, Aylie waited outside the classroom for Ren so they could walk back to her dorm together. She was curious about Eli and wondered what her friend thought of him. Lacey had volleyball practice after school so it would be just the two of them, which was rare. They went straight to their lockers to get their things and Aylie dropped off her textbooks, tugging her wool coat on over her navy blue uniform sweater. She draped her scarf around her shoulders without bothering to wrap it around her neck. She was anxious to put the school behind her and embrace ten days of absolute freedom.

Ren was right behind her. They both breathed a sigh of relief as they left the classroom buildings behind and made their way toward the dormitories on the other side of campus. It was officially fall break and they were carefree! The mile-long walk felt exhilarating, and the two girls chatted excitedly about their plans.

Aylie purposely slowed their pace to prolong their time together, glancing sideways at Ren. "So…tell me about Eli."

Ren blushed. "I don't know much about him, really."

"Well, you seemed to have quite a interest in him, unless I misunderstood the looks," Aylie teased.

"I've only met him once before. He's practically Derek's best friend, though, so he's going to be around a lot for holidays and things like that. I guess Switzerland's too far to travel for short holidays."

Aylie smiled. "Yeah, sounds like you're really broken up about that."

Ren's brown eyes were practically glowing. "He's SO handsome, Aylie."

She chuckled. "I can't disagree with you there."

"How did he and your brother become close friends so quickly? They've only known each other for a little over two months, right?"

Ren's expression changed slightly. "They're in a lot of classes together, I think."

Aylie's powers of perception were tingling. "And?"

"And...they have similar interests."

Aylie could sense her friend's hesitation, which piqued her curiosity even more. She stopped, just before the dormitory came into view, forcing them to go their separate ways.

"Ren—you know I can sense when there's something you're not telling me."

Ren looked around nervously. "I know."

"So?" Aylie waited expectantly.

"They're in the same...fraternity."

"Why is that a secret? There are several on campus."

"It's kind of a secret fraternity—no one officially knows they exist, except the students who are chosen to join. It's kind of an ancient tradition."

Aylie frowned. "Are they involved in anything illegal?"

"Of course not!" Ren exclaimed. "Derek would never be part of something like that."

Aylie couldn't help feeling a little suspicious. "Of course."

"Well, I should probably go inside," Ren said, changing the subject as they approached the sidewalk leading to her dorm. "I'll call you tomorrow, okay?" She took the sidewalk and quickly disappeared from sight before Aylie could ask any more questions.

Aylie turned away from the dorms and found the main road, which eventually turned into the long gravel road that led out of the city limits. From that point, the Ranch was only a couple miles away. She hadn't gotten very far when she saw something emerge from the edge of Silvervane Forest. It was definitely a person, which was a small relief.

Ryder. She recognized him instantly. He was wearing a black leather jacket over a solid gray t-shirt, and his jeans were wrinkled like he'd just picked them out of the dirty laundry pile. His dark hair was mussed and there was a shadow of stubble along the edges of his jawline. She felt silly when her heart skipped a beat and was glad he couldn't read her mind. She was actually relieved to see him, but she wasn't ready to admit it to herself or to him.

He waited for her, arms folded across his broad chest.

Aylie took a deep breath. I guess this is happening, she thought. Ready or not.

"Are you stalking me?" He asked, when she had finally caught up with him. A smirk was playing on the corners of his lips.

She rolled her eyes. "I'm pretty sure you're the only stalker here."

He chuckled and Aylie resumed her pace. She focused on the gravel beneath her feet, pretending not to care whether he followed or not. She didn't want to seem too eager to talk to him.

He kept in step with her, glancing sideways. "How's Silvervane Prep?"

"Great, now that exams are out of the way. Not that you'd know anything about that." It was her turn to scrutinize. "Where have you been?"

His lips curved into a roguish grin. "Sounds like someone missed me."

"I just wanted to make sure you were still alive, that's all," she replied defensively. "With your luck, you could've been buried under the floorboards days ago and no one would even know." She regretted saying the words the moment they left her lips, but she couldn't take them back now.

A flash of pain crossed his face before dissolving behind a smug rebuttal. "What does it matter to you?"

Aylie stopped and turned to face him. "I didn't mean it like that, Ryder."

"Sure you did." He shot her a pointed glance. "Your friends are probably betting on whether or not I'm going make it to the end of Fall Break without handcuffs."

"I don't care what my friends are saying—I wouldn't be talking to you if I did."

He looked at her skeptically. "Why are you talking to me?"

Aylie bit her bottom lip. "I already told you…I was concerned about you."

"Right, but you only care about whether I'm dead or alive?"

"Well that, and you still owe me an explanation for the little werewolf incident the other night."

Ryder laughed out loud. "Werewolf incident?"

"Don't you DARE pretend like you don't know what I'm talking about, Ryder Payne!" She exclaimed. "I'll go straight to chief Blair if I have to."

Ryder cocked an eyebrow. "Really? How do you think that conversation will go, Aylie? Do you honestly think he'll believe anything you say?"

Aylie's cheeks flushed and her heart was beginning to pound. "You owe me an explanation—I saved you from doing something stupid, remember?"

"That's not what I remember."

"Let me refresh your memory, then." Aylie retorted, blood rising. "You started freaking out, thrashing like you were possessed by something...sound familiar?"

"Hmm," he pretended to ponder. "Doesn't ring a bell," he said with maddening calmness. He picked up his pace, leaving her behind.

Aylie was furious. You're not getting off the hook this easily. She reached for his arm, catching him by the wrist. The moment she touched him she felt a jolt of electric current shoot through her veins, nearly knocking her to the ground. She stumbled backwards and dropped his wrist, staring at him in wide-eyed disbelief.

"What was that?" She exclaimed.

He held his wrist as if he'd been burned, but tried to keep his composure. "I don't know what you're talking about."

"You electrocuted me!" She said, drawing in a ragged breath. "Did you do that on purpose?"

"No, of course not." He spat on the ground. She could see a trace of blood in his saliva as it seeped into the gravel at his feet.

"Ryder, what is going on? Do you need help?"

He glared at her. "No. I just need to stay away from you."

Aylie ignored the stinging remark. "Well I'm not leaving Silvervane, so you're just going to have to pick up your Mansion and move somewhere else."

"Actually, I've decided to leave that behind," he said, matter-of-factly. "I might even burn it down."

Aylie stared at him. He looked entirely sincere. "I can't tell whether you're joking or not."

"I'm being completely serious."

"You're leaving Silvervane?" The thought filled her with unexpected sadness. Or maybe it was more like disappointment. She wasn't sure what she felt. She'd only met him a couple of weeks ago but it seemed like she'd known him for years.

Ryder nodded. "You won't have to worry about me or my haunted castle anymore."

"When?" She asked quietly, forgetting how angry she'd been only moments before.

"As soon as I graduate."

The news was like a punch in the gut. Sure, she'd been angry enough to slap him a moment ago, but she hadn't really wanted him to leave Silvervane forever. In that moment, Aylie realized she didn't want him to leave, and the revelation overwhelmed her. With an irrational burst of emotion, she started walking away blindly, putting one foot in front of the other without thinking about what she was doing. She didn't know why those words had affected her so strongly, but an odd sense of loss had gripped her and she wanted to get away from Ryder Payne as quickly as possible.

The wind picked up suddenly, blowing her hair every which way and biting at the exposed skin at her throat. She'd draped her scarf haphazardly around her shoulders when she'd walked out of the school and the breeze violently ripped it from her neck, tossing it to the ground several feet away.

Ryder had been following slowly behind and the scarf landed at his feet. He retrieved it and caught up with her, stopping silently in front of her. She reached out to take it from him, but he ignored her outstretched hand and moved closer to put it around her neck himself. Wordlessly, he proceeded to even out the lengths of both sides so that they were matching, and then twisted it once, pulling the ends through the knot he had created. He was concentrating intently, his fingers gently brushing the skin on her neck as he did it.

Aylie felt a slight tingling sensation where he'd touched her. She shivered, but it had nothing to do with the cold. She tried not to look into his face—that would only make things worse.

He finished and turned away, looking off into the distance. "I can see your ranch from here," he murmured.

Aylie nodded, dumbfounded. Ryder Payne was a paradox...cold as ice one moment and excruciatingly gentle the next.

"Do you mind if I walk you home?" He asked.

Aylie shook her head. "No, thanks—it's not that far from here."

Ryder looked into her eyes with solemn determination. "My asking was a formality. I'm going to walk you home whether you want me to or not."

They continued on in silence for several minutes, until the Ranch came into full view. Aylie could see the dark, paneled siding of her house in the distance; the chimneys were sending up smoke and ash, the bright afternoon sunlight beating down on the light colored solar-paneled roof and dormers. Shafts of sunlight glistened off of the bright, fall-colored leaves that were still clinging to the trees along the edge of the property, and the mountains beyond it were breathtaking in their rocky, rugged expanse.

The puffy white clouds and patches of blue sky overhead were a stark contrast to the deep green of the pastureland beneath their feet. The horses were grazing contentedly, scattered across the acres of farmland that spread out in all directions in front of them. Once they cut through the acre of tall grass leading to the pasture gate, Aylie would be home and their walk would be officially over. She tried not to let her disappointment show. She kept her eyes on the foot-worn path in front of her, trying not to be aware of how closely Ryder was following behind her. She could feel the intensity of his eyes on her and it wasn't an entirely unpleasant sensation.

Ryder unlatched the metal gate, holding it open for her to pass through. Aylie thanked him timidly, as she took a step into the tall pasture grass and then hesitated. She looked over her shoulder at him. "Thank you for walking me home."

"No problem."

He looked off into the distance, waiting for her to pass through the gate, but Aylie allowed herself to linger for a moment. She found herself longing to say something that would make him change his mind about leaving Silvervane, but refrained, feeling a little ashamed of how attached she'd become to him in such a short period of time. I wish you weren't moving. She thought wistfully. I wish I had met you sooner, before things got so complicated.

Ryder's eyes snapped to her face, like he was suddenly intrigued by something written on her forehead. He narrowed his chocolate eyes, studying her so hard that she started to squirm under the intensity of his gaze.

She cleared her throat uncomfortably. "Well, I guess I'll see you around?"

Ryder's full lips slowly spread into a grin. "You certainly will."

Chapter Eight

Aylie hardly ate anything at dinner. She had no appetite and couldn't force herself to eat another bite of her mom's spaghetti. She told her parents that she wasn't feeling well and went straight to her room. She didn't need to think about what was bothering her. She knew why she wasn't hungry and was thoroughly annoyed with herself for it. She should never have let herself get attached to Ryder in the first place and she inwardly chided herself for being so careless with her heart.

Her mom had always emphasized the importance of protecting her heart and her emotions when it came to the boys she allowed herself to like. She knew better than to let feelings based on shallow attraction and hormones cloud her judgment—that's how most girls ended up with broken hearts and a trail of short-lived, emotionally damaging relationships. But she hadn't meant to develop feelings for Ryder…she hadn't even realized it was happening until this afternoon.

She tried to figure out when it had started. Was she feeling this way about him because she felt sorry for him? Was she drawn to him because he was mysterious and rebellious, or was there something more? She tried to sort through all of the confusing new emotions by writing in her journal. Sometimes getting everything out on paper was the best way for her to figure out what she was feeling and why she was feeling it. This seemed like a much safer option than confiding in Lacey or Ren. They were her closest friends and she trusted them, but she didn't want to be teased about this right now.

Besides, Ryder was leaving town in a few months. There was no happy ending to this story. She needed to get over this little infatuation and move on before things got out of hand. She couldn't lose her head over a boy and let her feelings run away with her. It would be a recipe for disaster. She wrote until her eyes burned and fell asleep with the journal on her lap.

When Aylie awoke, she was standing in the middle of Silvervane Forest. The moon was standing high in the sky, casting its light in a wide pool all around her. There was snow covering the ground beneath her bare feet, but she didn't feel the cold. The stars were sparkling like crystals in the midnight sky overhead and she was enthralled by the beauty surrounding her. She had no idea how she'd gotten there or what time it was. She knew instinctively that she should be afraid of the forest at night, but she felt fearless. Safe. Protected. She glanced around at the snow-kissed fur trees and saw something moving among the branches. It was large and white, and it was coming toward her. She watched its every move—not in fear, but in anticipation. She wanted it to come closer.

When the animal finally emerged from the shadows, Aylie gasped. She wasn't sure what she had expected—a fox or a wolf, perhaps, but never this. A great, white lion was approaching her, its piercing blue eyes fixed on hers. Its fur was brighter than snow and it glistened in the moonlight. Its eyes were the most striking blue she'd ever seen, but they were burning like flames of fire. She was completely transfixed and utterly unafraid. She had never seen anything so magnificent. It stopped right in front of her, straightening to its fullest height—only then did Aylie feel fear. It wasn't the kind of fear that most humans experience when they are in danger, but the kind that fills you with awe and makes you aware of your own fragile humanness.

Are you ready? It asked her.

The animal had not opened its mouth, but Aylie understood what it was thinking.

"Ready for what?" She asked. She longed to reach out and stroke the lion's regal head, but she held herself in check.

It is time. The lion said.

"Time for what?" She looked into its eyes imploringly.

It is time for you to take back what belongs to you.

"What do you mean? What belongs to me?" She asked, wanting desperately to understand. "What do you want me to do?

Find me.

The lion looked deeply into her eyes and Aylie felt she might melt under their fiery gaze. Suddenly, the creature began to vanish right before her eyes, fading away into the darkness, piece by piece.

"Don't go!" She shouted.

Suddenly, Aylie awoke with a start and realized it had been a dream. She was breathing hard and her comforter was lying on the floor next to her bed. Beads of sweat gathered on her forehead, but she couldn't move a hand to wipe them away because her body felt somehow paralyzed from the intensity of the dream.

It was several minutes before she could finally summon the strength to sit up. Then she reached for her journal, trying to capture every detail of the dream. She didn't understand it at all, but she felt innately sure that it was somehow significant. After she had finished, she set the journal back down on the nightstand and slowly crawled out of bed. She tiptoed quietly over to the window, careful to avoid the loose floorboards that sometimes creaked, betraying the fact that she was awake.

She gazed out of her second story window at the snowy

landscape below and up into the night sky glittering with stars. The moon was full and at its peak, just as it had been in her dream. She glanced toward the forest, almost expecting to see the snowy, white lion of her dream emerge from it. To her astonishment, she saw—not the magical lion, but the shadowy figure of Ryder Payne making his way through the tree line. He was trudging through the freshly fallen snow as if it were broad daylight. He was too far away to see her yet, but she could tell that he was headed toward the ranch even from a mile away.

Aylie spun on her heal to see what time it was. The alarm clock revealed that it was only a little after midnight. She turned back to the window and watched him draw closer with alarming speed. Then she hurried to get dressed. She wasn't sure whether he intended to make her aware of his presence or not, but she was determined to find out why he was here, regardless. She ripped off her nightshirt and pulled on her silk thermals, jeans, and a hoodie, grabbing a pair of wool socks from her drawer before tiptoeing down the stairs. She paused by the backdoor to put on her barn boots and carefully pushed it open, closing it again quietly behind her.

Aylie had never attempted to sneak out of the house at night before and she wasn't sure what her parents would say if they caught her now. She knew she wasn't thinking clearly, but the dream had left an impression on her and it seemed like Ryder's sudden appearance was a strange coincidence.

She trudged through the snow, wishing she had thought to grab her heavy winter coat. Flakes were still falling steadily and it was only a matter of time before her sweatshirt would be soaked through. She walked around the barn in the direction she had last seen Ryder, but he was nowhere in sight. She couldn't even seem to find the trail of footprints he had left in the snow, which was a little unsettling. She looked around for some sign of him, unsure of which way to look. He couldn't just vanish into thin air.

Suddenly a branch in the tree above her snapped and fell at her feet, barely missing her head. Aylie jumped back in dismay. The branch was quite large and heavy, and could easily have given her a concussion or broken bones, had it landed on her. She peered into the darkness, trying to figure out what had caused the branch to break.

"Looking for something?"

Aylie was so startled she nearly shrieked as she spun around in the snow to face Ryder. "I was looking for you," she hissed, "and this branch nearly knocked me out!"

He looked up at the tree, as if he could see into its branches clearly in spite of the darkness. "You should probably be more careful. What are you doing out here, anyways?"

Aylie wrapped her arms protectively around her torso, trying to keep some of her body heat from escaping. "I saw you headed this way."

Ryder quirked an eyebrow. "You saw me coming?"

Aylie nodded. "I was looking out the window and saw you come out of the forest."

He furrowed his brows with an amused expression. "Why were you staring out your window in the middle of the night?"

"I had a weird dream and it woke me up."

"Do you have nightmares often?"

Aylie shook her head. "It wasn't a nightmare…exactly, but I couldn't go back to sleep afterwards."

"Hmm." Ryder smirked. "And then you saw me headed this way and just couldn't resist."

Aylie rolled her eyes. "Give me a break, Ryder."

"Can you offer another explanation for why you're standing out here, knee-deep in snow with nothing but a sweatshirt on?"

"I have thermals on underneath," she retorted, trying to keep her teeth from chattering as she said it.

Ryder chuckled. "You're freezing."

Aylie ignored the observation. "What are you doing out here, anyway?"

"I'm not stalking you, if that's what you're worried about."

"I'm not worried—just curious."

He took a step toward her, leaning in as he spoke. "Are you sure you really want to know?"

Aylie's heart skipped a beat. She nodded.

"I like to hunt at night, especially when there's a full moon."

"You hunt at night?" She looked at him skeptically. "Where's your gun, then?

His eyes danced mischievously. "I think we've already established the fact that I don't need a gun to hunt effectively."

Aylie's eyes widened. "Oh... I didn't think of that." She tried to wrap her brain around the concept. "So...you turn into some kind of werewolf creature somehow and hunt down innocent animals in the middle of the night for sport?"

Ryder laughed. "Not for sport—I eat what I kill."

"But you do turn into a werewolf-type creature?"

"I'm not a werewolf."

"But it's something other than human...," Aylie hedged, trying to get a confession out of him.

Ryder took a deep breath and let it out slowly. Aylie could feel his warm breath on her face and it smelled pleasantly like mint leaves. She shivered involuntarily.

"I don't know if I can trust you," he said, looking at her seriously. "I've never told anyone about any of this before. It's forbidden."

"What's forbidden?" She felt a prickle of fear in the back of her mind, warning her to be careful.

"Let's just say my family has a very complicated history."

Aylie was getting impatient. "I know all about the murders."

"There's a lot more to it than that," Ryder murmured. Without warning, he reached for her hand again. This time there was no glove separating his skin from hers and he reached for her wrist, turning it over like he had before. He stared at it with such intense concentration that Aylie felt like the blood in her veins was going to burst through the pores of her skin at any moment.

"Why do you keep doing that?" She asked, studying her own wrist as if there was something she must be missing.

Ryder hesitated. "You say that you know nothing about your family's history."

"I only know what I've already told you."

"I have a strong feeling there are some very significant details your parents have left out, but I can't be sure yet. I'm still trying to figure it out."

She saw his eyes flicker back to her wrist. "How is this supposed to help?" She asked, as snowflakes began to melt into the exposed skin of her forearm.

Ryder shook his head. "Its too soon for me to answer that question. There's a lot I don't know and I'm still searching for the answers myself."

Aylie pulled her wrist away, balling her fist inside the sleeve of her sweatshirt. "This is ridiculous!" She exclaimed. "You're acting like you know something I don't, but you can't answer a single one of my questions."

He looked away without answering, staring off into the forest for several minutes, as if debating something in his mind.

"If you're not going to answer me like a decent human being, then I'm going back to bed. I'm freezing, I'm wet, and now I'm pissed off."

"You don't understand," he said, shaking his head. "It's dangerous."

"What's dangerous?" She asked, feeling cold and angry and exasperated all at once.

"If I tell you, there's no going back."

"That's totally ambiguous."

"Maybe. But you're asking for answers that are far more complicated than you could ever imagine—they could put you and your family in danger."

Aylie took a step toward him. "Is it really me you're worried about or are you just trying to protect yourself?"

Ryder was thoughtful for a moment. "A little of both, I think."

She sighed. "Look, Ryder—either you trust me, or you don't. It's up to you. I'm not going to force you to confide in me, but if there's something I need to know, I hope you'll have the decency to tell me. Especially if it concerns my family." She turned to walk away, but the sound of Ryder's voice stopped her in her tracks.

Tomorrow night.

"What?" She turned around but Ryder had vanished. She was sure she'd heard him say it, but it was late and she was cold, and perhaps a little delirious. She trudged back to the house through the knee-deep snow and somehow managed to make it back to her room without anyone knowing she'd been gone.

CHAPTER NINE

Ryder practically fell into his king-sized bed when he finally reached the mansion. He had promised Aylie an explanation tomorrow and he knew she'd heard him say it—even though he hadn't spoken the words out loud. He'd developed a theory over the last few days that needed to be tested, and the fact that she'd heard his voice in her mind was proof that his theory was correct. What he didn't know for sure was how this revelation was going to affect him.

In the countless conversations he'd had with his father over the years about Edryd's Order, very few had been focused on their enemies—the Silver Veins. They were supposedly the direct descendants of the Lost Prince Rhydian, himself. Ryder's father had never met one, but he said they could be easily identified by the silver-colored veins in their right forearm. The town of Silvervane had been founded and named by the last known remnant of their kind, but they had died centuries ago.

This is why he'd insisted on studying Aylie's wrist—to see if she had the mark of a silver vein. Clearly, she had the ability to read minds, a telepathic gift that was a primary mark of both bloodlines. He didn't think she could be one of Edryd's descendants because she seemed ignorant of the things that came along with that heritage, yet the veins in her forearm looked absolutely normal. It was serious cause for concern. If she was secretly connected with the Order somehow, her family might know who was responsible for the death of his. On the other hand, if Aylie was a Silver Vein, she was a natural enemy of the Order and an even bigger target to them than he was.

The thought filled Ryder with anxiety. Despite his callous exterior, he had started to feel something for Aylie. It wasn't love…he wasn't even sure he had the capacity for that particular emotion. It was something along the lines of camaraderie or close friendship. He felt a protective instinct toward her that could end up being very dangerous if she turned out to be an enemy. He tried to picture her hunting alongside him as his brothers and father had done, but he couldn't quite wrap his head around the visual. If Aylie had Edryd's blood in her veins, she was totally unaware of it. She still thought he was a werewolf of some kind, which meant that she knew nothing of her heritage or ancestry, and certainly had no inkling of her own power and capabilities.

The most crucial question was, had her family purposely kept her in the dark, or were they also unaware of where they'd come from? Heritage had been so important to his father that Ryder couldn't imagine not knowing the significance of it. Good or bad, his bloodline was part of who he was and it was something that had to be preserved and protected.

And now he had more questions than ever. As much as he hated to admit it, Ryder could think of only one place to search for answers. If there was anything written in his father's journal about Silver Veins, he needed to know what it was. Aylie was in for a very rude awakening and she was going to need his help. Perhaps they could find his father's killer together…before he could even finish the thought, he fell into a deep sleep.

When Ryder awoke the next morning, the manuscript was the first thing on his mind. He dressed quickly and found his way through the passages that opened into the fake bookshelf, concealing the hidden entrance to his father's study. He locked himself in the room for the better part of the day. He skipped the stories he'd read a million times before and focused instead on pages his father hadn't discussed with him as often. It was astonishing how little information there was about the Silver Veins. He knew it was mostly due to the fact that the journal had been passed down from generation to generation among Edryd's descendants, but how did they expect to beat an enemy they seemed to have so little information about?

Ryder tried to pace himself to keep from getting frustrated, but the more he read the more questions he had, and the answers seemed to be coming up short. After several hours of fruitless research, he flipped back toward the front of the manuscript and read the poem again—maybe there was something he had missed before. He dissected the stanza one line at a time, studying each word carefully.

> *Two rivers of blood shall meet as one, In the chosen love of beloved sons. They, in nobleness and strength shall meet; In fiery protector and in harmony sweet. Through tumult and outcry and in loyalty bring, Fire and poetry that shall summon their King. And with the return of the true Prince comes peace—all pain and suffering and injustice shall cease.*

He read and reread the familiar lines again, pausing in different places for emphasis. The only thing the poem clearly suggested was the return of the Lost Prince, whom no one had seen for more than two centuries. There were no pictures of this so-called, immortal being, so there would be practically no way to identify him, even if you managed to come across his path. It was all so maddening to Ryder. He turned the page in frustration and his eyes landed on a small blotch of scribbling in the bottom, right-hand corner of the page. It looked like notes of some kind. His heart was beating with anticipation as he struggled to decipher the smeared ink. He could make out only partial phrases:

> *Rhydian – different forms? Elements, Guides,*
> *Wakened – walk through walls, healing, force fields,*
> *visions, telepathy*

The meaning of the words wasn't entirely clear, but it was obvious that whoever had scribbled these notes had some theories about what Silver Veins were capable of. He read the list again, intrigued. If Aylie was truly one of them, would she have the power to do these things? Were they abilities she was born with or did they have to be activated somehow? Suddenly Ryder was looking forward to his time with Aylie instead of dreading the explanation he'd promised. He didn't know how he was going to get the answers he was seeking, but he felt like he had a pretty good idea about where to start.

As the sun began to fade from the late afternoon sky, Ryder prepared to make the trek to the Bryant Ranch. He hadn't told Aylie when he'd be coming, but he knew she'd be waiting for him. He went to his bedroom and retrieved the ring from his dresser that his father had given him on his sixteenth birthday. It was a thick, iron band with a green emerald in its center, surrounded by an intricate Celtic knot—the symbol of Edryd's Order. Even though he wasn't a follower, he still had access to the power of his ancestors when he wore the ring. He slipped it onto the middle finger of his right hand and left the Mansion. He forced himself to walk slowly, waiting for night to fall.

A strong wind began to blow and the trees were swaying back and forth with fury overhead a he walked. Every now and then a branch would break, crashing to the earth with earsplitting force. But Ryder's reflexes were inhumanly fast when he wore the ring and he was able to dodge every single one without incident. By the time he cleared the forest it was after seven O'clock. He knew Aylie would probably be in the barn taking care of the horses for the night, so he steered himself in that direction as he crossed through the snow covered pasture. He was careful to make sure that he wasn't seen by anyone as he slipped through the gate and made his way toward the stables.

He had to dodge behind one of the stable doors when her little brother came out of the barn with an armload of firewood, and waited impatiently for the little boy to disappear into the house before he entered. He found Aylie draping a blanket over a large, black horse and listened as she whispered something to it.

"I take it that one's yours," he said, appearing from the shadows.

Aylie stood up straight, clearly unaware that he had been listening. "His name is Knight." She replied stiffly.

"I can see why," he murmured, sauntering over to her. "Do you mind?" He asked, lifting his hand to stroke the animal's sleek coat.

Aylie hesitated. "He doesn't usually let anyone touch him but me."

"There's a first time for everything."

Aylie took a step back, allowing him to get closer. He stood directly in front of the horse, allowing it to smell his hand. He moved with exaggerated slowness so that the animal could get used to him before attempting to touch him. Knight started to shake his mane, moving his feet restlessly, but then Ryder looked into his eyes and the horse immediately grew calm. They stood eye to eye for a solid minute without moving. Then Ryder gently began to stroke the horse's face, then his neck, and finally his shoulders and torso.

Aylie watched in amazement, seeing the way Ryder was able to gain her horse's trust so quickly. You can't be that dangerous, she thought. Knight is a good judge of character—he wouldn't let you touch him like that if you were a threat.

Ryder stopped stroking the horse and looked over at her. It's not always that simple. He answered her thoughts.

Aylie's eyes widened and she took a step back, stunned. "Did you just...say something?" She gasped. "How am I able to hear what you're thinking? How did you know what I was thinking?"

I told you that I would explain things to you tonight…this is me explaining.

Aylie took another step back. "How did you do that? Am I going crazy?" She chewed on her bottom lip, raking her fingers nervously through her long, blond hair.

I told you this was complicated.

"This goes beyond complicated," Aylie stammered, "this is impossible."

Obviously not. Ryder folded his arms, leaning against Knight's stable door as he waited for her to regain her composure.

"But how…how is this possible?" She demanded.

I'm trying to decide how much you can handle. I don't need you freaking out on me on top of everything else I'm dealing with.

"I'll be calm," she promised. She took a deep breath and closed her eyes for a moment. When she opened them again, she was very still, waiting for him to speak.

If I tell you what I know, you can't tell anyone else.

"Okay."

Ryder shook his head. That's not good enough—you have to prove to me that I can trust you.

"What do I have to do to prove it to you?" She asked warily.

You have to take a blood oath.

"A WHAT?" Aylie exclaimed. "That's barbaric!"

Ryder rolled his eyes. "It's not that big of a deal, Aylie." He said out loud. "My brothers and I used to make pacts like that all the time. It's just a drop of blood…not a gallon. It feels more like a pin prick than anything else."

"That seems a little extreme," she said furrowing her brows doubtfully.

"Maybe for you, but not for me. If I tell you what I know I'm putting my own life at risk—something I can't really afford at the moment, in case you didn't notice."

"I don't know about this…"

"If you want me to answer your questions, this is your only

option. It's up to you." Ryder uncrossed his arms and began stroking Knight's forehead, whispering to him to keep him calm. He knew he was putting Aylie in a difficult spot, but he had to make sure that she would keep his secret. This was the only way he could think of to do that without endangering himself and everything his father had worked so hard to protect.

Aylie started pacing the barn floor, raking her fingers through her long hair as she deliberated. He could tell that she was mentally running through her options, trying to decide if what he had to say was worth it. He waited patiently for her to make up her mind, giving her space to think it through. Finally, she stopped pacing. "You're sure it only feels like a pin prick?"

Ryder shrugged. "More or less."

Aylie frowned. "That's not very reassuring."

"Do you want to know or not?"

"You know I do," she said emphatically, locking eyes with him to show how sincere she was.

"Well, I'm willing to take the risk...are you?"

She bit her bottom lip. "Okay, I'll do it."

Ryder withdrew a small, black Swiss Army knife from the pocket of his jeans and snapped open the blade. He heard Aylie's sharp intake of breath and reached for her hand.

"Don't look at the blade," he said, gazing into her eyes. "Focus on me."

She nodded bravely, forcing herself to keep eye contact with him. Without hesitation, he took the tip of the blade and stuck her palm with it, drawing a tiny trickle of blood from the flesh in the center. Before she even had time to react, he did the same to his own palm, and then grabbed her hand so the blood in their palms mixed.

"Repeat after me," he said, without breaking eye contact. "I swear to protect your secret until the day I die or willingly accept the consequences of my betrayal."

Aylie narrowed her eyes. "It this really necessary?"

"Just say it."

Aylie sighed. "I swear to protect your secret until the day I die or willingly accept the consequences of my betrayal."

Ryder grinned. "See, that wasn't so bad, was it?"

Aylie quickly withdrew her hand, wiping the blood off on a barn rag. "Speak for yourself."

Ryder wiped the blood from his own palm off on his jeans, but the cut on his hand was a little deeper than he'd thought and a steady stream of blood began to pool in the center. "Damn it." He cursed. "I'm out of practice."

"You need a bandage," Aylie remarked calmly. "I'll go get something from the house."

"No. Your parents can't know about this. You promised—absolute secrecy."

Aylie put her hands on her hips. "Well what are you going to do about the blood, then?"

"I don't know." He looked around the barn. "You wouldn't happen to have healing superpowers up your sleeve, would you?"

Aylie shot him a look. "Yeah, sure."

Ryder shrugged. "It was worth a shot."

Aylie looked around the barn as well, spotting a tackle box full of horse supplies in the far corner. She walked over to it and started digging around for something. A moment later, she returned with a roll of ace wrap. "We can use this," she announced, as she began to uncoil the wrap. She took a long section and ripped it from the rest of the roll. Then she proceeded to wrap the material around his hand and secured it with a metal fastener to stop the bleeding. He couldn't help noticing how soft her hands were and how gently she wrapped the wound, careful to make sure the bandage wasn't too tight or too loose.

"You're good at this," he said, observing the way stray wisps of blond hair fell across her face as she worked. He felt her blood rise at his compliment and noticed her cheeks color slightly. It was intriguing how much she seemed to be affected by his words—especially when they were in close proximity like they were now.

When she had finished, he flexed his hand, checking to make sure he could still move his fingers. "Thanks.

Aylie put the remains of the roll back in the tackle box and stood in front of him expectantly. "Okay, tell me what you know."

Ryder quirked an eyebrow. "You're quite impatient," he observed.

"I just let you slice into my hand with a pocket knife—I think I have the right to be impatient."

He regarded her for a moment. "Are you sure about this?"

"Absolutely."

Ryder shook his head. "Just remember you asked for it." He moved toward the barn doors.

Aylie hesitated. "Where are you going?"

"Outside...I can't answer your questions in here."

"Why not?" She demanded.

"It's not really something I can explain with words...it's something I have to show you."

She bit her lip. "Where are we going, then?"

Ryder's mouth spread into an impish grin. "Are you worried I'm going to whisk you away to my haunted castle to eat you?"

Aylie frowned. "That's not funny."

"It's a matter of perspective," he replied with a smirk. "But don't worry, this won't take long." He smiled to himself as he led her away.

CHAPTER TEN

Aylie followed Ryder silently out of the barn and into the cold night. The thermometer said it was twenty-one degrees Fahrenheit, but she was guessing the wind-chill was much colder. She couldn't keep herself from shivering as they trudged through the snowdrifts to the pasture gate. "Seriously, Ryder," she complained, stopping short. "Where are we going?" Her teeth chattered.

"Into the trees."

"You mean into the forest?" She replied incredulously.

"Of course. I can't very well share my secrets out here in the open."

"You could've just explained everything back in the barn," she groaned. "Are you trying to give me pneumonia?"

"Are you trying to get us killed?" He replied rhetorically. He held the gate open for her and started walking again before she had a chance to respond.

Aylie pouted internally as she trailed after him, away from the ranch and into the Forest. This is seriously the perfect setting for a horror story. She thought, as they started to weave through the maze of fur trees. Attractive boy leads naïve, unsuspecting girl into the haunted forest to meet her death....

I'm surprised you would classify yourself as 'naïve and unsuspecting' Ryder replied in her mind. Although it is quite flattering to be considered the attractive villain of your internal monologue.

"Stop reading my mind!" she commanded, blushing in the dark. "You still haven't even explained to me how you're doing it."

"I'm getting there," he said, finally stopping in the middle of a small clearing.

Aylie was starting to feel extremely annoyed with his vague and condescending replies, but she was thankful for the chance to stop and catch her breath so she held her tongue. Ryder walked much faster than she did, but she wasn't about to admit that she couldn't keep up with him. She drew in several large breaths, despite the fact that her lungs were aching from the cold.

"You might want to stand back for this," Ryder announced, as he proceeded to take off his leather jacket. Then he peeled off the t-shirt he was wearing underneath and began to unfasten his belt buckle.

"What on earth are you doing?" Aylie exclaimed, feeling a little mortified.

"This is part of the answer to your question," he replied, as he dropped his jeans to his ankles and stepped out of them. Now he was standing in nothing but his boxers. "You might want to turn your head if you're afraid of seeing me in all of my glory."

Aylie turned the other way, closing her eyes. She was a little embarrassed at how uncomfortable this situation was making her. Many of her friends would've paid money to see Ryder strip down naked, but it wasn't really her thing and she was starting to wish that she hadn't forced Ryder to explain himself. She felt his hand on her shoulder but refused to look at him.

"I hope you're as good at fending off predators as you think you are," he murmured darkly into her ear.

Aylie's heart rate accelerated suddenly, slamming against the walls of her chest. It was a little hard to tell whether it was from fear or because she knew Ryder was standing so close to her—completely naked. She heard a familiar thrashing sound and a deep guttural cry, followed by that same eerie growling noise she'd heard several nights before. Chills ran down her spine as she turned slowly, opening her eyes one at a time. There, standing in front of her, was an enormous black panther with blood red eyes. He was barely visible in the dark, which made the situation even more terrifying. His eyes were glowing like fire and he looked unmistakably angry.

Aylie stumbled backwards in the dark, tripping over a thick tree root by her feet. She was too afraid to move, watching the panther as it began pacing slowly from side to side—sizing her up. She knew from childhood trips to the zoo that panthers were nocturnal and could see best at night. She also knew they were extremely fast and could climb trees, so escape was virtually impossible.

The panther suddenly advanced.

"Ryder—it's me, Aylie. I'm your friend, remember?" She tried talking to it to see if she could reason with him.

The animal paid no attention to her words and began to circle her menacingly.

"I'm not a threat to you," she coaxed. "You don't want to hurt me."

The Panther growled in response—a deep, bone-rattling sound that shook her to the core. It was no use. Ryder had completely lost touch with his humanity. He couldn't understand what she was saying and didn't seem to recognize her at all. He sank slowly into a graceful crouch, posing to strike. Clearly he had no intentions of leaving her alive. Frozen in terror, Aylie had nothing but her mind for a weapon. *Ryder—stop this! You're not a* killer…this isn't who you are.

The animal cocked its head to one side, looking at her like it was confused. Aylie let out a sigh of relief. He'd understood her on some level. She had to find a way to convince him to change back into his human form but she had no idea if she'd be able to do it. You morphed into this creature, now change yourself back. She demanded. You're human—just like me.

The panther suddenly sprang to its feet, walking toward her with slow, calculating steps. Aylie sucked in a breath and held it, trying to remain completely still. She knew this tactic sometimes worked with bears, but she wasn't sure how effective it was in fooling large wild cats. Ryder, think about what you're doing.

The large black cat stopped right in front of her, staring into her face with it's glowing red eyes. It's me…Aylie. She pleaded, hoping desperately that the animal would suddenly recognize her and retreat. Instead, it lowered its large head dangerously close to her face and sniffed, as if to catch her scent. She kept perfectly still, doing her best to conceal her fear. Animals could always sense fear, but predators fed on it.

The panther growled in her ear and Aylie closed her eyes, trying to mentally prepare herself for the worst. She would never see her family again—her parents, her brothers, her friends. Suddenly the things that had once seemed so important to her didn't matter anymore. Her grades, the universities she had applied to, the scholarships she was counting on…it was all a hallow dream. She felt the heat of the panther's hot breath on her face and lowered her head into her hands. This was not how she pictured her life ending—not that she'd ever imagined her death at all. She'd thought she would have the rest of her life to do the things she'd dreamed of, but now it was all over and she had no one to thank but herself.

Ryder had warned her. He had warned her over and over but she hadn't listened. He'd hinted to her that he was dangerous and capable of evil, but she hadn't taken him seriously. He'd given her every chance to change her mind, but she'd been stubborn and headstrong and too damn curious. She wallowed in her own misery, thinking of everything she wished she could have said to her family and friends. She was so wrapped up in the anguish of her thoughts that time seemed to stand still as she waited for her fate to overtake her.

Something touched her shoulder and she winced, waiting for the pain to start. She squeezed her eyes shut tighter. She didn't feel its teeth sink into her skin, which was a small relief. Maybe the panther would go for her jugular—that would be more merciful than a slow, torturous bleeding....

"Aylie, open your eyes."

She was startled by the sound of Ryder's human voice and her eyes flew wide open. He was standing in front of her again, fully human. He had already put his clothes back on and was kneeling on the ground in front of her with a curious look on his face.

"Are you okay?"

She swallowed and nodded, unsure of whether or not she could speak.

"You're not hurt." He sounded a little shocked. "To be honest, I'm a little surprised I didn't try to bite your head off."

Aylie felt her bottom lip quiver a little. "Good to know."

"Come on." Ryder stood to his feet and held out his hand.

She contemplated staying where she was on the cold, hard ground—afraid that the demon panther might reappear at any moment. She looked at him warily, her eyes darting around in every direction, searching for danger.

"You're safe now, Aylie—I promise."

"Are there more like you?" She asked, hesitantly taking his hand.

He pulled her to her feet. "Not anymore."

The sadness in his voice was unmistakable. Aylie tried to be sympathetic, though she couldn't say she genuinely felt sorry for him on that count after what she'd just experienced. "Your dad could do this, too?"

He nodded. "And my brothers. Gramps was too old there at the end, but I've heard stories about when he was younger."

Aylie shuddered. "oh." She turned around, scanning the trees for a way out of the forest. Her throat felt a little tight and her muscles were stiff from the strain of terror and tension. Her appendages were starting to feel numb, so the cold wasn't really bothering her anymore.

Ryder came up beside her. "The ranch is that way," he said gently, pointing in the opposite direction. "I'll take you home now."

Aylie had so many questions, but she was too shell-shocked to ask them right now. Ryder may not be a werewolf, but he certainly wasn't just an ordinary human. And if he wasn't what he seemed, there could be others just like him lurking out there somewhere in the forest. Was anyone in Silvervane truly safe with predators on the loose who could disguise themselves like regular people? Could someone with Ryder's abilities be murdering his family?

Aylie glanced sideways at him as they shuffled into the barn. She looked around to make sure no one was there before she spoke out loud. "Are there other people like you outside of Silvervane?"

Ryder nodded hesitantly.

Aylie swallowed. "I have a lot of questions."

He turned to face her, taking both of her hands in his as he looked into her eyes. "I can't tell you anything else tonight...it's too risky."

"Why not?" She frowned, feeling a little disgruntled at being so close to knowing his secret and yet so far from understanding it.

Just then her older brother Lucas appeared in the doorway. His eyes immediately fell on her hands in Ryder's and she quickly withdrew them, stepping away from him.

"Lucas—this is Ryder Payne," Aylie faltered. "He's our neighbor at the Mansion."

Lucas folded his arms across his chest, scowling. "I know who he is."

"He just came over to hang out while I was doing chores." She explained. She wasn't sure how convincing the lie was, but she had to say something to try and appease him. He was her protective older brother and he wasn't afraid to use a gun to frighten away undeserving suitors.

"What happened to your hand?" Lucas asked, looking down at the bandage wrapped around Ryder's palm suspiciously.

"Cut myself on the way here," he replied matter-of-factly.

Lucas didn't seem convinced but he changed the subject. "Mom was getting worried because the chores were taking so long," he said. "Better come inside before you get pneumonia."

Aylie nodded and turned to say goodbye to Ryder. Lucas waited impatiently for her in the doorway and she knew she had no choice but to let the conversation go for now. Ryder nodded in understanding and slipped past Lucas, out into the night. There was no telling where he'd gone or what he was about to do. Aylie shivered just thinking about it and followed her brother into the house.

Chapter Eleven

"Don't be mad, okay?" Ren's voice pleaded through the phone.

"Why would I be mad at you?" Aylie asked, holding the phone to her ear with one hand as she struggled to get dressed with the other. Lacey would be arriving to pick her up any minute and she didn't want to make everyone late.

"Well…I may have signed us up for something," Ren replied nervously.

"Okay, I'm sure it's not that bad." Aylie dropped the phone by accident and reached down to pick it up, hoping she hadn't missed anything important.

"…I don't know how Lacey will feel about it, though."

"You don't know how Lacey will feel about what?"

"About the tournament!" Ren exclaimed.

"What tournament?"

"The paintball tournament…I just told you that a second ago."

"You signed us up for a paintball tournament?"

"Aylie, weren't you listening at all?" Ren sighed into the phone. "There's a campus-wide paintball tournament today and my brother was trying to put together a team. You have to have an equal number of guys and girls. There are three guys, so they needed three girls..."

Aylie smiled. "Is Eli one of those guys, by any chance?"

"I didn't do it because of him," Ren replied defensively. "Besides, we would've spent the day at the mall or something boring like that anyways. We could use a day of fun, don't you think?"

"I highly doubt Lacey will consider being covered in paint a day of fun," Aylie laughed. "And her mom's the school principal so she practically lives there already. I don't think she's going to like the idea of spending the first day of break on campus."

"It's not on campus!" Ren qualified. "Maybe you could just mention the idea and try to convince her of how fun it will be?"

"Oh, no. I'm not going to be the one to tell Lacey that you canceled our 'girls day out' to play in a paintball tournament."

"But she likes you more than me!" Ren reasoned. "Please? She'll take it better coming from you."

Aylie sighed. "Okay, but I'm telling her it was all your idea."

"Fine. Meet us at the Silvervane Outpost in thirty minutes."

"The Outpost?" Aylie cringed. "We're playing in the forest?"

"Where else would we play? It has the best terrain for staging a battle, at least that's what I heard Derek say."

"Yeah, well...it's also the best place to meet bears," Aylie replied, secretly fearing something far worse. "I'm surprised the school is sanctioning this event."

"You're usually the brave one, Aylie—don't fail me now," Ren coaxed. "If you're not up for it, Lacey will never agree to play."

"I just think there has to be a better place," Aylie hedged, trying to think of an excuse that would get her out of going back into that forest.

"The decision's already been made, Aylie. The school approved it and the boys are already there setting up the course.

We can't back out on them now."

"I'll tell Lacey, but I can't guarantee she'll be willing to do it."

"Convince her, Aylie," Ren begged. "Please...do it for me."

Aylie rolled her eyes. "Lacey's not going to be happy about this."

"Thanks, Aylie!' Ren said, quickly hanging up the phone.

Aylie shook her head and finished getting dressed. After what happened with Ryder in the forest three days ago, she had been hoping to avoid it for a while. Apparently she was doomed to be forever reminded of what she couldn't understand or explain. She hadn't seen Ryder since he'd nearly ripped her head off in his panther-altered state, and she hadn't wanted to. His very existence now represented the impossible and the dangerous unknown—both of which seemed foreboding somehow. She only prayed they wouldn't run into him in the woods somewhere because she wasn't sure what she was going to do if they did.

Lacey was adamantly opposed to the idea of the tournament, just as Aylie had predicted. It took a lot of persuasion to get her to even agree to drive there, let alone play. She remained un-swayed in her resolve until they reached the Outpost and met up with the guys. The instant she laid eyes on Eli, she caved. The very next moment she was carrying a rifle full of paint balls and wearing enormous plastic goggles that would've horrified her fashion sensibilities to the core if she could've seen herself in a mirror.

Relieved that Lacey was no longer an obstacle, Aylie turned her attention to the tournament at hand. There were ten teams, each with their own 'home base,' which consisted of forts made from tree limbs, logs, and leafy branches. They were impressively constructed for having been built in only a few hours. They were spread out over a two-mile radius, giving the teams the ability to move around quite freely without being shot at close-range. There was plenty of cover from the dense trees and shrubs, and the tall underbrush was easy to manipulate, if necessary.

Aylie had played only once before, in a tournament like this one with her brother Lucas, but that had been near Silver Lake and not in a forest. This felt like a totally new experience and she was nervous for some reason. She tried to focus on Derek—he was their team captain and was giving everyone tips and pointers before launching into an all-out tactical strategy. She glanced around at the rest of the team. She was standing between Lacey and Ren, across from Derek, Eli, and Chance.

She was surprised to see Chance with the post-graduate boys instead of his hockey buddies. "How did you end up on this team?" Aylie asked him when they had been given their posts. "Why aren't you playing with Marcus and Kyle?"

"Derek asked me to be on his team almost a week ago," Chance replied, giving her a flawless, yet boyish smile. His perfectly styled blond hair was crushed beneath his paintball helmet, but his green eyes were un-obscured by the plastic goggles resting on top of his head. "Blake Kavanagh is playing with them instead."

"Don't forget your goggles," she reminded him, tapping the clear plastic mask covering her own eyes.

"Oh, thanks." He grinned, pulling the goggles down over his eyes as he crept toward his post several hundred yards away.

Aylie looked at the map Derek had given her. It was a hand-drawn sketch of the entire playing field. The spots each person had been assigned to cover were marked with personal initials. The drawing was very detailed and it wasn't hard for her to locate the area she had been assigned to. She maneuvered her way quickly through a patch of thick underbrush, along one of the dirt trails that followed a creek bed. A set of steps had been cut from the side of a dirt-covered hill, curving upward toward a manmade footbridge. There was an opening beneath the bridge on the opposite side, which provided her with a perfect view of the clearing, while still giving her cover. The sunlight was streaming through the trees, casting leafy shadows all around her.

It was very quiet as Aylie crouched down to fit into her spot beneath the bridge. She had checked the area for spiders first and was satisfied that nothing too large or creepy was lurking there. The opening was shallow, so there wasn't enough room for anything larger than a scary insect, anyway. She scanned the clearing in the distance for approaching threats. Far off, she heard the sound of a paintball rifle and shrieks of laughter, followed by the sounds of swearing and pounding feet. She was on the edge of the course, so she was unlikely to catch much of the action, which was fine with her. She wasn't really in the mood for anything intense.

After nearly forty-five minutes had passed without any excitement, Aylie's legs started to cramp. She crawled out of her hiding spot to stretch her stiff muscles and caught the unmistakable sound of a snapping branch close by. She whirled around, holding her rifle up to her shoulder blade, as she scanned the trees for the intruder. She couldn't see anyone within range, but some people had taken the tournament seriously enough to dress in camouflage. It wouldn't be impossible for someone to sneak up on her if they were able to blend in with the foliage. She glanced up at the sky to see what time of day it was getting to be. The sun was almost directly overhead.

It's almost noon already, she thought. I wonder if they've considered pausing this tournament for lunch?

Then she saw something dart through the trees up ahead. She couldn't see what it was, but it looked big. She couldn't tell whether it was a person or not. She squinted to see further into the trees on the other side of the clearing. A moment later she saw it again, but this time it was much closer, and it was unmistakably inhuman. Her heart pounded, but only for an instant, as she realized it couldn't possibly be Ryder. This creature was white. Pure white. It was far enough away that she was sure it wasn't something she needed to worry about...at least not yet.

As Aylie turned to crawl back into her hiding place, she felt someone grab her from behind, covering her mouth with their hand. She screamed in surprise, but the sound was muffled by her abductor's palm. The paintball helmet kept her from being able to see who it was, so she did the only thing she could think of and jabbed the culprit in the chest with her elbow as hard as she could. Her assailant stumbled backwards pulling her to the ground on top of him. Yanking an arm free, she ripped her helmet off. When she finally looked over her shoulder, Ryder was laughing with his arms still locked around her, pinning her to his chest.

She didn't know whether to feel angry or relieved. "What the heck are you DOING?" She cried. "You scared me to death."

Ryder grinned, releasing his hold on her so she could sit up. "Top secret strategy," he winked.

Aylie surveyed him skeptically. "Oh yeah? Where's your paintball gun, then?"

Ryder laughed. "I don't need such a primitive weapon, as you well know."

"You're not even part of this tournament, are you?"

"Maybe I am—maybe I'm not."

"If you're not playing then you shouldn't be here."

"You're in my neck of the woods, might I remind you," he said. "Literally."

"You don't own the entire forest," Aylie retorted, standing to her feet as she attempted to wipe the dirt from her knees.

Ryder looked up at her from his spot on the ground. "I didn't mean to scare you."

"Yeah right."

He grinned. "Okay, maybe I meant to scary you a little bit, but I wasn't trying to give you a heart attack."

Aylie heard a rustling sound behind her. Before she had time to react, someone shot her twice in the back and ran off, leaving her covered in blue paint. She was officially out of the game and hadn't gotten a single shot in on her opponent. Derek was going to give her a hard time about this and she wasn't looking forward to the teasing that would undoubtedly follow. "This is all your fault!" She accused, sounding more upset than she really was.

"I'll make it up to you, then." Ryder stood to his feet.

"How do you plan to do that?" She asked, turning her head to assess the paint splattered all over the back of her jeans. She couldn't see what the back of her jacket looked like, but she'd felt the hit, so she knew it was probably covered with paint as well.

"I'll take you back to my place and help you get the paint out of your clothes so no one will even know how close the shooter got."

"I can't leave in the middle of the tournament—my teammates would be furious."

"They won't even know you're gone. Besides, the tournament usually lasts till sundown. That's hours from now."

"What if they come looking for me?"

"They won't," he assured her. "I've seen them play for years."

Aylie raised an eyebrow. "You've watched them play for years? Nothing creepy about that."

Ryder rolled his eyes. "Not like that. This was the one school-related activity my brothers and I used to participate in."

Aylie felt bad for jumping to conclusions and looked at him apologetically.

"Do you want to get that paint off your clothes or what?" He asked, nodding toward the mansion.

Aylie looked up at the sky. Sundown seemed a long way off. Maybe Ryder was right. Maybe no one would even notice she was gone. "Okay." She agreed.

Ryder led her through the forest to the gravel road she'd taken with her mom when they'd visited the Mansion the week before. "How far is your house from here?" She asked.

"Only about two miles. We're more than half-way there."

That was a relief. She followed him down the long, winding road, doing her best to keep up with him. She still had questions to ask him, but she was trying to decide where to start first. She never knew what kind of mood he was in or how likely he would be to give her a straight answer, but she had to try. "So...that thing you did the other night...how do you do it?"

"That's a very vague question," he replied, without looking over his shoulder.

"You know what I mean."

"I suppose you're asking how I'm able to transition."

"Is that what it's called?"

"Changing from a human form to a genetically altered state is called transitioning."

Aylie furrowed her brows. "I thought it was called 'phasing,' or 'morphing,' or something like that."

Ryder laughed. "Maybe if you're watching a sci-fi movie."

"So how does it work?"

"It requires a certain genetic disposition—a chain of DNA capable of being split and rearranged into a very specific pattern."

Aylie was good at biology and physics, but they weren't her strongest subjects. "How do you force your DNA to split and rearrange like that?"

"Well, you have to have the genetic disposition, as I said, but it also requires an outside force of manipulation."

"Like what?"

"I'm not sure if you'd believe me if I told you."

Aylie rolled her eyes at him even though he couldn't see it. "Are you serious? I've already seen you transition into a savage panther and experienced your mind-reading skills. I think I can handle whatever explanation you have to offer."

"It requires the ability to harness the elements of another metaphysical dimension."

Aylie's brows pulled together in confusion. "Speak normal English, please."

"It requires magic."

"What?" She narrowed her eyes at him skeptically.

"Just what I said. The DNA is split and rearranged by pulling power into this dimension from a supernatural dimension. Most people just call it magic—it's a much more simplified explanation."

Aylie tried to wrap her brain around what he was saying. "So the panther I saw was some kind of optical illusion?"

"No." He said with exaggerated slowness. "The DNA is altered by a supernaturally derived source of power."

Aylie bit her bottom lip. Certainly Ryder wasn't trying to convince her that magic was a real thing. There must be a more scientific explanation behind what he was saying that wasn't registering. She could tell that he was getting annoyed with her lack of understanding, so she decided to let the subject go for now.

They were finally approaching the Mansion and the apprehension Aylie had felt when she'd last visited was beginning to return. She swallowed hard, remembering how lightheaded and dizzy she'd been inside the vault…the thickness of the air that had constricted her windpipe. She started to feel those same sensations again before they'd even reached the front door.

"Do you ever feel like it's hard to breathe inside the Mansion?" She asked, hesitating in the doorway.

Ryder reached for her hand to pull her through. "Every day."

Chapter Twelve

Ryder closed the heavy door behind them and ushered Aylie into the Great Hall. The butler appeared almost immediately and Ryder requested that he summon Bridgett to the hall right away. While they waited, he asked Aylie if she was hungry and gave instructions for the chef to prepare a light lunch as soon as possible.

Moments later, Bridgett entered the room. "You wanted to see me, sir?" She asked, looking up at him shyly.

"Yes. Would you please take Miss Bryant's clothes and see to it that all traces of paint are removed as quickly as possible?"

Bridget nodded. "What will she wear in the meantime, sir?"

Ryder was perplexed for a moment. "Wait here," he said, disappearing from the room. The only thing he could think to give her was a pair of his gym shorts with a drawstring that she could synch to prevent them from falling down. She might not like the idea, but it was better than walking around naked while she waited for her clothes to be cleaned. He returned with the shorts and gave them to Aylie. He watched the horrified expression cross her face as she realized his intentions, but she took the shorts and followed Bridgett silently out of the room.

"I'll be waiting here," he called after her, unable to hide his amusement.

When Aylie returned, she was dressed in the long-sleeved t-shirt she had been wearing underneath her paint-soiled jacket and the black gym shorts he had given her. They were extremely long and baggy, and he couldn't help chuckling at the look of chagrin on her face. "It's not that bad, Aylie."

She held up her hand to silence him, shaking her head.

"Alright, now that your clothes are being taken care of, I will try my best to answer your questions."

Aylie nodded in silent resignation, as he led her through the west wing corridor, at the end of which, was a long, spiraling staircase. He took each step with ease, forgetting how awkwardly narrow and steep they were for people who weren't used to climbing them everyday. It was dark and there were no railings. He was completely oblivious to the possible dangers of falling until he heard Aylie's gasp behind him. He whirled around just in time to catch her as she missed a step and slipped, nearly falling a full story to the stone floor below. He steadied her and waited for her to catch her breath. He felt her shiver. Whether from fear or cold he couldn't tell, but the look in her eyes when she glanced up at him stopped his heart for a second.

"Do you climb these stairs everyday?" She asked slightly winded.

"Yes, but you get used to them after eighteen years or so."

She shook her head. "I don't know if I could ever get used to taking my life into my hands like this on a regular basis."

Ryder smiled at the irony of her words. She was about to discover far worse dangers than stone staircases. He released her from his steadying grip and proceeded to lead her up the stairs. This time he slowed his pace, looking over his shoulder every few seconds to make sure that she was okay. When they had reached the door of his father's study, he pushed it open and signaled for her to enter ahead of him. Even though it was broad daylight outside, it was still hard to see inside the four walls of this room and he wanted to light a few oil lamps so they could see each other more clearly.

Then he proceeded to light a fire in the hearth so Aylie could warm herself. He pulled one of the wing-backed armchairs closer to the fire and motioned for her to sit down, which she did without protest. He walked over to his father's desk and retrieved the journal. He felt a spasm of fear at the idea of sharing something so precious and sacred with an outsider, but Aylie was the closest thing to a friend he had and if he couldn't trust her, whom could he trust? After all, she'd taken a blood oath and that was no small thing.

He sauntered over to the fireplace, journal in hand, and stood next to the hearth. She looked up at him expectantly, as she rubbed her hands together to soak in the heat from the dancing flames. "I know what you're waiting for," he said, gazing into the fire, "but there is no logical explanation."

She seemed to be formulating a reply. "So...you're asking me to believe that you have magical powers?"

"I'm not asking you to believe anything, I'm simply answering your questions."

Aylie leaned back in the chair, putting her hand to her forehead. "I want to understand this—I really do, but there has to be more to it than what you're telling me. There's no such thing as magic."

"The fact that you've never seen it before doesn't' mean it can't exist."

"Yes, but Ryder...magic?"

"How else would you account for my ability to transition into the panther that almost chewed your head off? What scientific argument could explain my ability to read your mind?"

Aylie shook her head slowly. He could see her brain fighting to find a more rational answer and watched as the battle in her mind raged, first one direction, then another. He could see the war between skepticism and childish belief behind her eyes and he was fascinated with the way her mind worked. She was both extremely logical and sincerely trusting at the same time. She wanted to believe him.

After several moments had passed, Aylie finally spoke. "Let's say for the sake of argument that I believe your theory," she said hesitantly. "Where does this magical power come from?"

Ryder was thoughtful. "That's a little complicated to explain."

Aylie let out a laugh. "How could anything be more complicated than what you've already told me?"

He looked down at the manuscript he held in his hands. "There are two possible sources—two bloodlines. They were once one and the same."

Aylie lifted an eyebrow. "I don't understand what you're saying."

Ryder took a deep breath, trying to figure out where to start. "It's an ancient magic that has been passed down through certain bloodlines for centuries. According to the legends of my ancestors, the magic originated from a single, powerful, immortal being—Ruardian, who had two sons. Both sons had different mothers and each inherited half of their father's supernatural abilities. The other half of their DNA was human—which made them demi-gods in their own right. The name of the oldest son was Rhydian. He was the rightful heir to his father's throne but he disappeared before he could be crowned king and was never heard from again. Some believe that his bloodline still lives on and that there are descendants alive who still have access to his powers. The younger son was named Edryd. He was jealous of Rhydian's power and claim to the throne and wanted the kingdom for himself. He murdered his father and took the throne by force, destroying the rest of Rhydian's bloodline to eliminate any future threat to his rule. He also invented dark magic—the very first druids came from his bloodline. My bloodline."

Aylie's eyes widened in shock. "You're a druid?"

Ryder shook his head. "Not by choice, but their ancient power flows through my veins."

"How many of your people are there?"

Ryder stared at the roaring flames in the fireplace hearth. "Thousands."

A knock sounded at the door. Bridgett came into the room, carrying a silver tray with several sandwiches and two steaming bowls of soup. She set the tray down on one of the coffee tables and went back to the silver cart in the hall to retrieve a ceramic teapot and two old fashioned teacups. There was an assortment of herbal teas on the silver tray from which to choose and she asked them both what they preferred.

Aylie murmured that anything would be fine, and Bridgett poured the steaming hot water over a bag of peppermint tea, bringing it to her on a matching saucer. She did the same for Ryder and quickly disappeared from the room, closing the door behind her. They sipped their tea in silence. Ryder didn't know what else to say. He was still debating whether or not to let her read his father's journal. He wasn't sure whether this would bring more clarity or greater confusion, the latter of which he feared. He set it down on the fireplace mantel and went over to the tray of food. He handed a sandwich to Aylie and took one for himself. They nibbled on them until they had both had their fill.

When Aylie found her voice again she was very calm. "Should I be afraid of you?" She asked, looking up at him imploringly.

Ryder shook his head. "You have nothing to fear from me, unless you know who's been murdering my family."

Aylie's forehead creased. "How could I possibly know who the murderer is if you don't?"

Ryder took another sip of his tea and set the cup down on the fireplace mantel. "Are you sure you're ready for this?"

"Just say it…whatever it is. I can handle it."

Ryder smiled. "I know you can, but I wanted to give you a chance to change your mind if you're ready to let all this go."

"No, I want to know the truth. You said it might affect my family."

Ryder nodded. "I have Edryd's blood in my veins—that's why

I'm able to transition into the panther you saw and it's how I'm able to read your mind."

Aylie nodded impatiently. "You already told me that."

Yes. But Aylie—how is it that you are able to read MY mind?

The horror on her face was unmistakable. Ryder saw her hands begin to shake as the implications of the question sank it. Her face turned pale and she looked like she might faint. He quickly went over to the silver tray Bridgett had left and poured her a fresh cup of hot tea, handing it to her. "Breathe, Aylie." He said, forcing her to take a sip.

She took a second and a third sip, staring wordlessly into the fire. Eventually, she set the cup down on the saucer in her lap. "So you're saying that I can read your mind because I'm a druid, too? That I have Edryd's blood in my veins, just like you?"

Ryder sat down in the chair beside her, inhaling the comforting scent of his father's pipe tobacco that still lingered in the chair's upholstery. "That's one possibility."

"What other possibility could there be?" She asked, unable to conceal her mild despair.

"You could be a Silver Vein."

"A what?" She leaned forward in her chair to study his face. He could feel the desperation in her gaze and felt helpless to offer relief.

"A Silver Vein...one of Rhydian's descendants."

"He was the older brother who went missing?"

"Yes. As I said before, some of my people believe his bloodline still exists, though I've never met anyone belonging to it."

"How can you tell which bloodline you belong to?" She asked, sounding hopeful.

"There are certain traits or characteristics that are common to each bloodline—specific 'powers,' or 'abilities,' if you prefer to call them that."

"What traits or abilities does a Silver Vein have?"

Ryder shook his head. "That's what I'm still trying to figure out. I know all about Edryd's bloodline, but very little about Rhydian's. I do know, however, that his followers have one defining physical characteristic—the central vein in the right forearm is rumored to be silver."

Aylie looked down at the teacup in her lap. "Hence the name, 'Silver Vein.'"

"Exactly."

"That's why you kept trying to study my wrist," she murmured. "It all makes sense now."

"Does it?" Ryder let out an awkward laugh. "Good. I was afraid I was scaring you off with all this talk of magic and ancient bloodlines."

Aylie laughed nervously. "I wouldn't rule out that conclusion just yet."

Ryder voiced the thought she was afraid to speak aloud. "You're hoping that you belong to Rhydian's bloodline and not mine."

Aylie looked away from him guiltily.

"That would make us blood enemies," he murmured.

"Would you try to kill me?" She asked, staring into the fire to avoid eye contact.

"Of course not. I'm not even part of Edryd's Order. My family defected almost a century ago."

"Is that what's causing all of the unexplainable deaths?"

Ryder smiled sadly. "I think it's safe to assume they didn't appreciate it."

"Isn't there someone you can ask for help?"

"Who would believe me?" He muttered, standing to his feet. He paced back and forth in front of the fireplace.

"This is a nightmare…a literal nightmare." She murmured shaking her head in disbelief. "Aren't you afraid that you'll be next?"

"Of course, but there's nothing I can do about it. I don't even know who's responsible for it."

Another knock came at the door and Bridgett entered again, this time carrying Aylie's freshly cleaned clothes. Ryder thanked the maid and took them, giving the jeans and jacket to Aylie so she could change out of the shorts he had loaned her. When she was once again dressed in her own clothes, she seemed uncharacteristically calm and resigned. "I think its time for me to return to my post," she announced, "but I want to talk more about this later."

Ryder nodded and agreed to take her back to the place where he'd found her in Silvervane Forest. They walked shoulder to shoulder along the winding, gravel road, back to her hiding spot under the wooden footbridge. To the place where her friends were waiting for her and the only realities she had to acknowledge were those of high school and the simple life of an innocent, teenage girl. He left her in the safe and predictable world of normal and hoped that somehow she could stay there a little bit longer.

CHAPTER THIRTEEN

When they had reached the perimeter of the paintball course, Aylie convinced Ryder to let her walk the rest of the way alone. She was extremely glad that she had, because her team was waiting there for her when she arrived and they weren't very pleased that she'd vanished. They had noticed she was missing about twenty minutes before she'd reappeared and they were about to contact the park rangers to send out a search team.

"Oh my gosh, Aylie!" Lacey cried. "Where were you? We thought something terrible had happened!" She looked like she was about to cry. She was covered in splotches of paint, from her kneecaps to her stomach, but she didn't seem to care at the moment.

"Where did you go?" Derek demanded, looking for traces of paint that might explain why she hadn't been at her post.

Aylie had to think fast. "I had to pee but I didn't know where the nearest outhouse was. I had to make sure I was far enough away that no one could see me."

"You must've walked quite a distance," Kyle mumbled, narrowing his eyes suspiciously. "You were gone for more than twenty minutes—longest piss I've ever heard of."

Ren giggled.

"Are you alright?" Eli asked, searching her face. He seemed less irritated and more concerned for her wellbeing than the others, with the exception of Lacey.

"Of course. Why wouldn't I be?" She asked, trying to appear normal. It's not like she'd just discovered that she might have the blood of a powerful, ancient druid sorcerer running through her veins or anything.

Eli didn't seem convinced. "You only left long enough to relieve yourself?"

Aylie nodded. She felt like such a liar that she couldn't look him in the eyes. She didn't like to deceive people, but she had to keep Ryder's secret safe. The secret that could very well end up being her own.

"I'm glad you're okay," Ren said, squeezing her shoulders.

"We lost, in case you were wondering," Kyle added, giving her a withering look.

"Did we lose because of me?" She asked, feeling guiltier than before.

"Not at all," Chance piped up. "Kyle's just a sore loser."

"Well now that the crisis has been averted, I say we all go out for ice cream!" Lacey suggested. "Derek and I can drive."

They agreed to meet at the Old Fashioned Ice Cream Shop downtown. It was the only ice cream place within a thirty-mile radius of Silvervane and a favorite off-campus hangout spot. It would probably be insanely busy on a Saturday evening, but it was still a fun place to mingle outside of school. Aylie tried to join in the narratives as everyone took turns sharing their dramatic paintball tales, but her mind was still preoccupied with everything Ryder had told her. She couldn't seem to make herself care about their paint-related woes, and no one seemed to notice how detached she was from the conversation…except for Eli.

Just before they left the ice cream shop, Aylie excused herself to use the ladies room—this time for real. She'd been holding it for more than an hour and it gave her the perfect excuse to skip her turn and avoid making up a story that was hardly believable. When she came out again, Eli was standing just outside waiting for the men's room. He put his hand on her shoulder as she passed by.

"Let me know when you want to talk about it," he said before disappearing into the restroom.

Aylie was a little caught off guard by his perceptiveness. It was almost like he knew where she'd been and who she'd been with. It wasn't possible, of course—no one even knew that she and Ryder were friends. Besides, Eli hadn't been stationed anywhere near the road when they'd walked to the Mansion, so he couldn't have seen where she'd gone. The feeling was strong, regardless, and she was relieved when Lacey finally dropped her off at the ranch. She fell asleep with Eli's words playing over and over in her mind until the lines between reality and her subconscious blurred together.

When Aylie opened her eyes she was standing in the forest again holding her paintball gun. The sun was still shining brightly overhead and she was waiting impatiently for something to come along. A person. A rabbit. A squirrel. Anything. She was so bored she could hardly stand it. Off in the distance she saw something moving back and forth through the trees. She squinted to see what it was. She couldn't tell from this far away, but it was large and white and familiar. She'd seen this animal somewhere before.

As she strained her eyes to identify it, someone grabbed her from behind, covering her mouth with their hand. She cried out, struggling to break free. Suddenly she realized it was Ryder Payne and her heart skipped a beat. She managed to free one of her arms and ripped the paintball helmet off so she could see his face. She whirled around with anticipation to wrap her arms around his neck and froze in shock. It wasn't Ryder.

It was Eli. His eyes were so full of compassion and concern that it caught her off guard. She stumbled backwards out of his arms.

"Are you sure you know what you're doing?" He asked, looking deeply into her eyes with both of his bright blue ones.

"Don't worry about me," she said, feeling awkward that she'd mistaken him for Ryder.

"Don't forget why you're doing this." He said solemnly.

"What do you mean?"

"It's time to take back what belongs to you."

"What are you talking about?" She asked, feeling more and more confused by the minute.

"Find me," he said. Then he took off running into the trees, leaving Aylie standing in the clearing with the paintball gun at her feet. She was determined to find out what was going on, so she ran after him. Forgetting about the paintball tournament entirely, she sprinted deeper and deeper into the forest. Every once in a while, she caught glimpses of him dodging branches and darting through the underbrush, but no matter how hard she ran, she couldn't seem to catch up with him. He was further away than ever and she was getting tired. She'd given no thought to how she was going to find her way back to the paintball course. She didn't know the forest well enough to navigate it without getting lost.

She stopped by a stream to catch her breath. The water looked cool and refreshing as she knelt down to splash some on her face. The pool was so clear that she could see her reflection in it. As she gazed into it, she began to feel it pulling at her to take a drink. It occurred to her then that she was extremely thirsty, but she had a strange feeling it wasn't safe to drink. There could be any number of germs or deadly organisms in this water that weren't visible to the naked eye. But the longer she gazed into it, the thirstier she became. She cupped her hands and lowered them into the water.

It's almost impossible to resist once you've felt its power, came a strangely familiar voice.

Startled, Aylie jerked back, letting the water slip through her fingers. There, standing on the other side of the stream, was the white lion. His eyes were even bluer than before...she remembered him now. She stared at him, wide-eyed and full of awe. Instantly she felt ashamed. "I wasn't even thirsty until I noticed how clean and clear it looked." She said, lowering her eyes. "I knew I shouldn't drink it."

Once your eyes have been opened, you begin to see things you didn't know existed, the lion said. It can be hard to know what is right and what is wrong.

Aylie allowed herself to look up at him from beneath her long lashes. He wasn't angry. His eyes were full of understanding. He knew exactly why she'd been tempted to drink the water.

You knew, for example, that it was okay to use the water to cool yourself, but you felt something telling you not to drink it. He continued.

Aylie nodded.

Look at the water again.

When she turned her eyes back to the stream again, it was dark and murky, like mud mixed with blood. Flies came up out of the water, drawn to its invisible stench. She wrinkled her nose, pushing herself away from the bank.

You knew something was wrong with the water even though you couldn't see it—that's because I gave you an intuition.

"But I didn't hear you say anything," she protested, a little confused.

In the core of your being, you have a spirit, the lion explained gently. You can hear the sound of my voice in your spirit. Sometimes it sounds like an intuition—a strong feeling or impression that you can't seem to shake. At other times, I give you dreams or pictures in your mind that stay with you long after you wake. The ones you can't stop thinking about. He took a step closer, looking down into the murky water of the stream. But if you ignore my warnings long enough, you'll stop hearing them altogether. You will no longer know be able to tell the difference between what is safe and what is not.

Aylie hung her head. "I shouldn't have touched the water at all."

The water itself is not bad, the lion replied, his voice soothing and gentle. You were not wrong to cool yourself with it. Your mistake was allowing your desire for it to become so strong that it overruled your better judgment—that is where most people go wrong.

"I'm sorry," Aylie murmured. The moment she said the words, she felt lighter. Freer. She felt as if he was smiling at her. She looked at him, full of gratitude. "What is your name?"

Ruah.

All at once, the ground beneath them began to quake. Aylie's body trembled, as the rumbling of rocks and trees stirred the forest around her, getting louder and louder. The sound of a mighty waterfall filled her eardrums until she could not bear it any longer. Ruah's name echoed over and over in the wind, as she buried her head in her hands.

Aylie jolted awake in her bed. To say that she was a little freaked out by the dream was an understatement. She felt around on her nightstand for her journal and clicked on the lamp by her bed so she could see. She remembered the first part of the dream, when she'd whirled around to find Eli behind her instead of Ryder. What was it he'd said to her?

She flipped through the pages of her journal until she found the previous dream she'd had about the white lion and compared what he'd said to her in that dream with the one she'd just had. Both Eli and the white lion had told her to take back what belonged to her. They both had piercing blue eyes, the same compassionate gaze....

Aylie rubbed her temples. She must be seriously affected right now to be comparing a real human being with a mythical creature from a dream. Could it be just a freaky coincidence? And what was the deal with the water in the stream? Why had it felt so wrong to drink it? She remembered the lion's name—Ruah. She recalled how the earthquake had felt beneath her feet. It had all seemed so real. It was almost as if she could feel her bed shaking underneath her at the memory of it.

Aylie raked her fingers through her straight, blond hair. What was happening to her? She wanted to dismiss the dreams...forget about them entirely. They were probably just stress dreams, anyway. The excitement of the paintball tournament mixed with impressions of Eli's concern coming out in her subconscious while she slept. Yet somehow, they felt like a warning. She didn't like the feeling, but she couldn't seem to shake it, either. There was something very pure in the lion's eyes in the dreams she'd had, and when she recalled the way Eli had looked at her outside the restrooms at the ice cream shop, she felt sure it had been the same look.

Maybe he really did know something. Not just about where she'd gone, but about Edryd's Order. Maybe he knew something that could help Ryder or prevent him from being their next victim. If nothing else, maybe he could tell her something about her own ancestry that would help her figure out which side she was supposed to be on. That, at least, would be a relief. She was sworn to secrecy about Ryder's identity and his connection with Edryd's Order, but she'd made no promises concerning her own personal background. She promised herself that she'd talk to Eli about it if the opportunity presented itself again. Eventually she drifted off to sleep, and this time it was blissfully uninterrupted.

CHAPTER FOURTEEN

Aylie sat on the iron park bench next to Ren, lacing up her ice skates. Figure skating was one of her favorite pastimes and she'd taken lessons since she was five. It had become a yearly tradition for her and the girls to go ice-skating at Silvervane's open-air rink on the last day of fall break and she could feel the anticipation mounting in the early December air.

Lacey plopped down on the other side of her, skates already perfectly laced. She crossed her ankles daintily, leaning back against the bench to wait for both of them to finish. "I think I might ask Marcus to the Winter Ball," she announced, sounding pleased with herself.

"Really?" Ren glanced sideways at Aylie, who was just finishing up the bow on her second skate.

Aylie looked up in surprise. "Are you interested in him?"

Lacey shrugged. "I'm not sure yet. He's funny and

charming…which you already know. And he's ridiculously attractive, so I'm considering it."

Aylie stood to her feet to make sure her skates were laced tight enough to provide sufficient ankle support. She rolled her ankles to the right and then the left and was satisfied.

"What do you think about that?" Ren asked, as Lacey sailed ahead of them on the ice.

"I don't know yet. I would never have pictured the two of them together."

"But how do you feel about the idea of Lacey having a thing for your ex-boyfriend?"

Aylie shrugged. "We broke up seven months ago, so I feel like he's fair game at this point."

"So you're totally over him, then?" Ren probed.

"I still care about him, but the break-up was a mutual decision. We're still good friends, we just want different things after high school. He wants a girl to carry on his arm, someone to cheer him on and make him feel like he's the center of their universe."

Ren snorted in disgust.

"He's a really good guy, Ren—he deserves to have what he wants. I liked him a lot, but I didn't want to make him the center of my universe. And I certainly don't want to follow him to the college that offers him the best hockey scholarship."

"That's very wise," Ren noted. "But are you ready for him to date someone else?"

"It wouldn't be fair of me to expect him to stay single when I'm not willing to give him the kind of commitment he's looking for. I have no choice but to be ready."

"Yeah…but with Lacey? She's your best friend."

"She's one of my best friends," Aylie corrected, smiling sideways at her as they took the curve. "And so is Marcus. I can't really see them working out, but I'd be happy for them if it did."

"That's very generous of you," Ren squeezed her hand and sprinted to catch up with Lacey.

Aylie skated by herself for a few minutes, taking each turn with ease, crossing one foot over the other and stopping to practice her spins and turns every now and then.

"You've always been a natural," said a familiar voice from behind.

Aylie smiled as Marcus skated up beside her. "Speak of the devil."

"Really? You were talking about me?"

Aylie laughed. "About you and Lacey, actually."

"Oh," Marcus smiled. "That. I'm still not sure about that."

"Well you probably should figure it out because Lacey is certainly thinking about it."

"What did she say?"

Aylie smiled. "My lips are sealed."

He grinned. Aylie had always loved his smile. It was the first thing she had noticed about Marcus when she'd met him in ninth grade. They'd dated for almost two years and had been pretty serious, up until seven months ago, when they'd realized there probably wasn't a future for them together. It had been a hard break-up for both of them, but time and a little space had made things easier.

"Are you okay with that?" He asked, looking sideways at her.

"Of course. Lacey is one of my best friends and so are you."

He nodded. "I'm still not sure if I feel that way about her but I wanted to know what you thought."

"You don't need my permission to date someone, Marcus."

"I know, but you're one of my best friends, too. Your opinion matters to me and I care about how that might affect our friendship."

"No worries," Aylie said. She looked around the rink. "Are you guys practicing here today?"

"Unofficially," he said, with a mischievous grin. "It's more like a pick-up game. Kyle, Chance, and Blake are all here. I don't know if anyone else is coming or not."

"Good luck then," Aylie said, punching him playfully in the shoulder. She sailed toward the other side of the rink to catch up with Lacey and Ren.

"Did you tell Marcus that I was planning to ask him to the

Winter Ball?" Lacey asked, the moment they were skating side by side.

"Of course not," Aylie assured her.

"Did he say anything about me?" She asked, looking anxious.

Aylie tried to think of how to respond without hurting Lacey's feelings. "He said he's trying to decide how he feels right now."

"So he's thinking about me, then?"

Aylie laughed. "I guess he is."

Lacey smiled, satisfied. "But what about you, Aylie? If I ask Marcus to the ball, who will you ask? You've always gone with him."

"I honestly haven't given it any thought," Aylie murmured.

"Oh, I know...you should ask Derek's friend. What's his name, Eli? That boy is FINE."

Aylie laughed out loud. "I think someone else might be planning to ask him," she hedged, trying not to glance in Ren's direction.

"Really, who?"

Ren blushed but didn't say anything.

"Never mind. Have you started to look for a dress yet?" Aylie knew talking about clothes was the fastest way to turn Lacey's attention away from something else. Ren shot her a grateful glance, as they made several more laps around the rink listening to Lacey's idea for her dress and plans for an after party.

After a couple of hours, their feet started to hurt and the girls decided it was time for lunch. Ren and Lacey turned in their skates, but Aylie always brought her own. She tied the strings together, putting rubber covers over the sharp blades. Then they piled into Lacey's sedan and drove to a small eatery called the Brown Bear Cafe. It was a cute and rustic little place, offering a full breakfast and lunch menu, along with various teas and specialty coffees. It closed at two O'clock in the afternoon, so the lunch crowd was always big. It took them nearly an hour to get their food, but it was worth it.

The hockey boys showed up just before they left, giving Aylie a chance to see Lacey and Marcus in action. It was a little weird at first, but she tried her best to get used to it. She could tell Lacey liked him a lot and wondered how long it had been that way. After they had eaten, Lacey offered to drive Ren back to her dorm and Aylie asked to be dropped off there as well. Lacey looked a little disappointed that she wasn't going to get a chance to talk to her about Marcus on the way to the ranch, but she seemed to recover by the time they climbed out of the car in front of the dorms at Silvervane Prep.

Ren waited until Lacey's car was out of sight before launching into a full-on interrogation. "Okay, what's up?" She asked, putting her hands on her hips.

"What do you mean? I just felt like walking home." Aylie answered matter-of-factly.

"I know you enjoy long walks and all, but that's not what this is about."

"What is it about, then?" Aylie asked, lifting an eyebrow.

"Was it hard seeing Marcus and Lacey together?"

Aylie shook her head. "It was strange, but I'll get used to it."

"I have another theory, then." Ren declared with a shrewd smile.

Aylie laughed. "Well?"

"First of all, you disappeared from the paintball tournament and were gone for hours." Aylie tried to protest but Ren held up her hand. "Don't try to deny it, Aylie. I checked your area at least three times while you were gone, so I know you didn't just leave to go pee. Secondly, you're somehow okay with the idea of Lacey dating the boy you were in love with for two years, which means you've suddenly gotten over him somehow."

Aylie was starting to hate how perceptive her friend was. What else had she noticed? "You didn't say anything to the others, though...about how long I was gone?"

"Of course not. I figured if you wanted to keep it a secret, there must be a reason."

Aylie smiled. "Thank you."

"But I can only think of one place you might've gone for that length of time in the middle of the woods."

Aylie felt her heart stop.

"Are you seeing Ryder Payne?" Ren asked pointedly. There was no mistaking the frightened and slightly terrified look on her sweet face.

"Depends on what you mean by, 'seeing.' "

"Are you secretly dating him?"

"No, not at all. It's nothing like that. We're just…friends."

Ren frowned. "So you two have been hanging out, then?"

Aylie knew she had to choose her words very carefully. She didn't want to lie but she didn't want to give anything away either. "Not exactly. We've run into each other outside of school a couple of times, that's all."

"Where have you run into him?" She probed.

Aylie sighed. "He's walked me home once or twice." It wasn't the whole truth, but it wasn't a lie, either.

Ren was silent for a moment. "Aylie, I know you're practically an adult and you're really smart, so I'm sure you're being cautious…."

"I am."

Ren frowned slightly. "I'm just wondering if he's the best person to be hanging out with right now, given the circumstances with his family and the murder investigation."

"He's innocent."

"But how can you be sure?"

The look of concern in Ren's eyes was so sincere and endearing that Aylie couldn't lie to her. "He thinks he might know who's responsible for the murders."

"Who is it?"

"I can't say. I gave him my word."

Ren's frown deepened. "Aylie, you don't know anything about this guy. What if there's more to the story than he's telling you?"

"I know a lot about him, actually."

"What has he told you?"

Aylie put her hand on Ren's shoulder reassuringly. "Don't worry, it's going to be fine." She promised to call in the morning and started to walk away before Ren could argue with her further. She felt bad for leaving her friend in the dark, but it couldn't be helped. She had given Ryder her word that she wouldn't tell anyone his secrets and she intended to keep that promise no matter what.

Chapter Fifteen

Aylie walked toward the ranch with her ice skates slung over her shoulder. It was a gorgeous, sunny day and she felt hopeful somehow. In spite of the shocking things Ryder had told her about her possible ancestry and the news that her ex-boyfriend was moving on with her best friend, she felt like something extraordinary was about to happen. She didn't know what it was, but she felt expectant. Her conversation with Ren had made her aware that her actions were being watched much more closely than she thought. It was lucky for her that Ren was intuitive enough not to bring it up in front of everyone else.

Aylie was going to have to be more careful from now on.
She found herself wishing there was a way she could bring Ryder into her circle of friends so that things didn't have to be so complicated. It would be so much easier to spend time with him if it weren't such a huge secret. If only her friends could see past the gossip and rumors concerning his father's murder. If she could somehow find a way to prove his innocence, maybe they would

be more accepting.

She chewed on her bottom lip. Ren's conjecture about her feelings for Ryder was more accurate than she would've liked to admit. She had done her best not to let infatuation for him cloud her judgment, but she couldn't eliminate her feelings for him entirely. In fact, they seemed to be growing stronger with each passing day. Every secret they shared and every moment they spent together seemed more significant than the last.

Aylie sighed. She really needed someone to talk to about all of this, but she felt trapped by all the secrecy. It seemed the closer she got to Ryder, the further from her friends she was becoming. It didn't seem right not to tell them what she had discovered—about herself and Ryder, but what other choice did she have? They probably wouldn't believe her, anyway. She hardly believed it herself; cursed bloodlines…magical powers…ancient druids…it was preposterous.

"You look deep in thought."

Aylie started. Her hand flew to her heart as she turned to face him. "Can you find a less startling way to get my attention next time?" She asked, forcing her breathing to regulate.

"I could, but it wouldn't be as enjoyable," Ryder said with a roguish grin.

Aylie rolled her eyes. "Stalking innocent animals this afternoon?"

Ryder shook his head. "No, I've decided to give that up for a while. I just felt like a walk and you happened along just at the right time."

"Lucky me."

He studied the side of her face. "How are you doing with…everything? I haven't seen you since I told you about the bloodline thing the other day."

"I haven't said anything to anyone, if that's what you're worried about."

"I wasn't worried. Besides, I'd know if you betrayed me."

Aylie raised an eyebrow. "How?"

He held up his hand, revealing a tiny scar in the fleshly part of his palm. "Blood oath, remember?"

Aylie nodded. "I don't see how that ensures my secrecy, but whatever."

Ryder shot her a look. "I assure you it's quite effective."

"I'll take your word for it."

Ryder chuckled. "We're just getting started."

Aylie stopped short. "What does that mean?"

"We have to figure out whose bloodline you belong to."

"How?"

"I've written a letter to my uncle Alexander. He and my cousins live somewhere in England. I used to visit every summer when I was a boy, but I haven't heard from them in years. They're the only relatives I have left, as far as I know. I'm hoping he'll agree to come for a visit during the holidays. He knows a lot about my…our background."

"Is he a…druid? I mean, one of them?" Aylie tried to make her voice sound as neutral as possible.

"Of course not. I'd be dead already if he was."

Aylie let out a slow breath. "Wow, they take the whole defection thing really seriously."

Ryder nodded. They had arrived at the pasture gate, but he hesitated. "Are your parents expecting you back at a certain time?" He asked.

Aylie shook her head. "They know I was planning to spend the day with my friends."

He looked at her curiously. "Why did you decide to come home so early? It's not even three O'clock yet."

Aylie looked away. "I don't know, I guess I just needed some time to think."

He grabbed her hand, suddenly pulling her in a different direction. "I hope you're done thinking because I want to show you something."

Aylie let him drag her away. She was secretly pleased that he wanted to spend more time with her, even though she had no idea where he was taking her. She'd learned that it was better not to ask questions when it came to Ryder Payne. He let go of her hand when they reached the forest so he could push through the maze of trees, vines, and thorny brush. He held them aside for her to pass through when they were too near the trail or likely to cause injury. Twice, he took her hand to help her over logs that had fallen across the path.

Aylie couldn't help noticing how much more caring and thoughtful Ryder was now than he had been when they'd first met. His mannerisms and behavior toward her had completely changed. And he'd held her hand at least three times now—never for long, but always longer than necessary. She wondered if it was something he was doing consciously or if it was just an impulsive behavior. She noted the confident way he walked, with his shoulders back and head held high…perfect posture. His messy brown hair smelled like mint leaves and mountain air, she could smell it wafting toward her in the breeze. Realizing that her mind was straying from anything helpful, Aylie mentally reeled herself back in. She forced herself to forget the sensation of his warm, strong hand when it swallowed hers and the way his presence made her feel completely safe. She attempted to redirect her thoughts. Ryder wasn't a big talker, so it was up to her to start the conversation if she didn't want to end up getting lost in her mind again. "How much further are we walking?"

"Not too far. Less than a mile from here."

"So we're not going to the Mansion?"

Ryder shook his head. "I'm taking you to one of my special spots."

Aylie felt her heart beat faster. She told herself not to read too much into it. Just because he wanted to take her to one of his favorite places didn't mean he had feelings for her. He was just being the friend she needed right now and she had to be smart about this. Getting too attached now would only make things harder later. Focus, she told herself. He's just a friend.

The trail dead-ended into an iron gate with a sign posted that said, DO NOT PASS THIS POINT - DANGER AHEAD. Ryder didn't even hesitate. He sailed right over the gate with one, long-legged stride.

Aylie stared at him with her mouth gaping. "What are you doing?"

"What does it look like I'm doing?" He reached for her hand.

Aylie hesitated. "The sign says there's danger ahead."

Ryder looked at her dubiously. "Seriously, Aylie? What could be more dangerous than me?"

She sighed. He had a good point. She looked at his outstretched hand and took it hesitantly. Not because she was afraid, but because she really wanted to hold his hand and she knew she shouldn't be so eager. He helped her over the gate and then guided her down a steep incline, steadying her until they reached the bottom. Now they were practically standing on the edge of a cliff, looking down over a ravine floor covered in boulders, hundreds of feet below. A massive waterfall jutted out from the ravine wall across from them, casting a misty rainbow over the canyon.

Aylie gasped. It was the most beautiful place she'd ever seen. She had no idea there were waterfalls like this in Silvervane. She wanted to climb down into the canyon and see it up close, but she knew it was too dangerous. She stood there looking out over it all in awe, completely forgetting for a moment that Ryder was standing beside her.

"Pretty amazing, isn't it?"

Aylie nodded, speechless. "How did you find this place?"

"My family has lived here for more than five generations. There was a time when we practically owned this entire forest."

Aylie tore her eyes away from the waterfall to read his facial expression. There was a mixture of pride and sadness in his eyes as he looked out over the canyon. She knew she was getting to see a side of him that no one apart from his family had ever seen before and she felt the sacredness of the moment in every fiber of her being. "And yet you want to leave it all behind," she murmured, almost to herself. She felt his gaze shift to her face, but she didn't dare meet his eyes. She knew he would be able to see right through her and she didn't want to feel exposed.

"Does that make you sad?" He asked, his gaze unwavering.

Aylie debated whether or not to answer his question. If she were honest, he'd know how she felt about him. If she lied, he'd probably be able to sense it. If she didn't give him an answer at all, he might just try to read her mind anyway. It was a no-win situation. "I'm sad that you're losing everything you loved because of a curse you have no control over," she answered diplomatically.

A gentle breeze stirred the air around them, blowing strands of her blond hair across her face. To her surprise, Ryder reached out and touched a strand. He rubbed it gently between his thumb and forefinger, before tucking it behind her ear. Aylie felt her heart accelerate, her cheeks flushing against her will. She turned away from him and looked down over the edge of the cliff. There was a steep decline of jagged rocks leading down to the bottom of the canyon in a zigzag pattern. It looked treacherous, but she wondered if it might be possible to make it to the bottom if she took her time and paced herself.

She felt Ryder's shoulder brush against hers, as she stood there contemplating her options. Even the smallest contact with him sent her heart fluttering and she hated how vulnerable it made her feel. She had to be stronger. She had to protect her heart. She had to remind herself that he was just a friend who would be leaving soon. But then he reached out and took her hand, this time for no apparent reason at all. There were no logs to climb over, no tree branches to dodge, and no gates to scale. She struggled to keep her mind from racing as he laced his fingers through hers, his palm pressing into hers.

Suddenly she wanted to cry. Being with Ryder felt like waking up for the first time. Everything inside of her came alive when she was near him. He made her brave and fearless. He understood her in a way that no one else ever had. She wanted to be with him like this forever—hand in hand, facing the uncertainties of the future together.

But it could never happen. He was only teasing her.

It's going to be okay, Aylie, his voice resonated in her mind.

It's so easy for you to say that, she argued. You're the one leaving.

I didn't think I had a reason to stay.

Aylie forced back the tears that were threatening to spill down her cheeks as she pulled her hand away from him. "I want to go home."

CHAPTER SIXTEEN

Ryder lay awake in his bed thinking about Aylie. He hadn't meant to overhear her thoughts as they'd stood side by side looking down at the waterfall together. He'd been completely caught off guard by the onslaught of emotions she'd unknowingly disclosed. Up until that moment, he'd had no idea of her true feelings for him and he felt guilty that he'd invaded her privacy by reading her mind. She'd gotten so quiet all of a sudden that he'd been curious to know what she was thinking about.

Hearing the thoughts in her head made him question his own feelings. He had no experience with the emotions or sentiments of love, apart from the affection he had for his deceased family members. He couldn't deny his attraction to Aylie, but he hadn't allowed himself to entertain anything more than friendship or gratitude toward her. Did he feel more for? He enjoyed being with her—she had been a source of strength and encouragement to him over the past several weeks. He was happy to have someone to share his secrets with and grateful that someone understood him, on some level. He had reached for her hand to comfort her when he'd realized how upset she was, but he wasn't entirely sure that had been his only motivation for doing it, now that he really thought about it.

So maybe he did feel more than just friendship, but he wasn't ready to call it love. Aylie intrigued him, by the way she'd responded when he'd turned into a crazed panther and had nearly taken her head off. She'd been so calm and rational, not at all like a girl of seventeen would normally react to something so insane and otherworldly. She believed there was goodness inside of him, in spite of the evil she knew he was capable of. She'd seen him transition and knew about his tainted blood, and yet she insisted he was innocent. She trusted him almost completely and her faith in him made him want to be a better person.

And yet there was a part of him that resisted her. Caring for Aylie meant opening up his heart to the possibility of being hurt yet again. If something were to happen to her he didn't know how he could bear it. He couldn't even finish the thought. The very possibility of her being mixed up in his fate made his blood boil. He couldn't allow anything to happen to her—not while he was alive and breathing. Admittedly, it seemed like there was very little he could do if he was the Order's next target, but he swore to himself that he'd find a way to keep Aylie safe, no matter what.

He continued to toss and turn until he finally drifted into a troubled sleep. The respite was short-lived when he awoke again two hours later to a strange sound in the hallway just outside his door. He lay completely still, listening to the sound of approaching footsteps. He had hoped at first that it might be the butler or a maid, but the person in question sounded as if they were stumbling around, unsure of where they were going. That could only mean an intruder had found his way into the Mansion. If it was someone from Edyrd's Order, Ryder wasn't exactly prepared to fight, but perhaps transitioning would give him an advantage if he were able to change before the intruder reached his door. He slid noiselessly from his bed and went over to his dresser to retrieve his ring.

Before he was able to slip it onto his finger, the prowler was at his door. Ryder grabbed one of the antique swords his father had mounted on his bedroom wall and crept over to stand behind it. As the doorknob slowly began to turn, he pulled the sword back, poising to strike as soon as his attacker was visible. The door creaked open slowly, revealing a pair of feminine bare feet. Ryder's eyes followed the pair of small feet to the dainty, white ankles and up the thin, bare skin of Aylie Bryant's legs. She was standing in his doorway, dressed in nothing but a long nightshirt. She appeared to be completely unconscious.

Ryder stepped back in shock and allowed her to enter. She walked right past him; unaware of the sharp blade he'd been prepared to slit her throat with. She drifted over to his fireplace and stopped right in front of it. She stood there for a moment, unmoving, as if she were deliberating something. Then she reached up to feel around on the cold, stone mantel. He held his breath as her hand stopped, resting on an ornately carved wooden box his father had given him for his sixteenth birthday. She lifted the lid and reached inside; withdrawing the dagger his father had presented to him the day he'd received the box. It was the same dagger his father had been murdered with, only he'd switched it out with a different one before the police chief had arrived that tragic morning. Now Aylie brought it down to eye level, gazed at it, and collapsed onto the cold, stone floor.

Ryder rushed over to her, unsure of what to do. If he woke her now she would have no idea where she was and might panic past the point of consolation. But if he left her where she fell, there's no telling what condition she'd be in when she finally awoke. He couldn't tell how hard she'd hit her head and he wasn't willing to take chances if there was the slightest possibility that she might have a concussion. He braced himself for the hysteria he knew was most likely coming and touched her gently on the arm. "Aylie," he said her name quietly. "Wake up."

She didn't open her eyes at first, and he felt his heart begin to sink as he struggled to wake her from her deep sleep. He shook her gently, saying her name louder and louder. Finally her eyelids fluttered and she slowly opened her eyes. "Ryder?" She gazed up at him, clearly confused as to why he was kneeling over her.

"Aylie." He breathed a sigh of relief. "You were sleep-walking."

"Sleep-walking?" Her eyes darted around the dark interior of his room, taking in the unfamiliarity of it as coherence began to return. She sat up, panic filling her eyes. She looked down at her half-naked body and her cheeks flushed crimson by the glow of the firelight. She was still holding the dagger in her right hand and dropped it on the floor in horror. "How did I get here?" She cried.

"I don't know," he stared at her in wide-eyed disbelief. "I heard someone stumbling around in the hall and I thought…." he looked at her apologetically. "I thought you were one of Edryd's Order coming for me."

Aylie tried to stand to her feet but lost her balance and landed on her butt. "Ouch," she felt a lump on the back of her head.

"I was afraid you might have a concussion, that's why I decided to wake you." Ryder stood to his feet. "I'll get some Advil, I think I have some in my medicine cabinet." He found the bottle of pain medicine and rushed back to the room. He usually always kept a glass of water on his nightstand and he reached for it now so that Aylie could take the pills he handed her. He watched as she swallowed them one at a time, washing them down with tiny gulps of water. She handed back the glass and thanked him. She looked around the room awkwardly.

"I'm so sorry," she murmured. "I have no idea what happened."

Ryder shook his head. "We can talk about that tomorrow. Right now we need to figure out what to do with you until morning."

"Until morning?" Aylie gasped. "I have to get home. My parents might wake up and realize I'm missing."

"Driving you home would wake your parents up for sure, it's deathly quiet out here in the countryside. And it's not safe in the forest this late at night, either—especially when you have no shoes on," he said ardently, "I would know." His eyes fell on the dagger she'd dropped on the floor and he picked it up, returning it and the box to the fireplace mantel where it belonged. Then he turned to face her.

Aylie looked like she was in utter shock. She was staring down at her nightshirt, which barely covered her underwear and left practically all of her bare legs exposed. "Can I at least borrow those gym shorts again?" She asked, trying to pull the hem of her shirt down in embarrassment. Ryder went over to his dresser and retrieved the shorts she'd worn the last time she'd visited. Handing them to her, he turned away as she stood to her feet to pull them on. It was hard not to stare at the shapely contours of her body and he found himself struggling to keep his thoughts on the problem at hand.

"Thank you," she said, signaling that it was okay for him to turn around.

When he faced her again, he felt something he'd never felt for her before. A kind of fascination and desire. A desire he knew instinctively he had to keep in check. He could feel his body reacting to the sight of her and he forced himself to think rationally. He had to figure out what to do with her until it was light enough to drive her home without waking her family in the dead of night, and he had to keep her from falling asleep in the meantime in case she had a head injury.

"I'm so tired," she said, yawning into her hand.

"You can't go to sleep, Aylie. It's too risky."

She sank down onto the cold, stone floor, wrapping her arms around her legs to keep herself warm. He realized she was cold and went over to his bed to pull the comforter off of it. He carried it over to where she was sitting on the floor and handed it to her.

"What will you sleep with?" She asked, looking over at the messy sheets on his bed.

"I'm not going to sleep," he remarked, as if it should be obvious. "Someone has to make sure you stay awake."

Aylie put her head in her hands. "This is so humiliating. I really don't understand how this could have happened."

"You couldn't possibly have walked here, Aylie."

She stared at him not comprehending his meaning.

"You couldn't have come five miles through the tangled forest while sleep-walking, for one thing." He lowered himself onto the floor beside her, staring vacantly into the fire. "You couldn't have gotten past my gate without climbing it or being let in, for another."

Aylie stared at him, waiting for him to finish his train of thought.

"And…not to be blunt, but you're half naked and the ground is covered in snow. You would've gotten frostbite if you'd walked that far with bare feet."

Aylie shivered. "How did I get here, then?"

"I honestly don't know. I've never had a half-naked girl show up at my door in the middle of the night like this before, believe it or not." He said with amusement in his dark eyes.

Aylie slapped him on the arm.

"I have something I want to show you, though," he said, standing to his feet again.

She huffed. "Another waterfall?"

"No. Wait here." He started for the door and then paused to look over his shoulder at her. "Stay awake until I get back, okay?"

Aylie nodded.

He sprinted down the hall and through the adjoining corridor, reaching one of the staircases on the west side of the Mansion. He took the stairs two at a time and crossed through the passageway leading to his father's study on the second floor. He pushed the heavy door open and went straight to his father's desk. The waning moon sent a small stream of light through the high, stone window, giving him just enough light to see where he was going without having to use a candle. He grabbed his father's manuscript and sprinted back through the mansion to his bedroom where Aylie was waiting for him on the hard floor, just where he'd left her. She was huddled into a ball beneath his comforter in front of the fireplace. She looked so small and helpless sitting there—it made him want to scoop her up in his arms, but he refrained.

"You look really uncomfortable," he said, staring down at her.

"Stone floors aren't made for sitting on," she mumbled.

He was thoughtful for a moment. There was a loveseat on the opposite side of the room that he never used. It was an antique and existed merely for decorative purposes. It was sitting against the wall in a dark corner and he knew Aylie wouldn't want to be that far from the fire. It was clear that she was freezing, even with his down comforter wrapped around her. "I can move that loveseat over here," he said, nodding toward the antique. "But it will be much quieter if you help me move it...I don't think it would be good to wake the housekeeper."

Aylie stood to her feet, dropping the comforter to the ground where she'd been sitting. She shivered and practically sprinted over to the loveseat. He had to stifle a laugh as he hurried to lift most of the weight on his end, maneuvering it over to the agreed upon spot. Then she sat down on it, pulling the comforter onto her lap and all the way up to her chin. He sat down beside her, journal in hand.

"This is what I wanted to show you."

"You want me to read your journal?" She raised a questioning brow.

"Well, it's kind of a like a journal, I guess—but it's not mine. It's been passed down in my family for several generations." He handed it to her.

She touched the worn leather cover carefully, running her fingers across its tattered edges. Then she opened it, letting her eyes fall on the inscription on the inside cover. "How much do you want me to read?" She asked.

"All of it."

Chapter Seventeen

The tales recorded in Ryder's journal were very similar to popular Greek mythological legends like those of Zeus, Achilles, or Hercules. She tried to read them with an open mind, but couldn't help noticing the obvious parallels. It seemed all too possible that everything Ryder's father had believed was nothing more than a retelling of famous stories imagined long ago. She tried to mask her skepticism from Ryder, however, pausing frequently to ask him questions. By the time she'd reached the end, she found herself so fascinated with the legends that she wasn't even tired anymore. Even if none of it was true, it was still an interesting narrative.

When she had finally finished reading, more than three hours had passed. Ryder was sitting next to her on the loveseat, his shoulder pressed against hers as they examined the pages together. She secretly wished there were more so they could continue on this way forever. She felt perfectly content just being close to him, though how she'd gotten to the Mansion in the first place still remained a mystery. She closed the manuscript carefully and handed it back to him. "It's almost dawn," she murmured, gazing up at the fading glow of moonlight that was streaming in through the high window.

Ryder nodded. "I'll be able to take you home soon."

Aylie stared solemnly into the fire. "How do you think I got here tonight?"

He shook his head. "I don't understand it." He relaxed his shoulders, leaning against the back of the loveseat with his legs stretched out in front of him. "If you didn't walk here, you must have transported somehow."

"Transported?"

"It's basically the science fiction concept of teleportation."

"Oh!" Aylie's eyes widened. "Is that something you can do?"

His eyebrows puckered. "Usually you can't transport unless you have an enchanted ring, like the one I wear when I transition. Mine was supposedly made by Edryd, himself—those tend to stay in the family." He smiled darkly.

"Can you transition without one?"

Ryder shook his head. "Without it, the urge can be present, and my body might even try to undergo the change, but I can't fully transition without the ring. It's the way Edryd maintained control of his followers, I suppose."

Aylie yawned. "Do you believe everything written in this journal?"

"I didn't used to—my dad and I got into arguments about it all the time."

"And now?"

"I'm not so sure anymore."

Aylie hugged her knees to her chest, wrapping her arms around them. "What else can you do?"

"Besides transitioning when I hunt, transporting is the only other thing I've ever really attempted, with regard to my inherited abilities. I've probably only done it three or four times in my entire life. Transporting is extremely difficult, and my dad discouraged my brothers and I from practicing it. He said it drains your body's physical energy to an extreme breaking point and is usually very difficult to recover from, unless you do it constantly and build immunity to the aftermath of the metaphysical changes. "

"So, you can change into a demon creature and teleport from one place to another—that's it?"

Ryder laughed. "You sound so disappointed."

Aylie shook her head. "I just wondered if there was more."

"If I were to fully embrace my druid roots by binding my spirit—or life force—to Edryd's, I would be able to conjure dark curses and manipulate molecular structures and other elements, but that kind of magic always leaves a mark on a person's soul. If you practice it long enough, it dulls your conscience completely and eventually destroys both your physical body and your mind.

Aylie shuddered. "I can't believe this stuff is real."

Ryder looked down at the journal on his lap. "I wish it wasn't. My family would still be alive right now if it weren't for the Order."

"I'm so sorry, Ryder."

He set the journal aside. "Hopefully my uncle will come visit. He's managed to stay alive all these years, as far as I know. He must know something that could help us."

Aylie's heart skipped a beat when he said the word, "us," but she knew it wasn't really something to be happy about. The danger he spoke of was real and she couldn't afford to take any of this lightly. They had to find the killer soon or her own family could be in danger.

"Come on, Aylie," Ryder said, standing to his feet. "Let's get you home before sunrise."

He offered to let her borrow a pair of his shoes, but they were so much larger than her feet she refused them. All she had to do was make it to his car and then into her house...she could handle the snow if it was only for a moment. She followed him out of his room, through passageways and down several flights of stairs through the mansion's front entrance. Just before her feet touched the snow, he came up behind her, scooping her up into his arms. Aylie flailed in surprise, demanding that he put her down, but Ryder only laughed. He carried her through the long courtyard into the garage where he kept his cars and set her down. She was flushed with embarrassment and climbed into his silver Camaro feeling like a two-year-old.

He took the drive back to the Ranch slowly, maneuvering snow drifts and rockslides simultaneously. The gentle, swaying motion of the car was the perfect rhythm to rock her to sleep. She didn't even realize she had fallen unconscious until she felt someone touch the side of her face. Her eyes flew open as Ryder's cool fingers traced the warm skin of her cheek. Her breath caught in her chest. His eyes were piercing into hers and his face was so close she could hardly stand it. Her stomach was doing somersaults as she gazed back at him. She couldn't remember ever feeling this way about a boy before—even Marcus. She tried to force herself to look away to break the spell and end the unbearable tension between them. Before she could summon the willpower to follow through, he leaned over and kissed her.

Ryder Payne was kissing her. It was the only thought in her head. She felt like her heart would burst. It was like being kissed for the very first time, only better. This kiss was long, but gentle. She felt it in every part of her being. When he pulled away, she stared at him in astonishment. He must've read her mind, because his mouth broke into an extremely satisfied grin.

"What was that for?" She breathed, in a voice hardly above a whisper.

He smiled again. "In case I don't get another chance."

"Why would you say that?" She asked, finding her breath.

"I'd rather be safe than sorry."

He leaned forward and kissed her again, a light brushing of his lips against hers, before reaching across her to open her car door. She climbed out feeling a little shaky and out of sorts. The frozen snow beneath her bare feet was a jolt of reality that gave her the incentive to tear herself away from him. She darted through the snow, around to the back of the house where the door was usually unlocked.

Aylie looked out her bedroom window as the morning light slowly began to creep into the sky. She watched Ryder's silver Camaro disappear down the winding, forest road until it vanished completely into the trees. Sleepiness washed over her, but it was almost time for her barn chores and there would be no chance for sleep now. She wearily changed into her warm clothes and headed for the stairs, just as her brother Sam appeared in the hallway.

"Where did you go this morning?" He asked innocently, rubbing his eyes. "I heard you come in."

Aylie felt a spasm of panic. "I thought I heard something outside, so I went to check and make sure the animals were okay," she lied. "But I haven't finished my chores yet."

"I bet it was that grey fox again," Sam said with conviction in his brown eyes. "Wake me up next time and I'll bring my BB gun."

Aylie smiled, grateful that he'd believed her. "See you in the barn."

It took her longer than usual to finish her chores. Yawning through most of them, she dragged herself and the pails of goat's milk back into the house two hours later. Her mom was just starting on breakfast. She was so tired she wasn't even hungry, but she knew she had to be present at the table or people would start asking questions.

Tomorrow morning she'd be back at school again. It was strange how different she felt after the events of the last few days. She and Ryder were becoming closer; they potentially shared a cursed bloodline that entitled them to unknown supernatural powers and abilities. Ren was half in love with Eli, who had appeared to Aylie in a dream and seemed to be hiding a few secrets of his own. And let's now forget the fact that the former love of her life was about to start dating her best friend, Lacey. Could life possibly get any weirder?

Aylie pushed all of these thoughts aside and got cleaned up for breakfast. There was no time to contemplate the future now. Her family was spending the day together before Lucas returned to the dorms and they probably wouldn't see him again until the Christmas holiday. He popped his head into her room just as she finished getting dressed to tell her that the food was ready. She reluctantly followed him down the stairs and they sat down at the table together. Aylie forced herself to participate in their conversations. Sam mentioned the noise she'd heard outside and told them all about his plans to catch the grey fox. Lucas glanced at her suspiciously but said nothing during Sam's narrative. Mr. Bryant smiled at his youngest son, praising him for his well-thought-out plan, while Mrs. Bryant fussed about the food getting cold.

It was a typical Sunday morning like any other at the Bryant Ranch. Even though everything was as it should be, Aylie couldn't shake the feeling that something bad was about to happen. She could tell that Lucas wasn't buying the lie that she'd gone out before sunrise to catch a thieving fox. Could he have seen Ryder dropping her off? Or worse, did he know she'd been missing in the middle of the night? She stared down at her plate, waiting for everyone else to finish. She was so tired she could hardly think straight and the last thing she wanted to do was sit through an interrogation from her older brother. He had become much more cynical and distant since going away to post-graduate school. Even though the campus was only twenty minutes away, he rarely came home to visit and didn't associate with any of his old friends. He was like a completely different person—one that Aylie could no longer connect with and she hated it.

They had been nearly inseparable as kids. They were less than two years apart, and Lucas had always been her affectionate older brother. He had looked out for her, no matter what situation she'd gotten herself into. He always bailed her out. He'd taken the fall for things she'd done on countless occasions, even accepting consequences that were harsh and unfair at times.

She looked up at him from beneath her lashes to see him staring at her with his eyes narrowed almost accusingly. She dropped her eyes instantly; afraid that he might be able to see in her face the secrets she was fighting so hard to keep hidden. She hated to admit it, but she felt instinctively that she could no longer trust Lucas and it was killing her inside.

After they had all finished eating, Aylie helped her mom clear away the table and wash the dishes, while the boys went outside to chop and stack a fresh cord of firewood. They carried in armloads to restock the fireplaces in both the living room and the den. Then they all gathered in the living room to spend the rest of the morning together. Sam wanted to play Monopoly, so they quickly set up the board while Mr. Bryant turned the news on quietly in the background. Being one of the town's officials, he always made it a point to keep up with politics and current events. He rarely talked about what went on behind closed doors at the government building, but at home, he was a loving and affectionate husband and father.

Sam went first, landing on Reading Railroad, which he purchased grudgingly. Lucas took the next turn, smiling at his good fortune as he landed on the Boardwalk. It was Aylie's turn to roll the dice. She threw them across the surface of the board and moved her token to the Chance space, which required her to draw a card. She groaned, moving her token to the corner spot marked "In Jail."

"Looks like there's a lot of that going around today," Lucas commented with a smirk, his eyes fixated on the television.

Aylie glanced over to see what he was talking about and gasped. Mr. Bryant turned the volume of the television up with the remote, as a picture of Ryder Payne in handcuffs flashed across the screen, followed by footage of him being escorted from the mansion by the police chief.

"When did this happen?" She asked, trying to fight the hysteria rising up inside of her.

"About an hour ago," Mr. Bryant replied, indifferently. "Looks like they might've found the real murder weapon, too. Apparently the one they confiscated a few weeks ago was a decoy."

Aylie swallowed the lump in her throat. Her heart started pounding and she couldn't breathe. She thought she was going to be sick. She ran out of the room and locked herself in the bathroom. She fell on her knees in front of the toilet, lifting the lid as quickly as she could in case she vomited, but nothing happened. She leaned over the toilet seat in total shock, as tears began to stream down her cheeks. She hovered there for what felt like several minutes before her mom started knocking on the bathroom door.

"Aylie, what's going on? Are you okay?"

"I'm...fine," she managed. "I think I might have a stomach bug or something." She wiped the tears from her face and attempted to pull herself together.

"Do you need me to call the doctor?"

Aylie could hear the panic in her mom's strained voice. "No, mom. I think I just need some rest." She forced herself to stand up, unlocking the bathroom door.

Mrs. Bryant stood back, allowing her to pass. "I'll make you some soup," she offered. "I'm sure your father and brothers will understand."

"I'll be up in a little while to check on you," Mrs. Bryant called after her.

Aylie crawled into her bed. She had no idea what happened or why Ryder had been arrested out of the clear blue, but she was afraid for him. She couldn't hold back her tears. The secrets she had been carrying were catching up with her. She felt completely overwhelmed and helpless. Pulling her comforter up over her head, Aylie cried herself to sleep.

Chapter Eighteen

For the next two weeks, Aylie walked the halls of Silvervane Prep feeling the emptiness of Ryder's absence. She missed him terribly. He had no family to speak up for him and no alibi for the night his father was murdered. The story was all over the news again, as if his father's murder had just happened. The pictures of Ryder's arrest were front-page news in every paper in the county. They were labeling him a danger to himself and others, claiming to have diagnosed him with a mild form of psychosis. Since no one but Aylie really knew him, there was no one who could argue to the contrary. His court hearing was scheduled for the day after Christmas.

Aylie was so miserable she could hardly hold herself together. There was no one she could turn to for help. She needed to see Ryder somehow, but there was no way for that to happen without her parents finding out and she knew they wouldn't agree to let her go by herself. She was trying to work up the courage to ask her mom to go with her to visit him in jail, but she hadn't been able to find the right opportunity. She had to make sure the moment was right.

In the meantime, she had to find a way to finish out the semester without losing everything she'd worked so hard for. The last thing she wanted to focus on was school, but since it was the only thing, she had control over, she threw herself into her studies with a vengeance. She skipped lunch nearly every day, working through her study breaks. She started going home right after school instead of sticking around to hang out with her friends. She ignored their calls and avoided them in class as much as possible.

A few days before Winter Break began, Aylie was just about to leave the school when Marcus stopped her in front of the lockers.

"Hey Ayles" he said, his brows knitting together in concern. There was no trace of his usual, disarming smile. "How are you doing?"

"I'm fine," she said, attempting to brush past him.

He grabbed her arm gently, preventing her from getting to her locker. "I don't think you are," he said. "Your friends are really worried about you. Hell, I'm even worried."

"There's nothing to worry about," she said. "I'm just trying to finish the semester well so I can get that scholarship."

"You're avoiding everyone, Aylie. Lacey and Ren are beside themselves with worry. They've tried calling you at least a dozen times in the last two days, alone. You haven't returned a single call."

"What are you, the sheriff?" She retorted.

Marcus looked hurt and shocked. "Aylie, this isn't like you at all. What's going on?"

"Nothing," she said, pulling her arm out of his grip.

Just then Ren and Lacey came around the corner. They saw her talking to Marcus and stormed over. "Why haven't you answered any of our calls?" Lacey demanded, hands on her hips.

"I've been really busy," Aylie defended. "You know, end of semester exams and all—they're kind of important."

"You have straight 'A's," Ren pointed out. "You don't need to spend every waking minute studying when you already know everything."

"You know how much that scholarship means to me," Aylie said, trying to convince herself as much as them. "I can't be stuck here in this crappy town forever."

Lacey raised her perfectly sculpted brows. "Where is this coming from, Aylie?"

"Nowhere," she said, rolling her eyes. "And I don't appreciate being ganged up on by my best friends."

"We're just concerned," Ren said softly. "You haven't hung out with us since the ice-skating rink and that was almost three weeks ago."

Aylie realized how much she was upsetting them and felt a little guilty. It wasn't their fault Ryder was gone. They deserved better from her. "Okay, how about tonight?"

Lacey perked up. "How about the Gathering Spot?"

"Sure," Aylie agreed. "What time?"

"Ren and I will pick you up at six O'clock. We can grab something for dinner and maybe see a movie afterwards."

Aylie nodded, promising to be ready on time. She hurried out the door to meet her dad in the parking lot. He'd been taking her and Sam to school for the past week, now that the snow was knee-deep, and the roads were too icy to walk on. The sun was setting earlier too, making the days seem much shorter. She climbed into the passenger seat, tuning out Sam's recount of the day's activities. Fourteen days. She thought. It's been fourteen days since I last talked to Ryder...since he kissed me in his silver Camaro. Fourteen days since his arrest. Fourteen days since my life turned upside down. How could everything get so messed up in only fourteen days?

Aylie stared blankly out the window of her dad's Silverado. Sam was still babbling on about the basketball team and the fundraiser that was taking place over the weekend. She couldn't wait to get out of the truck and escape to the solace of her bedroom for a few hours before Lacey and Ren arrived to drag her out of the house for an evening of fun. She bolted for the stairs the instant they got to the ranch, slamming her bedroom door behind her. A few moments later, she heard a knock at her door. She ignored it at first, but the knock came again.

Ugh. "What is it?" She called.

"It's your mom, Aylie. Open the door."

Annoyed, Aylie stamped over to the door and unlocked it, returning to sit cross-legged on the end of her bed.

Mrs. Bryant came into the room, carrying a plate of chocolate chip cookies covered in plastic wrap.

"Thanks, but I'm not hungry," Aylie muttered.

"They're not for you," Mrs. Bryant said, with a wag of her blond head.

"Who are they for, then?"

"I thought maybe we could take these to Ryder. He's been locked away in that rusty old jail for two weeks now, with no friends or family to visit him. After all he's been through, I think it's the least we can do."

"Really?" Aylie tried not to sound too eager. She didn't want her mom to get suspicious.

Mrs. Bryant nodded. Aylie slid off of her bed and went to get her shoes, stopping to check her reflection in the mirror before following her mom down the stairs. She was so happy at the thought of seeing Ryder that she didn't even care about the fact that her friends would probably find out about it. If they wanted to gossip—let them. Besides, it had been her mom's idea, so she was technically in the clear.

They got into the suburban and drove toward the Silvervane County Jail. Aylie was trying to maintain her composure as they navigated slowly through stoplights and snowdrifts all the way there. She was impatient to see Ryder, but she knew that she had to keep calm, or she'd blow their cover.

"How long have you been seeing him?" Mrs. Bryant asked softly.

Aylie's head jerked around. "What?"

"I wasn't born yesterday, Aylie." Mrs. Bryant replied with a knowing smile. "I know what lovesick looks like…you've hardly eaten since Ryder's arrest."

Aylie started to protest.

"I don't need to know all the details, but I'd like to know how long it's been going on."

"We're not dating," Aylie insisted. "That's the honest truth."

Mrs. Bryant glanced fleetingly at her daughter, quickly returning her gaze to the road. "How long have you liked him, then?"

Aylie blushed. She'd never talked to anyone about Ryder before and the timing of this conversation couldn't have been worse. She tried to think back to when she'd realized that she had feelings for him, but it all seemed like a blur. "I don't know, maybe a month ago?"

"Have you two been spending time together outside of school?"

Aylie wasn't sure how to answer that. If she said yes, her mom would want to know where and when—both incriminating answers. If she said no, she'd be totally lying. She looked down at her hands, twisting them nervously in her lap. "I thought you didn't need to know the details?"

"I just want to make sure you're being safe. This boy has a very troubled background."

"So, you think he's guilty?"

"If I genuinely thought he was guilty of murder, I wouldn't be taking my daughter to see him, now would I?" Mrs. Bryant replied pointedly.

Aylie turned her gaze back to the passenger window, watching the cars whiz by impatiently.

"You need to be careful, Aylie—even if Ryder is cleared of all charges, which I firmly believe he will be."

"Why?"

"I know Ryder is charming, but that boy has secrets. Dark secrets, I suspect."

Aylie studied the side of her mom's face. It was the first time she had ever alluded to being concerned about Ryder's background. There was something about her warning that made Aylie wonder if she knew things about his notorious ancestry. And if she knew things about Ryder's bloodline, maybe there were things about her own that she wasn't sharing.

"Why are you so supportive of this?" Aylie asked suddenly. "Of my visiting Ryder in jail, I mean?"

Before Mrs. Bryant could answer the question, they were pulling into the parking lot of the county jail and courthouse. They had to pass through security at the gate and again on their way to the front desk of the reception area. They passed through metal detectors and were screened at another checkpoint before they were given a chance to sign in and state whom they were there to see. The officer at the front desk looked at them curiously when she saw Ryder's name on the line.

"You can have a seat right over there," she said, pointing to the gray, plastic chairs in the waiting area. "We'll let you know when you can see him."

Nearly twenty minutes later, another officer appeared at the door on the other side of the waiting room. He called their names, escorting them into a small room with a large window and a table in the center. They sat down in the metal folding chairs on one side of the table and waited. Aylie nervously clasped her hands in her lap. She had no idea what she was going to say to Ryder, especially with her mom in the room. She wasn't even sure if he'd be happy to see her, but she had to know how he was doing. She had to make sure he was okay.

Just before they brought him in, Mrs. Bryant signaled to the officer watching on the other side of the window. He entered the room immediately.

"I'm sorry, officer," she said. "But I really need to use the restroom. Will my daughter be safe here with the boy if he comes in while I'm out of the room?"

"Of course, Ma'am," the officer replied. "He'll be escorted into the room in handcuffs. There will be two of us watching right here on the other side of this window," he said, pointing to the large pane of bulletproof glass on the left. "We can wait until you return, if you'd prefer."

"That won't be necessary," Mrs. Bryant said with a wave of her hand. "I trust my daughter will be in safe hands." She smiled and followed the officer out of the room.

Aylie stared after her, knowing that she'd made up an excuse to give her a chance to talk to Ryder alone. Tears came to the surface, but she held them back. She didn't want Ryder to see her crying when he came in.

When the door opened a moment later, Ryder walked into the room wearing a faded orange jumpsuit. His hands were cuffed in front of him, with two large guards positioned on either side. They made sure he was seated on the opposite side of the table before asking if she was okay to be left alone with him.

Aylie nodded.

"You brought cookies," he said out loud, with only a slight smile. In her mind he said, What are you doing here, Aylie?

"My mom baked them, actually." I had to see how you were doing. It's been two weeks and I was getting worried about you.

You shouldn't be here, he said, the tone of his thoughts alarmingly insistent. They have the dagger you were holding—the one above the fireplace in my room.

Aylie swallowed, her eyes growing large. She hadn't even realized the dagger they'd recovered was the one she had touched when she'd sleepwalked. The shock of what he'd just told her was slowly sinking in. Her mind spinning, but all she could focus on was the boy in front of her. Well they haven't arrested me yet.

"Did your mom come with you, then?" He asked out loud, keeping up the charade.

When they check it for fingerprints, Aylie—yours will be on it. You need to get out of here.

"Mom's here somewhere. Visiting you was actually her idea," Aylie replied. I don't care about me. It's been miserable for the past two weeks, she admitted.

Ryder smiled. You must miss me pretty bad.

Aylie sighed, resisting the urge to roll her eyes. This isn't funny, Ryder. You're in jail for a murder you didn't commit.

"How's school going?" He asked, locking eyes with her reassuringly.

"I've been really busy—exams start Wednesday." Is there anything I can do to help, Ryder? Anything at all?

You can contact my uncle. I wrote to him, but I don't know if he's written back yet. His address is on a piece of scratch paper on my father's desk. Write to him and tell him what happened. Maybe he can get me out of here.

Aylie was slightly alarmed. You want me to go to the Mansion—alone?

You don't have to, he replied silently. But my uncle might know how to get me out of here.

Aylie took a deep breath, nodding almost imperceptibly. I'll do it.

Just then Mrs. Bryant walked into the room. She smiled pleasantly at Ryder. "How are you holding up?"

"Not too bad, all things considered." He said. "Thank you for visiting and bringing...cookies." His eyes lingered on Aylie a second too long.

Aylie blushed, looking down at her hands.

Mrs. Bryant smiled warmly. "I'm so sorry all of this has happened to you," she said. "We've all been worried—especially Aylie. I brought her to see you, hoping you might be able to convince her to eat something and maybe relax a little. She's not been herself lately. I figured she might listen to you since it seems you're one of her good friends now."

Aylie shot her mom a look.

Ryder seemed both pleased and amused. "I'm not sure anyone can tell Aylie what to do. She's got a bit of a stubborn streak, if you know what I mean."

Mrs. Bryant laughed out loud. "I know it well and it's probably my own fault, too."

"But seriously, Aylie," Ryder shifted his gaze, looking deeply into her eyes. He leaned forward in his chair. "Take it easy, there's nothing to worry about. You're going to do great on your exams."

She chocked back the tears that threatened to spill down her cheeks. Here he was, trying to comfort her, when he'd spent two weeks in jail for a crime he wasn't guilty of. All she could do was sit here and have a shallow conversation with him, pretending like his life wasn't hanging in the balance. It was so unfair she could hardly stand it. She longed to reach across the table and hold his hands, comforting him the way that he was trying to comfort her.

You forget that I know what you're thinking. His words interrupted her thoughts. It comforts me to know how you feel about me. His eyes were shining under the glare of the florescent lights overhead. The door opened suddenly, and two guards reappeared to escort Ryder back to his cell. He stood to his feet, following them to the door. He paused in the doorway, looking over his shoulder at her. Aylie, I....

She smiled sadly, returning the look as they led him away. Her heart ached when he disappeared through the door. She followed her mom back to the car, lost in thought. She didn't even know how to process the fact that her fingerprints were on the murder weapon. She knew she should probably be more concerned, but she just couldn't bring herself to care about that right now. She had to get Ryder out of jail. She didn't know how she was going to do it, but she was determined to track his uncle down if it was the last thing she did.

Chapter Nineteen

The next morning, Aylie came downstairs for breakfast earlier than usual. Her parents were talking in the kitchen in hushed voices and it was obvious they didn't want anyone to overhear what they were saying. One of the most annoying things about living in an older ranch house was the way sound carried. She paused just around the corner, unsure of whether to make her presence known or to tiptoe back upstairs and give them a little more privacy.

"I just wish you would have talked to me about it first," Mr. Bryant murmured.

"You knew this time was coming, Lawrence. It's inevitable at this point—there's nothing we can do to stop it." Her mom's voiced argued back. "We agreed to this."

"There's no need to encourage it," he replied sternly. "It'll happen with or without our help."

"Exactly," Mrs. Bryant whispered. "And I'd rather she felt supported by us. It's going to be hard enough when she finds out that we've been keeping this from her for so long."

Aylie's blood was rising. She couldn't help thinking their argument was about her. She rounded the corner, purposely cutting their conversation short. "Good morning," she said, pretending not to sense the tension in the air as she moved to pour herself a bowl of cereal. "I need to know how to track down someone's telephone number," she said, directing the question to her dad. Her parents looked at each other awkwardly. Her mom turned to make a fresh pot of coffee.

"Whose number are you trying to find?" He asked, furrowing his dark, bushy eyebrows.

"It's an international number," she said, ignoring the question. "Can you help me?" She didn't know what their conversation had been about, but she was guessing now was the perfect time to enlist her dad's help.

He looked a little baffled but nodded. "Do you have an address?"

"I'll have it by tomorrow," she informed him, taking a bite of her cereal. "Oh, and I'm hanging out with Ren and Lacey today after school, so I don't need a ride this afternoon," she said, walking out of the kitchen to avoid further questioning.

After school Aylie made up an excuse to ditch Lacey and Ren and headed straight for the Mansion instead. It was an absurdly long walk that left her feet aching and blistered. She didn't even want to think about walking five miles back. She couldn't get her parents' conversation out of her head. What had they been talking about? What were they hiding from her? She was beginning to feel like things were unraveling all around her and she didn't understand why. She reached the tall, iron gate that guarded the Mansion and stopped, staring up at the hulking outline of the gloomy, stone-faced castle. Ryder is worth it, she told herself.

She pushed the call button and waited, but the gate didn't open. She pressed it again and waited for another minute, before deciding to climb it. Fortunately, she was a good climber or the whole plan would've fallen apart before she'd even reached the house. She jumped down on the other side of the gate, avoiding the sharp points of the spires, and followed the gravel drive up to the front door of the Mansion. Even in broad daylight it looked haunted.

Aylie gathered up her nerve and knocked on the door, softly at first, then harder. She waited several minutes but no one answered. She knocked again as loud as she could—still no answer. She knew the housekeeper and butler were there, at the very least. Either they were too busy to answer the door, or they were ignoring her knock on purpose. With everything that had happened at the mansion lately, perhaps they were leery of strangers. She wanted to give them the benefit of the doubt, but she also really needed to get inside to find that address.

She walked around one side of the Mansion, peering in through the only window that was low enough for her to see through. She couldn't tell what she was looking at, but the furniture seemed to indicate that it was some kind of sitting room. She cupped her hands around her eyes so she could see better. The young maid Aylie had seen on her first visit to the mansion walked into the room with a duster in her hand. She began to dust the surface of one of the coffee tables, but was interrupted almost immediately by the grim housekeeper. The old lady looked cross, like she was about to scold the girl for something. Aylie ducked to avoid being seen.

"What if the master sent her here to fetch his clothes or something he needs?" The girl protested loudly.

"It's none of your concern. If the master wants something, he has the right to a telephone call. Until I hear from him myself, you are not to answer that door."

"But why can't we just ask her why she's here?" The maid argued.

"I don't want strangers poking around here without the master home," the housekeeper said sternly. "Especially people like the Bryants."

"But what if she isn't one of them?"

"If you disobey my orders, you'll be out on the street looking for a new job before the master even hears of it, do you understand?"

The maid nodded sullenly, leaving the room.

Aylie's mouth fell open in shock. Had she really just heard what she thought she'd heard? What did the maid mean by, "one of them?" This was the second conversation she'd overheard today that made absolutely no sense. Her head was swimming now, and she was no closer to getting that address than before. She forced herself to focus on what she had come here to do, pushing the conversation from her mind.

Clearly no one was going to let her in, so Aylie was going to have to come up with a different plan. The sitting room window was the only one low enough to climb through. She'd have to break the glass from the outside to attempt it, which would be pretty risky. She crawled out from under the window and took a step back, surveying the side of the Mansion. Even if she managed to break in somehow, she didn't know her way around and was likely to get lost. She knew firsthand how maze-like this castle could be.

Suddenly she heard a door slam on the other side of the wall. She started to tip toe back toward the front of the Mansion, hoping to escape undetected. The sound of her name stopped her in her tracks.

"Aylie," the maid whispered.

She spun around on her heal.

The maid motioned silently for her to come back and Aylie obliged, trying to avoid being seen from the many windows covering the face of the mansion. The housekeeper could be watching her from any one of those windows and she'd have no way of knowing. Was the butler in on this, too?

"Did Ryder send you?" The maid asked, talking so low Aylie could barely hear her.

Aylie nodded. "He needs an address from his father's study…an uncle he thinks might be able to help him. He sent me here to get it."

The maid looked nervous. "I'm not allowed in there while Mr.

Payne is away. If I'm caught in that wing of the house, I'll be fired."

"Can you find a way to get me inside, then?" Aylie whispered back.

The maid nodded. "If you come back tonight I can let you in."

"I don't know my way around..." Aylie hedged.

"I can draw you a map."

Aylie smiled at her gratefully. "Thank you for helping me."

"I'm Bridgett," the girl said, returning the smile.

"Aylie Bryant."

"I know. My mom and I used to buy eggs and butter from your ranch."

"I remember now," Aylie exclaimed. "That's why you looked so familiar the first time I saw you here."

Bridget looked at her curiously. "The master must trust you an awful lot to send you here by yourself."

"I think he's a little desperate to get out of that prison cell at this point," Aylie replied modestly.

Bridgett smiled. "He respects you, I've seen it in his eyes. He's never treated anyone the way that he treats you."

Aylie thought she almost saw a hint of envy behind Bridgett's innocent, brown eyes. She smiled awkwardly. "I guess that's a good thing."

"I hope so." Bridgett glanced over her shoulder anxiously. "Be here after ten O'clock—that's when the housekeeper goes to bed. Meet me at the door on the other side of the cellar," she said, pointing to the one she'd come from.

Aylie groaned inwardly at the thought of having to walk all the way home and back again, but it was her only option. She thanked Bridgett and started for the ranch, hoping fervently that she would be able to get out of her house undetected again tonight. Sneaking out was starting to become a habit and she wasn't proud of it. Maybe when she got Ryder out, he could teach her how to transport.

It was well after ten o'clock when Aylie was finally able to sneak out of her house, and she still had a long walk ahead of her. She hoped Bridgett would wait up for her—otherwise the long journey would be wasted. She wished fervently there was another way to get the address from Ryder's study. The moon had waned and was almost non-existent in the evening sky, leaving only tiny pinpricks of starlight to guide her through Silvervane forest. She'd brought a flashlight, but the tiny beam did little to illuminate her path. She swallowed her fear and forced herself to keep moving forward. She missed Ryder, now more than ever, as she followed the winding gravel road in the dark. What would he think if he knew she was out here in the middle of the night? Had he known the housekeeper would refuse to let her in?

Surely not. Ryder would be furious if he knew what she was doing right now. It warmed Aylie's heart to think of how protective he'd become…not that it did her much good right now. She ignored the painful blisters on her feet and the weariness in her bones and forged ahead. Ryder had been right about one thing—there's no way she had walked there the night she'd appeared outside his room. She could hardly make it through the woods with her eyes wide open and shoes on her feet. She stopped for a moment to catch her breath. She bent over, sliding her hands down to her knees. Thankfully some of the snow had melted over the past two days, or she would've been standing in it over her ankles right now. If there was one thing she hated more than anything else, it was being cold and wet at the same time.

Above the familiar rustling of trees swaying in the cold, night breeze, Aylie heard the sound of feet crunching through the snow not far behind her. The hair on the back of her neck stood up, as she looked around frantically to see who was trailing her. How long had she been followed unaware?

She started moving again, this time much faster than before. She hadn't thought to bring a hunting knife or anything to defend herself with. She was so used to being safe with Ryder in the forest that she hadn't been thinking clearly when she'd agreed to meet Bridgett in the middle of the night. She'd been more concerned with the possible dangers inside the mansion, rather than outside. She chided herself for being so foolish. She could almost picture Ryder's reaction to this scenario and somehow it comforted her in a weird sort of way.

Aylie wanted to run, but she forced herself to maintain an even stride. If it were a wildcat of some sort, running would incite a chase, which she had to avoid if she was going to survive this little excursion in one piece. Perhaps her stalker would keep its distance if she just kept an even pace and maintained a calm presence. She still had so far to go it seemed a little hopeless, but she focused on the path in front of her, choosing her steps carefully to avoid twisting an ankle.

The darkness seemed to be closing in around her. Fear was becoming palpable. She imagined that she saw moving shadows all around her and her mind was beginning to fall for the delusions perpetuated by her terror. She could remain calm no longer. She took off down the road in a dead sprint. Suddenly, something was standing in the middle of the path ahead of her. She stopped in her tracks—it was the white lion from her dreams. His fur was even more luminous in real life than it had appeared to her in her sleep—a pure, glistening white.

She rubbed her eyes, questioning her senses. "You're the one who's been appearing in my dreams," she whispered aghast.

I Am.

Just as she'd been able to understand him in her dreams, she could hear the lion's thoughts in her mind, loud and clear. She was so taken aback by his presence that her knees began to buckle. She tried to keep her lips from quivering. "Why are you here?"

To help you. He started walking toward her. With each calculated step, Aylie's lips began to tremble. She wasn't afraid that he would harm her, but she felt something very similar to fear and didn't know what to make of it. She couldn't take her eyes off of him. It was as if her feet were glued to the earth. She didn't know how she was ever going to make it to the Mansion at this rate. He reached the place where she was standing, his shining, blue eyes gazing into hers with unwavering intensity. Touch my forehead, he commanded.

Aylie didn't even hesitate. Her hand shook as she reached forward, placing her fingers on his large, white forehead. The moment she touched him, she saw a montage of images flash before her minds' eye. They moved too quickly for her to comprehend, but each image left an impression somewhere deep in her soul. She couldn't explain what was happening, but before she knew it—she was standing in the center of Ryder's study. She blinked, coming back to full consciousness, and looked around the room. She didn't know how she'd gotten there, but she didn't have time to worry about it now. She went straight over to the desk and searched for the piece of paper with uncle Alexander's address. She found it beneath a pile of unopened mail and stuffed it into the pocket of her jeans.

She looked around for an exit and realized she had no idea how to get back to the cellar door Bridgett had told her to use. There were so many passages and stairways; it was like trying to find her way out of the world's largest labyrinth. She thought about the lion and wished he were here to show her how to get out. She closed her eyes, trying to remember what
he'd told her in the dreams. Ruah. Her eyes flew open, as she suddenly remembered his name. Then the lion's words came flooding back to her, 'You can hear the sound of my voice with your spirit.' Aylie closed her eyes again. "Ruah," she whispered, feeling a little silly and unsure. "How do I get out of here?"

Instantly, the knob of the study door turned and Bridgett peaked in. "Aylie?" She whispered, wide-eyed. "How did you get in here? I was waiting for you by the cellar door just like we talked about."

Aylie hurried over to her. "I'm so sorry…I got in another way, but now I'm not sure how to get back out."

Bridgett motioned for Aylie to follow her. They crept through a long corridor that led them down three, steep flights of stairs. Aylie remembered how easily she'd nearly slipped and fallen the last time and walked as close to the wall as possible; Ryder wouldn't be there to save her this time. They took another long passageway, crossed through a hall of some kind, and came out in the wine cellar.

"That's the door," Bridgett whispered, nodding with her head.

Aylie smiled gratefully, clasping her hand for a moment. "I don't know what I would've done without you," she whispered back, as quietly as possible.

Chapter Twenty

Ryder lay back on his cot reading an old copy of Robinson Crusoe. He'd always been an avid reader and Daniel Defoe's work was a classic. His cellmate had fallen asleep on the cot across from him out of sheer boredom. They weren't given liberties in the dayroom for another two hours, so they had to make do with what they had in their cell for entertainment. He wished he had thought to ask Aylie to bring him some of the volumes from his father's study, but that had been the last thing on his mind when she'd shown up at the jail unannounced.

He still couldn't believe she'd brought her mom to see him, although she had claimed the visit was her mom's idea. He'd gotten the feeling that Mrs. Bryant knew exactly what was going on between them, but she'd kept it to herself and had appealed to him as Aylie's friend, which he appreciated. She didn't look down on him for his family's misfortune or fear his influence over her daughter. On the contrary, she seemed to be encouraging him to associate with Aylie, which puzzled him.

If Aylie's parents had been secretly involved with Edryd's Order, they would never have allowed their daughter to consort with him in any way. Rather, they would have kept her as far away from him as possible and would probably have finished him off themselves by now. He couldn't tell from his brief interactions with Mrs. Bryant if she knew anything incriminating about his ancestry or not. He'd noted her reaction to the sword in his vault. It was a ritual sword that had belonged to his great grandfather Payne—the last of his family to serve the Order. The significance of the weapon would have been obvious only to someone who understood its origins. Perhaps she had simply been fascinated by it.

Ryder sighed. It had been almost a week since he'd seen Aylie and he wasn't sure whether or not she'd been able to get his uncle's address. On top of that, it was the day before Christmas Eve, so mail was likely to be slow even if she had been able to write. This wasn't where he pictured himself spending the holidays, but at least there was someone on the outside who cared where he was.

His thoughts were interrupted by the sound of approaching footsteps outside the cell. He glanced up from his book to see the Corrections Officer drop an envelope through the bars. It landed facedown on the dirty cement floor. Ryder eased himself off of his cot to see who the letter belonged to. To his astonishment, it was an expedited letter addressed to him and bore a postmark from the First United Kingdom. He ripped it open with his index finger, extracting a letter from his uncle.

Dear Ryder,

Your friend, Ms. Bryant, has notified me of your situation. She found my address and was able to trace my telephone number. I have contacted your attorney on your behalf and you should be released any day now. No need to worry about bail—I have taken care of it and look forward to seeing you very soon.

Yours Truly,
Uncle Alexander

He let out a deep breath. It was only a matter of time before he would be released from this cold, lifeless jail cell. It was the most welcome news he'd received in almost a month and his heart swelled with gratitude—both to Aylie and his uncle. He wondered how she'd been able to track down his uncle's phone number, but there would be time for questions later. He returned his attention to his book with a new enthusiasm, breezing through page after page until he was escorted to the dayroom. There were men playing cards, chess boards, a bookshelf covered in dust and dirty magazines, along with a few discarded books with tattered covers, like the one he'd borrowed. There were two small televisions hanging from the ceiling—one at each end of the long room. Around one screen, a large group of inmates crowded to watch basketball, while the news channel played on the other.

Ryder sauntered over to one of the unoccupied chessboards and sat down on a stool, glancing over at the television broadcasting breaking news. There was a report of an air raid over a foreign country, and two people were arguing back and forth about whether the strike had been ethical. Then the news anchor returned, turning the discussion toward local news. His report began with the story of a local business that had burned down during the night—investigators suspected arson. After that story had concluded, the news anchor introduced a second reporter filming from a remote location, queuing her to reveal the topic of the next segment. The reporter thanked him for the introduction and began describing an attempted robbery of the area's most prestigious home, followed by the shocking news of yet another tragic murder connected with the robbery.

Ryder's stomach lurched when he saw footage of the Mansion flash across the screen. The pictures of the murdered victim revealed only the top of Bridgett's head and the tips of her toes sticking out from beneath a white sheet, as her lifeless body was carried away on a stretcher. They showed an old high school photo of the girl in her Silvervane Prep uniform, offering their condolences to her family and friends.

"Is Ryder Payne innocent?" A picture of Ryder in handcuffs flashed on the screen. "Could the real killer still be out there?" The reporter asked dramatically, looking into the camera for effect. Ryder's attorney appeared in front of the camera next to make a statement. "Ryder Payne has been declared innocent of all charges at this time and will be released from Silvervane County Jail later this afternoon."

Ryder stared at the screen in shock, as several of the inmates in the dayroom turned to glare at him.

"Lucky break," one of the men spat, rolling his eyes.

"He couldn't very well have murdered someone out there while he was in here, now could he?" Another inmate retorted in Ryder's defense.

"Maybe he had someone on the outside working for him," the first man said, squaring up to the second.

"Or maybe he's innocent, like the lady said."

A fight nearly broke out, but one of the guards intervened before it came to blows. He escorted Ryder out of the room and back to his cell, commanding him to get his things together. It would be safer for him to remain behind bars until his release, as some of the men would love nothing more than to send him home with a beating to remember them by. He followed the officer's orders, though there was a part of him that wanted that group of thugs to cross him and get what they deserved.

It was the thought of seeing Aylie that kept him in check. The last thing he wanted to do was give the Corrections Officer a reason to delay his release. He did as he was told and waited impatiently, sitting on the edge of his cot. His mind was racing. How did Bridgett get mixed up in all of this? She had nothing to do with Edryd's Order…at least, not that he was aware of. She was an innocent young girl with all of her life ahead of her. Anger welled up in him with every passing moment. It was one thing for the Order to come after his family, for they had defected and retaliation was a natural consequence. He seethed inwardly as he waited for his release.

More than two hours later, an officer finally appeared outside his cell to escort him out. His uncle had arranged for someone to meet him and make sure that he got home safely, though how safe he could really be inside the Mansion was questionable. He followed the procedure to get his clothes and personal items back and was released to the lobby. The only person in the waiting area was a hockey player from Silvervane Prep that he hardly recognized.

Blake Kavanagh stood near the door, arms folded across his broad chest. He looked extremely uncomfortable and hardly made eye contact with Ryder as he passed through the security checkpoint. "Hey," the boy said awkwardly. "I'm Blake."

Ryder nodded. "Nice to meet you," he replied, a little confused.

"My mom's Judge Kavanagh," the boy said, as if that explained everything. "She was assigned to your case and she knows your uncle. She's the one who got your charges dropped."

"How does she know my uncle?" Ryder asked.

Blake shrugged. "Beats me. Come on, she's waiting for us out in the car."

Ryder followed Blake to the parking lot without question. He was a little disappointed that Aylie wasn't there to greet him, but even more confused about what was going on. How did his uncle know the judge, and how had he managed to get her to drop all charges so quickly without a trial? It didn't make sense. He climbed into the back seat of her luxury sedan feeling a little uneasy.

"Good afternoon, Ryder. I'm Judge Kavanagh, it's nice to officially meet you," she said, looking over her shoulder to smile at him.

He forced a smile. "Thank you for coming to get me."

"I talked with your uncle Alexander—we're old friends."

Ryder nodded mechanically.

"He has asked that you stay at my house until he arrives, just to keep an eye on you and make sure you're safe."

"I appreciate it, Judge Kavanagh," Ryder replied, trying not to show his chagrin, "but that's really not necessary. I can take care of myself."

"I'm sure you can," the Judge replied, looking at him through the rearview mirror as she pulled out of the parking lot. "But I would like to do my due diligence to keep you from harm until your uncle arrives. He should be here in a few days and he's bringing your cousins with him for an extended stay."

Ryder shifted uncomfortably in the back seat of the Lincoln. Something about this arrangement didn't sit well with him. It felt like he didn't have much of a choice in the matter, even though he was a legal adult. Was he being put on house arrest? He was tempted to demand that she let him go, but since his uncle had gone to such trouble to take care of things, he agreed to stay with her until he could come up with a different plan.

The first thing he had to do was find a way to see Aylie. It would be much harder to sneak out of the Judge's house in the middle of the night than his own. He would have to invent a reason to visit the Bryant Ranch. It would mean facing the rest of her family, however, and he wasn't sure how they would feel about him showing up at their house after everything in the news. Perhaps her father would be as empathetic as her mother was…that would make things a little easier.

He brainstormed reasons to visit the Ranch all the way to the Judge's house. He said very little unless asked a direct question and refused dinner, saying that he was tired and needed to lie down. He was shown to the guest room and given towels for the bathroom he would be sharing with Blake—a scenario he had never encountered before. The house would probably have been considered large to most people, but to Ryder, who was used to living in a castle, this place felt almost as confining as his prison cell. He fell asleep early, hoping to awake from the ever-evolving nightmare that had somehow become his life.

When he opened his eyes, Ryder found himself standing in the middle of the courtyard at his own mansion. He looked around, noticing how dark the sky was. Must be just before dawn, he thought, turning to walk into the house. A black cat darted in front of him with a screech, making him pause. He laughed as he reached for the doorknob. Out of nowhere, something lunged at him from behind. He staggered backwards, blood dripping from the claw marks raked across the back of his right shoulder. He whirled around to see the silhouette of a large black wildcat bearing its sharp fangs. It gave an eerie, high-pitched shriek that made him cringe inwardly. There were two more panthers flanking it, ready to strike when commanded. Ryder winced, as the pain spread through his shoulder and down his arm. He stared at the panthers in alarm and confusion. They were just like him. Why were they attacking him without cause? Their eyes glowed with the same, red-orange light he'd always known. Their presence should've been a comfort to him, not a terror. Before he could wrap his brain around what was happening, the panther lunged for his throat....

Ryder jolted awake, sitting upright in a strange bed in an unfamiliar room. He was breathing hard, trying to remember where he was. It took a few minutes before he realized he was at the Judge's house. It hadn't been a dream then, after all. For some reason he almost preferred being attacked by ferocious panthers, as opposed to being trapped in this house with strangers who knew nothing about him and cared little for his well-being. Something told him not to trust these people. He considered trying to sneak out but knew there would be hell to pay if his uncle found out. He forced himself to lie back down and tried futilely to go back to sleep.

Chapter Twenty-One

"Did you hear about Ryder?" Lacey railed through the phone with disgust. "He's been cleared of ALL charges."

"Really?" Aylie tried to disguise her excitement. "How did that happen?"

"I don't know. Something about new evidence or some nonsense like that." Lacey was unabashedly skeptical.

"Well…that's good news, don't you think?"

"He didn't even have a trial, Aylie. There's something suspicious about that, if you ask me."

"How do you know all this? I didn't hear anything about it," Aylie said, trying to keep her voice as neutral sounding as possible.

"Blake Kavanagh was the one who had to get him out of jail," Lacey replied dramatically. "He told Marcus all about it. Apparently, Ryder has to stay with them until his uncle gets here."

"Seriously? Why the Kavanagh's? I didn't know Ryder and Blake were friends…."

"Oh, they're definitely not friends. His uncle knows the Judge somehow and she agreed to keep Ryder as a favor."

"Poor Ryder," she murmured.

"You mean poor Blake," Lacey huffed. "He's having a Christmas Eve party at his house tonight and now he has to deal with that loser hanging around."

"Are you going to the party?" Aylie asked, trying not to sound envious.

"Of course, Marcus invited me." She replied with a laugh. "You should come, too—check out the escaped convict. I'm sure it'll be loads of entertainment."

"I don't know…" Aylie wasn't sure if her parents would let her go somewhere else on Christmas Eve.

"Come on, Aylie. You only live once."

"I'd have to convince my parents."

"Put your mom on the phone," Lacey replied confidently. "I'll convince her."

A few hours later Aylie was standing on the front porch of Judge Kavanagh's house. She'd caught a ride with Marcus and Lacey and had been forced to watch them make eyes at each other all the way there. She kind of wanted to vomit but kept her feelings to herself. She knew she should be happy for them, but it was hard when she couldn't be with Ryder that way.

Sophia Kavanagh answered the door, greeting them less than cordially. She was Blake's older sister and had dated Aylie's older brother a few months back. She wasn't sure what had happened between them, but judging from the superficial greeting she'd just received, Aylie guessed the break-up must've been Lucas's idea. She followed Marcus and Lacey inside, determined to find Ryder as quickly as possible.

The Kavanagh house was decorated to the hilt, with artificial Christmas trees in every room. There were long strands of garland with big red bows hanging festively along the tops of the walls and the wooden railings of the bannisters. Every fireplace had stockings dangling from it. White Christmas lights hung from the ceilings, while holiday music played softly in the background. It seemed like every room was filled with pockets of hockey players and their girlfriends or other athletes Aylie didn't really know. She used to be part of this crowd but now she felt sorely out of place.

She was starting to wish she hadn't come. She couldn't seem to find Ryder anywhere and wondered if he'd found another place to crash during the party. She walked down one of the halls, glancing in each room as she passed by. Chance was playing his guitar for a group of girls in a room on the left and he looked up at her and smiled as she passed by. Kyle high-fived her as she squeezed by him and the circle of guys who were chugging Red bulls. She had reached the end of the hall and there was only one room she hadn't looked in yet. The last door on the right was open just a crack and seemed to indicate that whoever was behind it wanted some privacy.

Aylie deliberated whether or not to peek inside. It could be Ryder's room, or it could be a couple making out or something more intimate, which would be extremely awkward to walk in on. She stood outside the door for what seemed an eternity trying to decide what to do. Just before she'd made up her mind to knock, the door opened wider.

Ryder stood casually in the doorway, wearing a fitted, dark blue long-sleeved T and a pair of dark wash jeans. His hair was sticking up in all of the usual places and his dark eyes were locked on hers. There were bags beneath his eyes and he looked like he hadn't slept in days. Aylie's heart stopped at the sight of him and he pulled her inside, closing the door quickly behind her. He wrapped his arms around her, pulling her to his chest. "I had no idea you'd be here," he murmured into her hair.

"I had no idea they let you out," she said, trying to keep her voice from shaking. "My parents have been careful to keep me away from the news, I think."

He held her tighter. "Thank you, Aylie. I would still be in that cell if it weren't for you.

She buried her head in his chest. "I'm so sorry, Ryder."

"What on earth do you have to be sorry about?" He asked softly.

"I just can't believe you were stuck in that jail for three whole weeks for a crime you didn't commit—you almost had to spend Christmas in there." Her eyes teared up.

"But now I don't, thanks to you." He whispered. He lifted her chin and kissed her lips, gently like a soft caress. Then he led her over to his bed and sat down beside her. "Thank you for contacting my uncle. I take it you found his address without any trouble?"

Aylie hesitated. She wasn't sure how much she should tell him. Did he need to know about the conversation she'd overheard between Bridgett and the housekeeper, or would that only make him angry? And how could she possibly explain the whole lion thing and how she'd been able to transport to his father's study without a ring? She looked into his eyes and felt the tension of the last three weeks begin to fade. "Bridgett let me in. The housekeeper told her not to, but she helped me anyways. I couldn't have gotten the address without her." It wasn't the whole truth, but it was enough for now.

Ryder's jaw clenched visibly, his eyes flashing with an anger Aylie hadn't seen in a while. She pulled her head back to look at his face more clearly, confused by the sudden change of emotion. "Have I said something wrong?" The last time he'd been this angry he'd transitioned and had nearly taken her head off.

"You haven't heard the news yet," he said sadly, looking down at her fingers interlaced with his.

"What news?"

"Bridgett is dead. She was murdered. It happened early yesterday morning before I was released. I think it's one of the reasons they let me out. I couldn't have been the one who murdered her because I was locked up at the time of the incident."

Aylie's eyes widened in horror. "No. That's not possible. I just saw her a week ago." She shook her head in denial.

"It's true, Aylie. It was all over the news yesterday. I guess your parents kept that from you, too."

Aylie's eyes welled up with tears. They started to stream down her cheeks. "She helped me, Ryder. The housekeeper warned her not to but she did it anyways. This is ALL my fault!"

"What do you mean?" Ryder asked, jumping to his feet.

"I...I overheard them arguing when I got to the mansion the day after I visited you. The housekeeper told Bridgett not to let me in. She threatened to fire her if she disobeyed, but I never imagined something like this would happen. I swear!"

Ryder paced back and forth in the tiny bedroom, his hands balled into fists by his side. "The housekeeper threatened her?"

Aylie nodded and the tears kept coming. Ryder stopped pacing and sat down beside her again, pulling her close to his side. "It's not your fault, Aylie. None of this is your fault."

"But if Bridgett hadn't let me in...."

"You don't know if that's why she was murdered. We can't assume anything without proof." He gently wiped the tears from her eyes with his thumb. "We're going to find out who did this," he vowed. "I promise."

"But how? These murders have been happening for years...you could be next," she breathed, trying to prevent a fresh batch of tears. And what about the dagger? The police chief still has it and my fingerprints are all over it. Why haven't they arrested me yet?"

Ryder shook his head with a troubled expression. "I don't know. My uncle will be here in a few days," he said, stroking the side of her face. "He'll know what to do. He's managed to keep his family in tact all this time and I trust him."

Aylie took a deep breath, regaining her composure. She wiped away the traces of her tears and sat up straight, pulling away from him to comb through her disheveled blond hair. "There might be someone else who can help," she said, just as the bedroom door flew wide open.

Lacey's slim figure loomed in the doorway, staring at them with a look of shock and betrayal. She folded her arms across her chest, waiting for an explanation. Ren, Derek, and Eli stood close behind her, looking extremely uncomfortable.

"Does someone want to tell me what's going on here, or should I assume it's what it looks like?" Lacey said.

"What exactly does it look like?" Ryder challenged.

"Like my best friend is hiding behind closed doors making out with a murderer." She retorted in disgust.

"Well, then it's not what it looks like." He replied coolly.

"We were just talking," Aylie interjected, embarrassed by Lacey's accusation.

"You really expect me to believe that? You're sitting on his bed," she hissed.

"I've never lied to you, Lacey. You have no reason to assume that I'm lying to you now."

"Well you certainly didn't tell me about your new boyfriend," she snapped, her anger dissolving into hurt.

"You weren't exactly open to the idea," Aylie said defensively. "It's not like you would've been supportive."

"So you've been dating this guy behind everyone's back?"

"No," Ryder interjected. "I didn't ask her to be my girlfriend until tonight. We made it official just a few minutes ago." Aylie glanced sideways at him, shocked that he had told Lacey they were dating.

"You were gone for three whole weeks," Lacey accused, "that was plenty of time for her to say something about your relationship." She turned to Aylie. "Why didn't you tell me this was going on?" Her eyes were filling with tears.

"You hate him, Lacey. I don't know why, but you do."

"Were you ever planning to say something?"

"Of course, but we hadn't made it official yet."

"Do your parents know about this?" Lacey questioned, biting back her tears.

Aylie nodded. "My mom does—she took me to see him about a week ago."

"Your mom took you to the jail?"

Aylie nodded.

Lacey pursed her lips. "And here I was, worried about how you were feeling with Marcus and I." She shook her head. "So much for best friends who tell each other everything." She stormed off, leaving Ren, Derek, and Eli standing in the hallway alone.

Ren stepped forward awkwardly. "I'm Ren," she said, introducing herself to Ryder. "I've never officially met you."

He smiled in spite of the tension in the air. "Nice to meet you."

Eli reached out next, shaking Ryder's hand firmly. "Any friend of Aylie's is a friend of mine," he said warmly.

"And don't worry about Lacey," Ren said sweetly. "She'll come around eventually."

Aylie smiled at her, mouthing the words, "Thank you."

"I'm sorry for bringing the mood down," Ryder said, trying to dissipate the tension. "I didn't mean to crash the party."

Derek snorted. "No worries. I think Lacey's the only one who' really upset about this."

"Should I try to go talk to her?" Aylie wondered aloud.

"I think it's going to take a little time for her to adjust to the idea," Ren said. "You might want to give her some space."

"Well...she was sort of my ride," Aylie said, biting her bottom lip.

"I'll take you home," Eli offered. He looked at Ryder as if checking to make sure it was okay.

"I think that's probably a good idea," Ryder agreed. He took both of her hands in his, drawing her closer and interlacing their fingers together.

Aylie looked up at him, blushing in surprise. She could feel the heat in her cheeks and the pulsing of her heart in her eardrums. She knew Ren and Eli were watching and it made her feel like a silly schoolgirl.

He bent down, resting his forehead against hers for a moment. "I'll call you when I get home," he murmured. He kissed her lightly on the forehead and let go of her hands. She followed Ren and Eli out of the room, pausing to smile at him over her shoulder before she disappeared.

CHAPTER TWENTY-TWO

Aylie slid into the backseat of Eli's car, replaying the part of the conversation over and over in her mind where Ryder had told everyone they were dating. She could still feel his lips on her forehead and she couldn't stop smiling. She was thankful it was dark outside so that Ren wouldn't see her stupid grin. She felt bad that she'd hurt Lacey but she was so elated about Ryder that she couldn't bring herself to worry about it. She knew her best friend would forgive her…eventually.

"Do you mind if we stop somewhere on the way home?" Eli asked, pulling off of Main Street to take an unfamiliar back road.

Aylie shook her head. "That's fine."

"So," Ren said hesitantly, turning her head to look sideways at Aylie as they drove down the long, deserted road. "Tell me about Ryder."

"There's not much to tell," Aylie replied. "We really were just friends."

"Are you in love with him?"

Aylie was silent, not knowing how to answer that question. She hadn't put a label on her level of affection for Ryder lately and she was a little afraid of what her answer might be if she really thought about it. "I don't know…maybe."

"Wow," Ren murmured. "I never thought you'd get over Marcus so quickly."

"It's been almost nine months."

"Yeah, but you and Marcus always seemed so perfect together. Seeing you with Ryder was a little strange, I'm not going to lie."

Aylie shrugged in the dark. "He's a really good guy, Ren."

"We're counting on that," Eli interjected, pulling up in front of an old, abandoned cabin in what looked like the middle of nowhere. There was no moon and the stars did little to illuminate the dark and desolate landscape.

"Where are we?" Aylie asked, peering out of the car window into total darkness. There were no other houses or buildings in sight and there was nothing but trees and forest in every direction. She had never been here before and had no idea where she was.

"I'm afraid that's classified information," Eli said, putting the car in park. He got out, moving his seat forward so that she could climb out, too. Ren and Derek were already waiting outside the car.

"What's going on?" Aylie asked, looking to Ren for answers.

"We'll explain everything when we get inside," Derek promised, steering her toward the front door of the cabin. Eli stepped in front of them, putting his right hand on the doorknob. Rather than using a key, he closed his eyes and leaned in, muttering something under his breath. Suddenly there was a clicking sound and the door opened from the other side. He ushered them through quickly, as the cabin door closed tightly behind them.

Aylie looked over her shoulder, feeling a little uneasy. She followed Ren and Eli through the dark interior of the empty house. It seemed like no one was home, but then who had opened the door for them? She felt her skin crawl as they stopped in the middle of what seemed to be the heart of the decrepit little house. She glanced around, noting pieces of old, broken furniture strewn about the room. The windows were boarded up in a haphazard fashion and there were no signs of electricity anywhere. Candles had obviously been used for light, and a few lumps of melted wax lay discarded in the crevices of the floor as if someone had dropped them in their hurry to get out of the cabin.

Eli knelt down on the dusty wooden floor. He placed the palm of his hands on the dirty floorboards at his feet and suddenly a trapdoor appeared. He opened it, motioning for Ren to climb down the ladder into the chasm below. She obeyed without question, waiting at the bottom of the ladder for Aylie to follow her. Slowly, Aylie climbed down into the chasm, resisting the urge to panic. Ren would warn her if she were in danger, right? She ignored the feeling that she was being led into a trap and waited for Derek and Eli to follow.

When everyone had reached the bottom, Eli led them through an extremely long underground tunnel, the opening of which was smaller than any Aylie had ever walked through before. The tunnels inside the mansion were nothing compared to this one in terms of length and lack of airflow. It must have been miles long, because Aylie's feet were beginning to ache and she felt the shallowness of the air around her. She forced herself to take smaller breaths so she wouldn't get lightheaded like she had in the passageways of the mansion. No one was talking and she didn't feel inclined to start up a conversation just now. She trusted Ren and she knew the explanation was coming, though it was getting harder and harder not to panic as they went deeper and deeper underground.

Finally, the tunnel opened into a larger chasm, with smaller tunnels branching off in several different directions. Aylie could hear the sound of people talking and laughing in the distance. They took one of the tunnels branching off from the center chasm and suddenly there was light everywhere, revealing a massive, underground city. Aylie looked around in awe. It was like nothing she had ever seen before. The walls were made of multi-faceted stones mixed with limestone. The ceilings were vaulted, providing plenty of space for the rows of storefronts, buildings, and apartment homes lining both sides of each tunnel. Here, Aylie noticed, there were street signs pointing in various directions to different archways and tunnels. The ground was cobblestone in some places and smooth clay in others. There were shops and cafes of every kind lining the alleyways with apartments above them, rising several stories high. The city was so developed and extensive that Aylie had almost forgotten they were underground, except for the dim glow of artificial light and the musty smell of earth all around her.

Eli led them through another, shorter tunnel, which opened into a massive, circular coliseum with large pillars and auditorium seating that stretched up almost to the ceiling. The seats were filled with people of every race and color, and it looked exactly like the pictures she had seen in her world history book of historic amphitheaters—the places where gladiators fought to the death in ancient Rome. The carvings on the pillars and walls were incredibly detailed, portraying wild adventures and battles fought long ago. Aylie's mouth fell open, as she gazed around the arena taking everything in.

Eli led her through the middle of the coliseum, directing her to sit in one of the seats in front of a raised platform located in the center. She complied, sitting down silently next to Ren and Derek. To her left, was a row of people dressed in dark brown cloaks with hoods drawn low over their heads. She watched in awe as Eli approached a man holding a similar dark brown cloak. He peeled off the sweatshirt he'd worn to Kyle's party and put the cloak on in its place before mounting the platform in the center of the arena. Suddenly the room fell quiet, as every person turned their attention to him in reverential silence. He didn't have to say a word. His very presence commanded respect, and it was very clear that everyone in the room esteemed him. He smiled, welcoming people who represented countries all over the world.

He greeted foreign dignitaries, diplomats, and even a few kings. His accent was thicker than she'd ever heard it before and she was astounded by how difficult it was to understand some of the things he was saying.

Aylie leaned over to whisper in Ren's ear. "This is Derek's roommate, right?"

Ren squeezed her hand. "You'll see."

Aylie listened as Eli addressed each people group in their own tongue and dialect. She was amazed that he knew so many different languages. Just how old was this guy, exactly? How could he know so much at the age of twenty, and why was everyone so captivated by him? When the greetings were finally over, two men in brown cloaks approached the platform, carrying what appeared to be a solid, marble chair. It looked extremely heavy, but they brought it to Eli so that he could sit down. They bowed low to the ground as they left the platform, backing away reverently. Eli pushed the hood of his cloak back, revealing his white blond hair, which looked luminescent in the dim coliseum light.

The people wearing brown hooded cloaks were council members, Ren informed her, though Aylie didn't understand what kind of council would meet underground like this. An aged council member with a long white beard stepped onto the platform next. He addressed the crowd. "The Prince has called this council to order. You have all been summoned here for this very sacred occasion. What is disclosed within these walls must remain sacred until the time the Prince chooses to reveal himself. All who will agree to fulfill this requirement and choose to remain, please respond with, 'I will.' "

Aylie's ears rang with the sound of the multitude shouting back their unified allegiance. Her heart began pounding wildly in her chest. She felt her head spinning, the knuckles of her hands turning white as she clenched the arms of her chair tightly. "Ren," she hissed, "Is Eli saying what I think he's saying?"

Ren beamed at her as Eli stood to address the crowd again.

"Brothers and sisters," he said with a smile that radiated like the sun, "to all of you who have followed me faithfully from one generation to the next and have not turned to the Order in despair—I honor you and thank you for your loyalty. For all of you who have lost friends and family for my sake—my heart grieves for your losses." Here he paused, overcome with emotion as tears streamed down his brilliant face. The entire room could feel the weight of his crushing sorrow, and no one made a sound until he had recovered himself. "And to all of you who have believed the legends about me and have awaited my return, even when there was no proof of my existence—you have my deepest respect and gratitude."

The room erupted in cheers, as the mood in the coliseum shifted from one of unbearable sorrow to uncontainable joy. Shouts rang out from every corner of the amphitheater and applause broke out like wildfire. It started out slowly at first, spreading through the arena as it grew louder and louder. The applause didn't die down, but continued for what seemed like hours. When Eli finally silenced the crowd, he said, "I have summoned you all here because Edryd's return is quickly approaching. His brutal assault on mankind will soon begin. Many of you have already sacrificed friends, family, and social status to protect our legacy and our way of life, but the days ahead will be unlike anything you have yet known. No matter what it looks like, you will never be alone. You will not be without hope. I am fighting with you and I assure you—we will be victorious!"

As he spoke, the floor began to quake, the ground beneath them rumbling like it was going to split apart. The pillars surrounding the platform shook and it looked as if the ceiling were about to cave in. Instinctively, Aylie covered her head with her hands. She heard Ren laughing and shot her a look. "How can you be so calm?" She demanded, her hands still cupping the back of her head.

"I've been waiting for this moment my entire life!" She cried, as tears filled her dark brown eyes. "My family has been looking for the Prince for centuries! He's alive, Aylie—he's here."

Aylie couldn't believe what she was hearing. She didn't have to be told who the Prince was, she had read about him in Ryder's journal. The legends had seemed far too fantastical to be true at the time, but listening now to the sound of Eli's voice—gentle as a summer breeze, yet commanding as thunder—she had no doubt that it was him. This was Rhydian...Eli was the lost prince. She felt the truth of the revelation in her bones, though she wasn't exactly sure how she knew it.

His words penetrated the atmosphere of excitement around them. "We know who our enemy is and we have suffered great loss at the hands of his followers, but their power is limited and their Order is not yet fully unified. As you know, the last high priest of Edryd's Order died many years ago. Edryd cannot return without the veneration of the next high priest and the unity that only he can bring. This gives us the advantage of more time."

"How can we prevent the next priest from being chosen?" A member of the council interjected.

Eli's uplifted expression melted into extreme sadness. "The next high priest has already been chosen. We cannot stop him from being venerated."

The crowd erupted in angry speculation and argument. People began to shout for justice and vengeance—the execution of Edryd's next high priest for the deaths of their friends and family.

With a compassionate gaze, Eli held up his hand and the crowd fell silent again. "Murder is Edryd's way, not mine."

"Then how can we prevent the next high priest from fulfilling Edryd's wishes?"

Eli looked out over the crowd. "Long ago, my father—the Great King Ruardian, spoke of One who could change the path of Edryd's high priest."

"Haven't you come to fulfill that prophecy?" Asked another member of the council, a woman with long, braided hair.

Eli shook his head with a knowing smile. "That is not my mission. I have come to help the person Ruardian has chosen to fulfill their destiny." The crowd began whispering, conjecturing about who would be given the honor of helping the Prince turn

Edryd's high priest away from the path of darkness and allegiance to the Order.

Aylie leaned over, nudging Ren in the arm. "Is he going to tell us who it is?" She asked, looking over at the council members in the row beside her. "It must be one of them."

"Who has been chosen to be Edryd's next high priest?" Asked an elderly council member seated next to Aylie.

Eli looked at the man solemnly. "All will be revealed in due time."

One of the councilwomen who had been silent suddenly stood to her feet. "Is there really no way to prevent the boy from becoming the next high priest?" She cried out in anguish. Her voice was strikingly familiar. Aylie furrowed her brows, waiting to see if the woman would speak again and confirm the alarming suspicion ringing in her mind.

Eli turned to the woman with a pitying look. "Ruardian's prophecy foretells that the boy will become the next high priest. No one can stop this from happening. But hope is not yet lost, there is one person who can change the young priest's course of action, which you well know."

The councilwoman began sobbing, the man beside her quietly entreating her to return to her seat. Aylie leaned forward, staring at her parents in wide-eyed disbelief. She shot an accusing look at Ren, who was suddenly fascinated with the floor at her feet and refused to meet her gaze. She snapped her eyes back to Eli, hoping for further explanation. He turned to face the crowd again, locking eyes with her instantly. "Some of you will be required to sacrifice everything to see mankind and the earth restored to its created order. Some of you will be required to help those who must make these sacrifices—to stand by them and lend them your strength. No one will be immune from what is coming, but the end will be glorious. It has already been foretold."

"Does the person Ruardian has chosen know of the role they are destined to play in all of this?" Asked the old man who had opened the council meeting.

Eli glanced at Aylie meaningfully. "She will soon enough."

Aylie shifted uncomfortably in her seat, as every eye in the arena was suddenly fixed on her. She stared back at him, shock and alarm coursing through her body. She couldn't be the one Eli was talking about...she had nothing to offer. No powers or special abilities. She didn't even have the mark of a Silver Vein! She stared at her parents, dressed in the brown hooded cloaks of the council members. Her mom was still sobbing, hood drawn over her face. Aylie was reeling from the shock of discovering that both of her parents had known about all of this, and now Eli was implying that she was the only one who could keep Edryd—an ancient druid and murderous sorcerer—from destroying all of mankind.

"I don't understand," Aylie whispered to Ren. "How am I supposed to do anything about this? I don't even know who the next priest is."

Ren turned to her with a tragic look, resting her hand on Aylie's shoulder. "Aylie," she said softly, "it's Ryder."

CHAPTER TWENTY-THREE

"No!" Aylie sprang to her feet. She refused to believe what Ren was saying. She wouldn't listen to another minute of these crazy theories.

She stormed out of the arena with all eyes watching. She didn't care what those people thought. She didn't even care what her parents thought. It was her life, not theirs. She knew Ryder better than any of them—he would never join Edryd's Order. Eli might be the great, immortal Prince returning to claim his lost kingdom, but he was dead wrong about Ryder Payne. And he was wrong about her destiny. She didn't know what she was going to do next, but she wasn't going to let a room full of crazy, sycophants decide her future for her.

She found her way back through the tunnels and out through the trap door, but then realized she had no idea how to get home from here. She stalked out of the cabin and went over to Eli's car, sulking angrily against the hood. She would have to wait for someone to take her home, but she had no intentions of discussing Ryder Payne or in being part of their little club. The only thing she cared about right now was getting home. She was so exhausted; she half hoped she'd imagined all of it. Maybe her tiredness had made her delusional.

Aylie looked around, surveying the gloomy mountains and thick trees enshrouding the lost little cabin. There was no starlight tonight, as clouds billowed in the dark night sky announcing a coming storm. It was very fitting weather for the mood she was in. Bring on the thunder and lightning—she was ready for it. As she stared out into nothingness, a familiar figure suddenly appeared before her.

Of course you would show up tonight. She thought accusingly, trying to avoid the lion's compelling blue eyes.

Do not reject your destiny. Ruah warned. For if you do, an even greater evil will be unleashed on the earth and the ones you love will be consumed by it.

Aylie frowned. "Ryder blames the Order for murdering his family—he would never join them…never."

Ruah's deep blue eyes were full of compassion. Ryder WILL become the next high priest. He communicated gently. And he will ask you to join him.

Aylie shook her head in disagreement. "You're wrong."

You can influence Ryder to turn away from the path of darkness, he continued un-phased, as if he hadn't heard her rebuttal. But you must also remember who you ARE. If you forget that, he will be lost.

"What do you expect me to do?" She asked, feeling helpless. "If I can't stop him from becoming Edryd's high priest, then how can I change his path?"

I cannot tell you how to fulfill your destiny, the lion said, though his eyes were full of kindness. That is something you must discover for yourself.

"What if I can't do it?"

I will help you, he promised. Whatever decision you make, I

will be with you. I am not asking you to do this alone. Listen for my voice…in your dreams, in your head, in your heart…listen with your spirit. You may not always see me, but I will always be there.

Aylie sighed, blinking back tears of frustration. "But why me?"

Do you love Ryder?

Ryder. Aylie remembered his lips on her forehead…the euphoria she'd felt only a few hours ago when she'd left Kyle's party. The way he'd held her close and thanked her for helping him. The way he'd comforted her when she'd blamed herself for Bridgett's death. She forced the memories out of her head. When she looked up, Ruah was gone.

"Aylie?" Her mom's voice called softly.

Aylie looked up miserably to meet her mom's worried gaze. "Nice robe."

"I'm sorry we didn't tell you about this sooner," she pushed her hood back, revealing her tear-stained face. "We didn't want to scare you or overwhelm you before the time was right."

Aylie shot her a condescending look. "Are we going to talk about the fact that you and dad look like ridiculous, wannabe Jedi's?"

"This isn't a joke, Aylie."

"You're right," she retorted. "It's my life." She shook her head. "But this explains why you didn't try to stop me from seeing Ryder—why you encouraged me to visit him in jail. You were using me to get to him."

Mrs. Bryant shook her head. "That wasn't our intention, Aylie."

Aylie glared at her. "You knew this was going to happen all along," she accused.

"We didn't know Ryder was going to be Edryd's next high priest until recently, but we knew it was someone in his bloodline. When all of his brothers died and his father was murdered, he was the only one left," she explained. "And we didn't know that you were going to fall in love with him."

"How could Ruardian choose me to influence Ryder when he's

been dead for a thousand years?"

"His body died a thousand years ago, but his spirit didn't—that part of him still exists."

Aylie shook her head in disbelief. "I can't believe I'm hearing this from you."

"His son Rhydian—you know him as Eli, never died. He escaped his brother Edryd's murderous reach. He's immortal, so he never ages. He's been hiding for centuries, moving from place to place. He takes on a new name and identity in every generation, that's why he's impossible to track."

"I know the stories already," Aylie muttered, folding her arms across her chest. "But why did he randomly decide to move to Silvervane, of all places, and take on the fake identity of a college student after all this time?" She didn't hold back her skepticism.

"He came here because Edryd's heir is here. Ryder's family was originally from England. If his family had stayed in Europe, that's where Eli would've gone. It doesn't have to make sense to be true, Aylie."

"Okay, that might explain how he ended up here, but it doesn't explain why he chose me."

"Ruardian knows what will happen in the future before the events ever take place—he must've known about your relationship with Ryder."

Aylie bit her lip, contemplating how to respond. "Mom, I don't want to question your sanity but this is really disturbing."

"What proof do you need, Aylie? Have you met Ruah yet?"

Aylie narrowed her blue eyes. "How do you know about him?"

"He appears to all of us when it's our time to be wakened."

"Wakened?"

"When Ruardian believes we are ready to embrace our unique destiny, he reveals himself to us in different forms—whichever form we will respond to best. The lion is just one of his many forms."

"Uh huh."

"When he appears to you, whether in a dream or in front of

your eyes, it awakens something inside of you. You feel drawn to something greater than yourself. You become aware of a higher power, for lack of a better phrase."

"A higher power...do you know how crazy that sounds?" Aylie asked, arching a brow.

"I remember feeling exactly what you're experiencing right now," Mrs. Bryant said, putting her hand on Aylie's shoulder tenderly. "I was a little older than you are now. But before you were born, Ruah appeared to me. He told me I would have a daughter who would one day have the power to change the course of history. I knew it meant giving life to a child that I might lose someday. That has been the hardest part of my destiny." Tears brimmed in her light blue eyes.

"Why didn't you tell me about any of this? I had to hear the legends from Ryder—the boy everyone believes is about to destroy the world by waking the devil's spawn from an enchanted sleep."

"Maybe we should have," Mrs. Bryant murmured remorsefully. "But we wanted you to have a normal life as long as possible."

"Does Lucas know anything about this, or is he exempt from this 'alternate reality' because he's not Ruardian's chosen?" She asked bitterly.

Her mom's face fell. "He knows."

"How long has he known?"

"About two years."

Aylie shook her head angrily. "Unbelievable."

They were suddenly interrupted by a mass of people emerging from the cabin. Most of them were unfamiliar to Aylie, but she spotted Ren and Derek in the middle of the crowd and waited for them to reach her. She had a few things to say to them as well. By the time they made their way over to her, she had decided to ride home with them. Her mom protested, but she stalked away, following them to the car.

"You owe me an explanation," she said, as they climbed into Eli's car. He had given Derek permission to drive back without him. He was going to be with the council for a few more hours and wouldn't be home until late.

"I know," Ren said, biting her lip. "Please don't be mad, Aylie. Your parents made us promise not to tell you. They said we had to wait until the time was right."

"But you're one of my best friends. I just don't understand how you could keep something like this from me." She didn't try to hide the hurt in her voice.

"I wanted to tell you so many times. I was waiting for you to tell me about Ryder so I would have a reason to confide in you about what I knew. You never gave me a straight answer about him, and you avoided me for weeks when I asked, remember?"

Aylie pursed her lips. She wanted to be angry with Ren and Derek, but part of her understood that they were respecting her parents' wishes. It wasn't their fault that her mom and dad had hidden their involvement with the council. In some ways, she was almost relieved that they knew about everything...the Order, Ruah, Rhydian—all of it. Finally she would have someone to talk to who understood the crazy world she'd unwittingly gotten sucked into. She didn't know how much she should trust them right away, but at least they had a grid for what she was dealing with.

The ranch was dark when she got home. Her parents were still with Eli at the council meeting and Sam was spending the night at a friend's house. She knew her parents were going to be home really late, so she turned the porch light on for them as she walked into the house. She shrugged out of her jacket and hung it on the coat rack inside the front door. She wasn't hungry after everything that had happened so she headed for the stairs, intending to go straight to bed. She stopped short when she saw someone sitting in the middle of the staircase.

"It's just me, Aylie," Lucas said quietly.

Aylie's heartbeat slowed. "Why are you sitting here in the dark?" She asked, flipping on the hall light.

"It wasn't my idea to keep everything from you," he said,

lowering his head into his hands. "I wanted to tell you right away, but mom and dad made me swear not to."

"How did you find out?"

"Derek told me when we were seniors in high school. We used to play hockey together, remember?"

"Is that why you're not friends with him anymore?" She asked, glaring down at him.

"Something like that," he replied gruffly.

"I guess that explains why you hate coming home so much."

"Yeah."

She paused, leaning against the corner of the railing. "Do you believe what they're saying?"

"I believe some of it," he said, lifting his eyes to hers. "I've seen things. But I don't believe you're doomed to sacrifice your life for the sake of some lame-ass kid who refuses to do his own dirty work."

Aylie was taken aback by his tone. "So you don't believe Eli's the Lost Prince, then?"

"He might be, but that doesn't mean he's the one we should all bow down to."

Aylie narrowed her eyes, trying to understand what he was saying. "What do you mean?"

Lucas straightened up, raking his hand through his dirty blond hair. "There are two sides to every story."

"Are you saying that you think Edryd is the good guy?"

Lucas shrugged. "I don't know...maybe he is. I've never heard his version of the story, have you?"

Aylie shook her head and fell silent. Was her brother actually defending the cruel and heartless murderer who had brought such violence and tragedy to their backdoor?

"You should think about which side of this you want to be on," Lucas said, interrupting her thoughts. "I know I have."

He stood silently to his feet and walked past her to the end of the hall, pausing to glance at her one more time before disappearing through the front door. She pivoted on her heel, watching him vanish behind it in shock.

Chapter Twenty-Four

Ryder stayed in his room while the Kavanagh's spent Christmas morning together as a family. He was thankful they didn't try to talk him into joining them—he'd never been much good at faking holiday spirit. At least, not since his mom and all of his brothers had died. His father had taken him on a hunting trip last year during the holidays and it had been a welcome distraction from memories that were too painful to relive. Christmas had become nothing more than a cruel reminder of everything he had lost and this year was even worse with his father now dead. If Aylie hadn't come into his life when she had, he would've been utterly alone.

He pushed the bedroom curtain aside and watched the sun rise up over the mountains in the distance. There was a fresh layer of snow on the ground, with a fresh shower of flakes still falling. There had been a storm last night and Ryder had hardly slept.

He'd been awake all night devising a plan to get home. He'd been locked up in Judge Kavanagh's house for three days now and he was going crazy. He wasn't used to such strict rules and constant observation. He missed the freedom of the Mansion and the mountains and the forest. He missed Aylie, and he planned to do something about it.

After lunch, the Kavanagh's would be visiting relatives in the next town over and would be gone for several hours. Ryder had already declined the invitation to go with them, much to Kyle's relief. He told them he didn't really enjoy being around people he didn't know very well and would prefer to stay in his room. The Judge had argued with him at first, but then she decided to let it go.

He waited until they'd been gone at least twenty minutes before he started his trek to the Bryant Ranch. There was no forest on this side of town, so he wouldn't be able to transition without leaving himself exposed. Without the swiftness of his panther form, it was going to take him a lot longer to get there than he would have liked. He found the nearest bus stop and hopped on, riding it to the edge of the city limits. From there, he took the gravel road out of town on foot. The scenery was so familiar and comforting, it soothed his soul in spite of the fact that he was being accosted by a swirl of heavy snowflakes.

Finally, Ryder reached the Ranch's back pasture. He trudged through the snow-laden grass, picturing the surprised look on Aylie's face. He sauntered toward the barn where he knew she was mostly likely finishing her morning chores. Apparently she wasn't exempt from her work, even on Christmas morning. He breathed in the fresh mountain air. This was going to be much easier than he'd thought. He crept around the back of the barn, peaking in through the crack in the sliding door. He saw Aylie brushing Knight's coat vigorously, like she had something on her mind. He smiled to himself, noiselessly sliding the door open just wide enough to slip through unnoticed. He stole up behind her without a sound, wrapping one arm around her waist. He covered her mouth with his other hand to keep her from screaming loud enough to alert her family of his presence. When he released her, she jumped into his arms, smiling up at him. She was practically glowing.

"How did you manage to get away from the Kavanagh's?" She asked, breathless.

"I have my ways," he replied mischievously, kissing her on the lips. She leaned in to deepen it, wrapping her arms around his neck. There was a fierceness to her kiss that set him on fire and alarmed him all at the same time. He didn't want to stop her, but he could feel something beneath the kiss that concerned him. He forced himself to pull back, just enough to look into her eyes. "Is everything okay?" He asked, searching her ocean-blue eyes. In his eighteen years of life, he had never felt this way about another human being before and he felt like his heart might explode at any minute.

Aylie dropped her gaze to his lips again with a hungry look that made his body come alive. "Of course, why do you ask?" She murmured, kissing him again.

Ryder felt like he was about to lose his mind. She was kissing him like her life depended on it and he was fighting the urge to take things to a level he knew he shouldn't. Not yet, anyways. She took a few steps backward and he followed, pressing her into the back wall, his hands on either side of her head as he kissed her back. He couldn't help feeling her desperation in every part of his body. He slid his hands down the sides of her neck, her arms—her waist. He didn't want to hold back, but something was pulling at his mind. Something wasn't right. He had to control himself…get her to talk instead of letting her push him over the edge. He tried to step back, but she held him tighter. He laughed into her mouth but she had no intentions of letting him breath anytime soon.

Desperate times call for desperate measures, he thought. He leaned in, kissing her so hard and fast that he felt a little lightheaded himself. Aylie gasped, breaking away for an instant to catch her breath. It was all he needed. He laughed, taking a deep breath of his own. He rested his hand lightly on her chest to keep her from crushing into him again before he had a chance to find out what was wrong.

"What's going on, Aylie?"

She frowned. "Nothing. Why do you keep asking me that?"

He leaned over, looking down into her eyes with his piercing, soul-searching gaze. "I know you, Aylie. We're connected. I can sense what you're feeling."

"I missed you," she said, gazing back at him innocently.

"I missed you, too," he smiled, kissing her lightly on the forehead. "But there's something else going on—I can feel it."

Aylie averted her eyes, looking down at his chest. "It's Christmas," she said, with a tortured expression. "Can't we just enjoy being together for one day?"

Ryder thought about it, noting the way she refused to give him a straight answer. Maybe she just needed time to process what was bothering her. Maybe she still felt guilty about Bridgett's death. Whatever it was, he would get it out of her eventually. "You're right," he said, lifting her chin so he could look into her eyes again. "What do you want to do then?"

She perked up suddenly, her lips breaking into a slightly mischievous grin. "I want us to spend the day with my family."

Ryder's eyes widened. "You want us to spend the day with your family, as in…me spend Christmas day with your family?"

Aylie nodded. "Yes, that's exactly what I want."

"I don't know if that's such a good idea…."

"It'll be great," she interrupted confidently. "My parents already know about us, anyway. I'm sure they'd love to get to know you better." Her tone was strangely condescending as she said it.

"Are you sure?"

"I'm positive." She took his hand, lacing her fingers through his. "Come on."

He followed her with trepidation, bracing himself for the cold reception he was sure to encounter. He hadn't met her father yet, but Lucas's opinion of him was quite obvious. He felt Aylie squeeze his hand reassuringly as she pushed open the front door, dragging him into the living room where the rest of her family was gathered around the television watching a Christmas movie. They looked up as he entered and the surprise on their faces was evident. Lucas didn't even attempt to hide his displeasure. He instantly stood to his feet and walked out of the room, glaring all the way.

Mr. Bryant reluctantly stood to his feet, crossing the room to extend his hand in a friendly gesture. "You must be Ryder," he said, attempting to smile politely.

Ryder nodded. "Yes, sir."

"It's very nice to meet you, Mr. Payne. My wife and I want you to feel welcome here at the Bryant Ranch." His gaze shifted to Aylie. "I know my daughter thinks very highly of you."

Aylie squeezed his hand again. See? I told you it would be fine.

"Do you really live in a haunted castle?" Sam asked, wide-eyed.

Ryder chuckled. "That's what they say."

"Have you ever seen a ghost before?"

"Sam," Mrs. Bryant shook her head disapprovingly. "Why don't you move over to the beanbag chair so Aylie can sit beside her friend?"

"You mean boyfriend," Sam muttered, leaving his usual spot on the loveseat.

Ryder followed Aylie over to Sam's vacated spot, sitting down beside her stiffly.

Relax, she thought, pressing her hand into his.

Mr. Bryant turned the volume down on the television, the sound of the familiar Christmas classic fading into the background. "So Ryder, what are your plans for the rest of the holiday? Do you have extended family in town?"

"My uncle and cousins should be here any day," he replied, uncomfortably. "I'm staying with Judge Kavanagh until they arrive."

"That's very kind of her," Mr. Bryant remarked.

Ryder smiled. "I'm very grateful for her hospitality."

"Where is your uncle visiting from?"

"England, I believe," Ryder looked down at Aylie's hand

inside of his. "I haven't seen him in a few years."

"Well, I'm glad they're able to visit. I'm sure you'll appreciate having them here." Mr. Bryant smiled, turning his attention back to the television screen.

Ryder breathed a quiet sigh of relief, glad that the worst of the interrogation appeared to be over. He relaxed his shoulders, leaning back against the sofa cushions, as Aylie pressed into his side. He noticed that Sam was staring at them and smiled, causing Sam to blush and look away.

Mrs. Bryant entered the room. "Would anyone like hot chocolate?"

"Yeah!" Sam exclaimed enthusiastically.

She carried in a tray of steaming mugs, balancing it on her forearms. She handed the first cup to Mr. Bryant, who preferred his hot chocolate mixed with a little coffee. She gave Sam the next mug, saving the last two for Aylie and Ryder. Lucas had still not returned and would have declined hot chocolate anyway, preferring something stronger.

Ryder reached for his mug, glancing down carefully at the tray Mrs. Bryant held as he did so. His eyes suddenly fixated on her wrist. The sleeve of her sweater had been rolled up to keep the fabric away from potential hot chocolate spills. The tip of the silvery, liquid vein pattern tracing down her forearm was impossible to miss. His hand stiffened around his mug, just long enough for Aylie to notice.

Her forehead creased. What's wrong? She asked silently.

Your mom's wrist...

He saw Aylie's eyes flash to the exposed skin on Mrs. Bryant's wrist as she pulled the tray away. He heard her sharp intake of breath and noticed the way she stiffened against his side. He felt her heart pounding and her hand shook a little as she attempted to lift her hot mug to her lips. He could feel the tension growing in her body.

You don't exactly seem surprised, he observed, glancing sideways at her.

A sudden knock at the front door startled Aylie, causing her to spill her hot chocolate on the carpet. She stared at the brown discoloration at her feet with a look of mild terror on her face. Mrs. Bryant was already armed with paper towels, kneeling down to blot the warm liquid from the carpet as Mr. Bryant moved to answer the door.

Ryder turned to Aylie. Okay, you have to tell me what's going on here. He thought sternly, forcing her to look up at him. Before she could reply, he was startled by the familiar sound of his uncle's voice

"I thought I might find you here," said Alexander Payne, as his tall, dark figure filled the doorway.

CHAPTER TWENTY-FIVE

Ryder reluctantly said goodbye to Aylie and followed his uncle out to the car parked in the driveway. He whistled, taking in the sleek, black finish of the limited-edition Audi.

"Nice ride," he remarked. "Where'd you rent this from?"

"It's not a rental," Alexander said, tossing Ryder the keys. "I bought it."

"You bought an Audi to visit for the holidays?"

"Consider it a Christmas gift," his uncle replied with a smile. "Try it out."

Ryder slid into the driver's seat. He put the key into the ignition and cranked it to life, listening to the purr of the engine in awe. He backed carefully out of the long driveway, checking to make sure he didn't hit anything on the way out.

"Oh, come on, Ryder—you can do better than that," his uncle

teased.

Ryder hit the gas hard, pushing the pedal to the floor as they flew to the Mansion in record time. Ryder zipped into the carriage house, putting the car into park. He climbed out, walking around the exterior of the car to admire it once more.

"Where are Roman and Colin?" He asked, realizing belatedly that his cousins hadn't been with them in the car.

"They're already inside," Alexander replied, retrieving a piece of luggage from the back seat. "We arrived a few hours ago. Your butler was kind enough to let us in and the housekeeper told me where I might find you. Your girlfriend seems like quite the catch," he winked suggestively.

Ryder grinned. "I wish you would've gotten a chance to talk to her a little more," he said, "she's been a lifesaver."

"So it would seem," Alexander said, carrying two large suitcases to the front door. He set them down to ring the doorbell and waited for the butler to answer the door. "It's lucky she reached out to me when she did, or you would've been spending the holidays in the slammer." His smile was thoughtful. "It was good thinking on her part, tracing my address to locate my phone number."

Ryder nodded. "She thought of that on her own."

"I wonder how she was able to do it," he mused, as the butler opened the door, greeting him for the second time that day. "Both my phone number and address are unlisted—I'm a bit of a stickler when it comes to privacy, I'm afraid."

The butler interrupted their conversation, taking the suitcases from them as he ushered them both inside. The old man seemed genuinely glad to see Alexander again, though he'd been the one to greet him when he'd arrived with his boys just a few hours before. "Glad you were able to track this one down," the butler said, nodding toward Ryder.

Alexander clapped the old man on the shoulder. "Couldn't have been easier," he smiled. He paused in the Great Hall, looking around at the massive interior and up at the high, domed skylight. "This place is still as beautiful as I remember it," he murmured aloud.

Ryder stood beside him, looking up through the skylight. His heart felt less empty with his uncle beside him. Even though Alexander and his father had fallen out and had not parted on good terms, Ryder still remembered the summers he'd spent with his uncle and cousins fondly.

"Well, if it isn't the infamous Ryder Payne," said his oldest cousin Roman, entering the Great Hall with a grin on his absurdly handsome face. They had very similar facial features, but Roman's hair was blond, and his eyes were an interesting shade of hazel-green. "You're practically a celebrity right now in the serial killer world."

Ryder grinned, reaching out to shake his cousin's hand firmly. "It's been too long."

Roman clasped his hand for a second longer. "I was sorry to hear about your father," he said, with a look of genuine sympathy. "I always looked up to him."

Ryder swallowed the lump in the back of his throat. "Thank you."

Colin sauntered in, wearing an absurdly bright purple, button-down shirt beneath a black silk vest with gray tweed loafers. "What's up, cuz," he greeted, with a handshake they'd used in their youth. "We came to crash the party, but it looks like we're going to have to bring the party to you." His raven black hair was slicked back, making him look older than he really was.

"Always the exuberant one, Colin," Ryder laughed, shaking his head. "It's good to see you."

The four of them talked over dinner, trying to catch up on everything they had missed in each other's lives over the past four years. Uncle Alexander's business had tripled, making him one of the wealthiest men in England, in edition to inheriting the title of Lord Payne after his father's death. He had managed to buy certain outlying properties that had added to his wealth and prominence on the European Continent. His sons had also been encouraged to invest and had unashamedly taken up illegal, off-book gambling to accrue their own small fortunes.

Ryder listened to the stories of their accumulated wealth and their claims to self-importance, all of which were a stark contrast to the quiet, unpretentious life of solitude his own father had chosen for his wife and sons. It made him miss his own family terribly, but at least he had blood relatives still living. Having them here in the mansion was still a comfort, even if it wasn't what he was used to.

After dinner, Alexander suggested they retire to the billiard room, pulling out an expensive box of cigars he'd purchased on one of his trips to South America. He passed one to each of his boys and then offered one to Ryder, lighting a match for them. Ryder was taken aback at first. His father had always smoked a pipe but had never allowed him to try it. He felt a little uncomfortable accepting the cigar from his uncle, not really knowing how to smoke it. Afraid that Alexander would think he was juvenile for rejecting it, he took the cigar hesitantly, doing his best to blend in.

"So, tell us about your girl." Colin said, crossing his legs as he leaned back against one of the gold-trimmed, upholstered couches in the long billiard room located on the second floor of the Mansion.

Ryder nearly choked as he inhaled a lung-full of cigar smoke before releasing it in one large puff. He coughed, trying to play it off casually. "What do you want to know about her?"

"Tell us about her family," Roman suggested, taking a seat next to Colin.

"Yes, we're all curious about the girl who rescued you from prison," uncle Alexander said with a smirk, seating himself in a wing-backed chair across from him.

"What's her name?" Colin asked with genuine interest.

"Aylie Bryant."

"Bryant," Alexander murmured. "That's an interesting surname."

Something in his uncle's tone made Ryder feel uneasy but he ignored it, determined to enjoy this visit as much as possible.

"How long have you two known each other?" Colin asked,

puffing his cigar like an old man, though he was the youngest one in the room.

"Only about three months," Ryder replied, inhaling another puff of his own cigar.

"Three months? That seems a bit fast," Roman said, tapping the end of his cigar on the ashtray sitting on the end table beside him. "Do you attend classes together?"

"We both attend Silvervane Preparatory Academy."

Alexander nodded. "At least my brother managed to make one good decision on your behalf—that school is one of the best in the world."

Ryder tried not to take offense at his uncle's insinuation. "I can pretty much choose any university in the country after graduation."

"And where exactly do you intend to go from here?" His uncle asked.

Ryder shook his head. "I'm not sure, that's something I wanted to talk to you about."

"You'll have to leave the girl behind, of course," Roman said, taking one last puff of his cigar before discarding it.

Ryder didn't respond.

"If you plan to come live with us in England, he means," Colin clarified. "Roman's not much of a romantic, I'm afraid."

"Staying with us would be the most logical choice," Alexander said, with a fatherly smile. "We would love to have you—on your vacations from University, at least."

Ryder smiled. "Thank you. That's exactly what I was hoping for."

Alexander finished his cigar and walked over to a silver tray with three glass decanters. He poured himself a glass of bourbon and returned to his seat. He took a sip, staring into the bottom of the glass afterwards, reflectively. "Of course, that would require you to accept certain family duties and responsibilities."

Ryder nodded, "I'm happy to assume any responsibilities you want to give me, uncle."

Alexander studied him carefully. "Did your father ever

mention anything to you about your inheritance?"

Ryder quirked an eyebrow. "If you're referring to this Estate, the paperwork has already been taken care of. My father's attorney has assured me there won't be any complications."

"Oh, of course. But I'm referring to a rather different kind of inheritance."

Colin shifted uncomfortably in his seat, glancing over at Roman who was leaning forward in anticipation. Ryder tried to ignore the growing sensation of uneasiness in the pit of his stomach, reaching out for the ashtray on the coffee table in front of him to discard the remains of his wretched cigar. "I'm not sure I know what you mean," he replied hesitantly.

Alexander smiled, taking another sip from his bourbon glass before explaining. "Being a Payne comes with certain obligations and social responsibilities. One of those obligations is to carry on the family line—to keep our traditions, our practices, and above all, to ensure that our bloodline remains unpolluted."

Ryder felt his jaw tighten. "What exactly do you mean by 'unpolluted?' "

"We are part of the Royal Family, Ryder. If you were to return to Europe, you would be required to accept the title that is yours by birth—you are a lord, and it is your duty to preserve the royal bloodline." He paused for a moment. "I'm sure my brother must have shared stories with you over the years about our family 'history.' He was obsessed with a heresy regarding our bloodline until his dying day, I daresay."

Ryder felt his blood begin to boil. He clenched the arms of his chair until his knuckles were white. He forced himself to keep a calm exterior. He didn't want to get into an argument with his uncle and cousins on Christmas Day.

"I don't mean to alarm you—I know how much you loved your father. But I must tell you that he was very mislead in his later years. He had a book that he claimed was a record of our family history, saying that it contained true accounts of an ancient king who was rumored to be murdered by one of our ancestors. He also ranted about an immortal prince who is roaming about on the earth somewhere, just waiting to save the world." He shook his head in dramatic sympathy.

Ryder sucked in a deep breath, trying to remain calm and open-minded, in spite of his uncle's harsh accusations.

"It was nothing more than your great-grandfather's personal journal, but your father read that book religiously after your mother was murdered—a tragedy that shocked us all. I believe he was looking for an answer to his suffering. He believed that someone in our family was to blame for your mother's death. It was a baseless accusation—nothing short of scandalous. We argued about it several times. I was concerned for his welfare and for the wellbeing of you and your brothers. I begged him to turn to the law for help in finding your mother's killer instead of fairytales, but he became consumed by the stories in that journal. He was deceived, Ryder. He renounced our family and our traditions. Eventually, we parted ways because of it." He looked at Ryder with tear-filled eyes, his voice wavering with strong emotion. "He was deeply disturbed, Ryder. I know it's hard to hear right now, but I don't want you to make the same mistakes and live to regret it."

Ryder cleared his throat, preparing to defend his father's honor and the manuscript he had cherished till his dying breath. Until today he would have taken his uncle's side without argument, but he'd seen the distinguished trail of liquid silver in Mrs. Bryant's wrist...he knew for a fact that Silver Veins existed. If that part of the legend was true, everything else in the journal could be true, too.

"Think about it, Ryder," his uncle continued. "Your father renounced our family and our heritage because he believed in some ancient, immortal prince who was meant to 'free mankind.' In all those years of searching and studying that journal, did he ever find any evidence that this prince really exists? Any proof of the legendary immortal kingdom? Did you ever encounter the crazed sorcerers your father claimed were trying to destroy the world?" Uncle Alexander's eyes filled with compassion. "Have you ever seen another of our kind here in Silvervane? And yet your father accused us of murdering your precious family."

Ryder cleared his throat, feeling confused by the raw emotion and sincerity of his uncle's argument. He genuinely believed the manuscript to be nothing but a hoax and a delusion that had led his poor, delusional brother to an early grave. It was such a rational argument that Ryder couldn't completely banish the feeling that his uncle could be right. What if everything written in that journal was a delusion? What if Silver Veins had murdered his family and not the Order? What if his father had it backwards?

"So...you're part of Edryd's Order?" Ryder asked, his head spinning with the implications.

"It's not what you think," Colin interjected. "My father is right. The Order would never murder one of their own, let alone the family of the next high priest."

"High priest?"

"Seriously, Ryder—what did your father tell you?" Roman sneered, shaking his blond head. "Of course, the Order will have a high priest, how else can they be unified?"

Ryder shook his head, trying to banish the confusion swirling around him. His mind felt fuzzy, as hazy as the cloud of cigar smoke filling his lungs. He dropped his head in his hands. He didn't know whether to believe his sympathetic uncle or remain true to his dead father. Their beliefs were diametrically opposed to each other...they couldn't both be right. He felt a hand on his shoulder and looked up wearily.

Alexander gazed down at him anxiously. "Are you okay, Ryder?" He asked with concern in his large, gray eyes. "I didn't mean to overwhelm you."

"I'm fine," Ryder mumbled. "I just need a good night's sleep in my own bed."

"Of course. We'll talk more in the morning."

Ryder nodded and stood to his feet, bidding them all goodnight as he slowly climbed the staircases to his bedroom on the third floor of the west wing. He couldn't stop his mind from racing from one thing to the next. If the journal was a hoax and Edryd wasn't the murderer and villain it made him out to be, then perhaps it wasn't the Order he should be fearing. Perhaps his family was murdered by Silver Veins who had managed to hide in plain sight, unthreatened because of his father's mislead loyalties.

He remembered Mrs. Bryant's wrist. He had never seen the mark of a Silver Vein in real life before today. That part of the legends was true, it would seem. But did that really mean Silver Veins were the innocent ones, while Edryd's Order was corrupt? Could it be the other way around? If it was, did the Bryant's have any connection with the people who had murdered his family? He was pretty sure they were innocent, but what about their friends? Their people? Their bloodline?

Chapter Twenty- Six

Aylie slept fitfully, tossing and turning as dream after dream flitted through her sleeping subconscious. Ruah stood beside her in a vast, desolate field. Storm clouds rolled across the angry sky overhead. Flashes of lightening and torrents of thunder shook the ground beneath their feet. The setting sun was an alarming shade of red as it disappeared behind a thick haze of black smoke.

Are you ready? The lion asked her solemnly, his electric blue eyes piercing her from the inside out.

The question struck her with invisible force, drowning out the sound of the thunder. She couldn't speak to reply. She looked over her shoulder, knowing that Ryder was waiting for her answer. He wore a somber black hooded cloak and his arm was outstretched toward her, beckoning for her to join him. Blood dripped from the palms of his hands, his eyes darker than coal. She stood transfixed, looking from Ruah to Ryder and back again.

How could she choose between them?

A sudden thudding noise awoke Aylie from her nightmare, sending her heart into wild palpitations. She gasped, trying to catch her breath, as she opened her eyes and searched the room for the source of the sound. A shadowy figure emerged from the far-left corner. "What are you doing here?" She whispered, forcing herself up into a sitting position.

Ryder glided over to her bed without a sound, sitting down on the mattress beside her. "I had to see you." He took one of her small hands in one of his larger ones.

"You're transporting now?" She asked, a little confused.

He nodded, a sly grin spreading across his face.

"Where have you been?" She frowned slightly. "I haven't heard from you in almost a week. I was getting worried." She looked down at his palm, tracing it with her fingertips.

He touched the side of her face with his free hand. "I'm sorry. My uncle's been keeping me busy," he replied, offering an apologetic smile. "It's been so long...we've had a lot to discuss."

She leaned into his hand, relishing the feel of his fingertips on her cheek. "Is everything okay?"

He smiled. "It's better than okay. It's been great having him and my cousins here."

Aylie felt a little disappointed. She had missed him every day, but it seemed like he hadn't missed her at all. Perhaps he no longer needed her now that he had family around. She stared down at their hands, feeling a little sorry for herself.

This doesn't change how I feel about you one bit, he answered her unspoken thoughts. He leaned forward, kissing her tenderly.

The fear and uncertainty she'd been wrestling with was dissolving as she lost herself in this passionate embrace. Ruah's words haunted her, echoing over and over in the back of her mind, but she ignored them. Ryder's kiss was long and hard and she felt completely intoxicated. Slowly, he opened his eyes and looked down at her, pulling back to look at her face. With what appeared to be great effort, he leaned away slightly, forcing himself to slow down. He gazed at her longingly like he wanted to consume her and Aylie's breath hitched in her throat.

"There's something I want to talk to you about," he whispered, tracing the outline of her lips with his index finger.

Aylie listened, closing her eyes to savor the sensation of his finger as it traced along the skin of her bottom lip.

"My uncle explained to me why he and my father parted ways four years ago," he began.

Aylie nodded silently, opening her eyes to study his face as he spoke. She was instantly overcome by the depth of his dark eyes and the gorgeous contours of his lips, cheekbones, and chin. The overwhelming attraction she felt for him was unlike anything she had ever experienced before, and she was finding it hard to keep herself in check. It took great effort to focus on what he was saying, but she sensed that it was important and fought her unruly emotions.

"Alexander thinks my father might have suffered from some kind of mental disturbance." He said somberly.

Aylie's forehead creased. "Really?"

Ryder nodded. "He says the manuscript was nothing more than a journal my great-grandfather kept and not an accurate description of my family history at all."

Aylie touched his lips with her fingertips. "Do you believe him?"

"I didn't want to believe it at first, but the more I think about it, the more I can see how it could have happened," he said, looking troubled. "My dad was destroyed when my mom was murdered. He would've believed anything at that point."

"But I thought those legends had been passed down for generations before your grandfather got ahold of them?"

"That's what my dad believed," Ryder said sadly. "But I think my uncle might be right about his mental state."

Aylie stared into his troubled eyes, sensing every emotion he was feeling. She wanted to cry and lose herself in kissing him all at the same time. She touched the side of face gently. "How do you feel about that?"

He tried to shrug it off. "I feel a little foolish for starting to believe the things in that journal," he murmured, running his fingers slowly down the side of her neck. "It changes things."

Aylie shivered, feeling on fire everywhere he touched her. "Like what?" She asked, fighting the temptation to pull him in for another long kiss.

He looked like he was struggling with himself, trying to decide whether or not to answer her question.

"Tell me," she coaxed, running her hand down his strong, muscular chest. She felt him tense under her touch and knew his body wanted to respond.

"My uncle and cousins have been explaining my heritage to me—the truth about my bloodline."

Aylie traced the lines of his abs through his white t-shirt, hearing him only a little through the haze of her own, raging emotions.

"They belong to Edryd's Order."

Aylie's fingertips froze on his chest. "What?"

"They're loyal to The Order."

Aylie's body tensed. She dropped her hand from his chest, pushing herself up to her elbows. She was nose to nose with him now, her eyes wide and fixated on his face. "What are you saying?"

Ryder cleared his throat. "I might have been wrong about Edryd...about who he was and what he did. That whole journal might have been a total fabrication."

"Why would someone want you to believe such awful, slanderous things about your own family?"

"Maybe they wanted us to be afraid so that we'd cut ourselves off from the rest of the family," he hedged, worrying his bottom lip. "We've been pretty easy targets out here all alone in this gloomy mansion without the protection of family and friends."

"But Ryder...."

"Think about it, Aylie. My uncle and cousins are still alive and well. No one has ever tried to murder them or harm them in any way. What if that manuscript was an elaborate web of lies to get my family out here alone, to isolate us so that the real enemy could get to us more easily?"

"If Edryd's not the real enemy, then who is?"

Ryder's expression turned dark. "If Edryd is actually the innocent one, Rhydian's descendants are the real enemies—the Silver Veins." He paused to let the revelation sink in.

Aylie swallowed. "Are you sure you should believe what your uncle says? He's accusing your dad of being mentally unstable...."

"I've been thinking about this all week," Ryder said solemnly, pulling himself up into a sitting position. "It's really hard to accept, I know, but it's the most logical conclusion. Nothing made sense before—all the stories about an immortal prince who could restore humanity...there's no proof the prince even exists! No one has ever even seen him."

Aylie swallowed hard. She sat up slowly, pulling the covers up around her arms. The room suddenly felt extremely cold. She couldn't believe what she was hearing. Her brain couldn't comprehend the words that were coming out of Ryder's mouth. Did he really believe what he was saying? Could he be so easily swayed by an uncle he hardly knew?

"I can guess what you're worried about," Ryder murmured, resting his hand on one of hers. "But I promise your family is safe. I know they didn't have anything to do with my father's death."

"What?" Aylie stared at him in confusion, her stomach doing frightened little flips.

"Your mom's wrist, Aylie—we both saw it. I know she's a Silver Vein."

Aylie felt her blood go cold. "What are you saying, Ryder? That we're your enemies now? Are you going to become one of them?"

Ryder looked her in the eyes. "Aylie, I already am one of them. I was born into this—it's my destiny."

Her eyes widened in horror. "No, it's not." She shook her head.

"It's going to be okay, Aylie. It's not what we thought it was at all. It's political more than anything—nothing to do with druids or sorcerers or anything like that."

She couldn't speak or form a coherent thought. She was in total shock and didn't know how to process any of this. Ruah had been right. Ryder was going to join the Order. He was going to become their next high priest and there was nothing she could do to stop him. Telling him what she knew would expose her family and the rest of the Silver Veins—which included Ren and Derek, among many others.

"Have you already joined them?" She asked, trying to keep the tears from her eyes.

Ryder shook his head. "Not officially. I told my uncle I had to talk to you first."

Aylie swallowed. "When?"

"Tomorrow night."

Aylie felt her eyes sting and she looked away, staring out the window beside her bed. She had never felt so helpless. Her heart ached for the boy sitting beside her...for his future...for his soul. She wanted to save him, but she didn't know how. Ruah hadn't told her what to do next.

"Come with me," Ryder murmured, breaking in on her thoughts.

"What?" Aylie jerked her head in his direction.

"Come with me. Join me."

"Become part of the Order?" Ruah's words rang in her ears.

"Why not? What do you have to lose?"

"You said it yourself—my mom is a Silver Vein, which means my dad probably is, too. Which means I'm meant to be a Silver Vein."

Ryder gently grasped her right hand, turning her wrist over to expose the veins. "See? There's only blue blood running through these veins—no silver." He lowered his lips to her wrist, lightly brushing them over the delicate skin covering her veins. "That means you haven't declared your allegiance yet."

"Joining you would make me an enemy to everyone else I care about," she said, shaking her head at the unbearable thought.

Ryder looked at her sadly. "If you become a Silver Vein you'll be my enemy."

A solitary tear trickled down her cheek. "So I have to choose between you and my family." It wasn't a question. She already knew the choice that lay before her. She had known since the day she'd been tricked into attending Rhydian's council meeting, but she'd been hoping to find a way to change her destiny before the time came.

I want you in my life, Aylie. He leaned forward to kiss her on the forehead. I don't want to do this without you.

Another tear slid down her cheek. I don't want to live without you, either.

Chapter Twenty-Seven

Aylie awoke early the next morning, feeling as if she hadn't slept at all. She'd lain awake all night thinking after Ryder had left. No matter what decision she made, everything was going to change after tonight. She dressed hurriedly and forced herself to choke down a bowl of cereal for breakfast. She rinsed the dish under warm water and set it in the sink.

Her mom entered the kitchen and squeezed her shoulders warmly. "Are you ready for today?" Mrs. Bryant asked.

Aylie raised an eyebrow. "What do you mean?"

"This is the first day of your very last semester of high school." Her mom said with a smile, pride shining in her clear blue eyes. "Soon you'll be moving away to college." Her eyes misted as she turned away to make a breakfast smoothie for Sam.

Aylie's heart skipped a beat. For a moment she'd feared that somehow her mom had figured out what she was about to do.

Her parents hadn't brought up the council meeting she'd crashed a week ago or the implications of her relationship with Ryder, and she wasn't about to fill them in on it now. Ren hadn't badgered her about it either and Lacey was totally in the dark about all of it, which was a small relief. She didn't want her parents or anyone else to try and change her mind.

She followed her dad and Sam out to the truck and climbed into the passenger seat, holding her book bag on her lap. She smoothed the folds of her pleated, uniform skirt beneath it and crossed her knee-high covered ankles. Sam hoisted himself into the backseat, his backpack carelessly strewn over one shoulder. His shoelaces were untied as usual, which made Aylie smile. Her dad walked around to the driver's side and slid into his seat, revving the engine to life.

Aylie stared out the window in silence as they drove. They stopped at Silvervane Elementary first to drop Sam off. He scrambled out of the truck and headed for the gymnasium, but he paused to look over his shoulder at her with a buoyant wave before skipping off to check in with his friends. She waved back, smiling sadly. Her dad attempted to make small talk as he drove her to Silvervane Prep, and she did her best to answer his questions without getting annoyed like she so often did. She smiled at him, squeezing his hand as she got out of the truck. Even though she wasn't leaving home, she knew everything was going to be different now. She had no idea what to expect when she and Ryder were initiated into Edryd's Order, but she was sure it involved oaths of some kind. Ryder had assured her that her family would be safe, but somehow knowing that things were about to change made every moment seem a little more precious.

She took a deep breath and pushed her way through the halls of Silvervane Prep, trying to get to her locker before the bell rang. She greeted Lacey and Marcus hesitantly, but her best friend smiled at her brightly, apparently having decided to forgive her for dating Ryder behind her back. She started gushing about how great Marcus's New Year's Eve party had been the moment they reached their lockers. Aylie smiled, feeling detached from the conversation but giving it her best effort. Ren sidled up next to her, shooting her an apologetic glance. Aylie nodded, trying to avoid a conversation with her at all costs—Ren would never understand what she was about to do.

At lunch everyone seemed excited to be back for their final semester at Silvervane Prep. Even the hockey players appeared to be more optimistic about their academic future. Many of them had already received scholarships to play for top universities and they were soaking in the glory of their last days as gods of the High School scene.

Aylie couldn't seem to connect with their energy, so she kept to herself, only speaking when she was asked a direct question. She noticed Kyle and Addison staring at her from across the table, but she didn't care enough to ask them why. Undoubtedly Kyle was still sore about having to pick Ryder up from the county jail, and now everyone knew she was dating him. Chance sat down beside her, smiling kindly to offer his emotional support, which she appreciated. Ryder hadn't shown up for homeroom this morning, and she wasn't sure if he'd be here at all. She knew how important this day was for him and school probably wasn't his top priority.

Suddenly the lively chatter in the dining hall died down, as everyone turned to stare at the door. Gasps and muted whispers broke out all over the room. Aylie was slow to realize what was going on and finally glanced to see what everyone was gaping at. Her mouth nearly fell open at the sight of Ryder and the two equally attractive boys who were flanking him, one on the right and one on the left. He locked eyes with her from across the room and sauntered toward her, the unfamiliar boys following his lead.

"Do you mind if we join you?" He asked, gazing only at her.

Lacey shot her a mildly frightened glance, but Ren smiled welcomingly. To Aylie's surprise, it was Kyle Kavanagh who moved over to make room from Ryder and his cousins to sit down across from her. He acted almost nervous, glancing sideways at Ryder with a look somewhere between fear and awe. Addison batted her eyelashes at him, as the three boys sat down together.

Some of the other hockey players looked confused, but no one objected to their presence.

Ryder nudged Aylie's foot under the table, smiling roguishly to set her at ease. It worked. She flashed a smile back at him, taking another bite of her chicken salad.

"These are my cousins—Roman and Blake," he said, introducing them to the table as if they'd all been friends for years. Everyone responded politely, welcoming him and his cousins without reservation. In fact, it was as if nothing could be more normal.

"My cousins will be finishing out the semester here at Silvervane Prep," Ryder explained.

Lacey stole a sideways glance at Aylie but said nothing. It was clear that she felt uncomfortable around them, but Marcus seemed to be okay with it, talking to Ryder's cousins for the rest of the lunch break. Kyle and Addison were practically groupies, enamored by every word that came out of their mouths.

Aylie watched the way they all interacted with Ryder in mild bewilderment, wondering what could have caused such a change of heart among the very students who had spread such awful rumors about him only a matter of weeks ago. It was like he had gone from zero to hero in an instant. She didn't quite know what to make of it.

When lunch was over, Ryder and his cousins walked her to her next class.

"We're so happy to finally meet you," Colin said, his gray eyes resting on her face. "We've heard so much about you."

"You'll be joining us tonight I hear," Roman said with a wicked sideways glance. "Good choice."

Aylie swallowed imperceptibly. Ryder squeezed her hand, rubbing his shoulder against hers as they walked slowly through the halls.

You're going to be fine, he assured her.

She took a deep breath and kissed him on the cheek, parting ways with them as she went into the French room.

Ren was waiting for her at her desk, "That was interesting," she mused, watching Ryder and his cousins as they disappeared down the hall.

"Yeah. I had no idea they were going to be coming here."

"They kind of gave me a weird vibe," Ren murmured quietly.

Aylie looked down at her French notebook. "Yeah."

Chapter Twenty-Eight

"You're doing the right thing," uncle Alexander said, smiling at Ryder approvingly as he drew the long, black cloak up around his nephew's shoulders. He allowed the hood to rest at his back until the ceremony started. "And might I add how glad I am to hear that your girlfriend will be joining us as well—it would have been a pity for her to reject us."

Uncle Alexander's twisted smile was unsettling. Ryder cringed inwardly, hoping that he hadn't unknowingly endangered Aylie by asking her to join Edryd's Order with him. If his uncle was hiding the true nature of what they were about to become a part of, both her and her family could be in a very perilous position. He could only hope that his newfound faith in his uncle wasn't misplaced and that everything was going to work out for both of them.

Ryder followed his uncle through the tunnels to the Order's

official underground headquarters. He ignored the uneasy sensations in the pit of his stomach and focused on the tunnel walls, which were covered in spray painted graffiti of Order symbols, sacred phrases, and ceremonial words known only by its elite members. He was impatient to reach his destination and make sure that Aylie had been escorted there safely. He had wanted to be the one to bring her through the tunnels her first time, but his uncle had forbidden it and had sent Colin instead. Ryder had been forced to relent, agreeing that it would be better for Colin to fetch her than for Roman to do it.

Ryder pictured Aylie in his mind. They had probably blindfolded her just like they'd blindfolded him when he'd come the first time. It was apparently their practice with anyone who was not officially part of the Order and it helped them maintain secrecy and discretion in the midst of outsiders. Their method made sense, but it seemed a little uncivil to him. He was sure Aylie would be scared and anxious, but his hands had been tied in the matter and he felt powerless to do anything about it.

When they finally arrived, Ryder scanned the room for Aylie frantically.

"Relax cousin," Roman said, sidling up next to him. "She's right over there." He pointed to a row of chairs in front of the low, wooden platform in the center of the room. A solitary cloaked figure was seated with her hood drawn over her head. He walked over to her quickly, sitting down beside her. He took her hands in his. They were as cold as ice. He reached for the hood of her cloak, pushing it back so that he could see her face. Her blond hair shimmered in a long braid down her back, but her eyes looked hallow and her lips were almost blue.

"Aylie," he said, staring into her eyes. "What's wrong?"

She lifted her gaze slowly from the floor to his face. The fear in her eyes was so pronounced that it sent a shiver down his spine. "Ryder," she said, her voice barely above a whisper. "Are you sure you want to do this?"

He felt the erratic beating of her heart, the fear flowing through her veins. He sensed the weight of her anxiety and his determination faltered. "I don't think we can back out now," he murmured, swallowing the lump in the back of his throat.

"Truer words were never spoken," his uncle said, approaching them humorlessly. "The ceremony is about to begin."

Alexander Payne took the platform, waiting for the crowd of hooded figures to find their places in the giant circle around the perimeter of the room. Ryder helped Aylie to her feet, leading her up to the edge of the platform. There was a wooden table in the middle of it, with a clay basin and a ceremonial knife wrapped in an ornate strip of cloth sitting on top of it. They stepped onto the platform and Alexander instructed both of them to kneel down in front of the basin. He unwrapped the ceremonial knife, holding it above his head as he began to chant. The circle of cloaked figures joined in, repeating the chant over and over, getting louder each time.

Finally, Alexander lowered the knife and the chant ceased. Everyone watched as he drew the tip of the sharp blade across the meat of his own palm. Then he reached for Ryder's hand, slashing his nephew's palm as he'd done to his own. Blood dripped freely from the gashes in their palms, flowing into the silver basin as they grasped each other's forearms in a ceremonial blood oath.

Next, it was Aylie's turn. Ryder was instructed to use the ceremonial knife to cut both of Aylie's palms, the flesh above her heart, and the skin at her throat. Since she was an outsider being brought into the Order, her blood was considered impure and would need to be cleansed in order for her to join their ranks. Ryder had known nothing about this part of the ceremony before he'd arrived and his face blanched as he realized what he was being asked to do. He saw the absolute loathing in Roman's eyes and the sneer of satisfaction on his uncle's face.

With a sickening wave of certainty, Ryder understood his uncle's intentions now. If he refused to carry out Aylie's rite of passage his uncle would, and he would probably bleed her to death on purpose. If Ryder agreed to do it, however, there was still a possibility that she would bleed out if he didn't cut her in exactly the right places and stop the bleeding in time. A sudden hatred for his uncle coursed through Ryder's body, but there was nothing he could do about it now. He could only guess at the depraved nature of his uncle's power and he didn't want to put Aylie in more danger than she was already in.

He understood now why her face had been so pale...why her blood had frozen in her veins. Colin must have warned her about what was coming, and she'd been trapped before Ryder had even known what was happening. She'd been willing to stay for his sake, and he loved her for it. He stared at his uncle, repulsed at the wicked gleam in the man's sardonic eyes.

"Well?" His uncle asked, his lips curing into a wicked grin. "Are you prepared to do what is necessary?"

Ryder took a deep breath and forced all emotion from his face. He knelt down in front of Aylie's rigid body. She was still on her knees and the fear on her face was evident. He stared into her scared eyes. Without blinking, he took the knife from his uncle's hand...the one still dripping with his own blood and grasped it firmly.

Are you ready? He asked silently.

She nodded, closing her eyes and tilting her head back slightly to expose her neck to him.

I'm so sorry, he thought, as he drew the blade of the knife across the skin of her pale, white throat.

Keep Reading for a preview of

CHOSEN

The Silvervane Chronicles

Book II

CHOSEN

- A Silvervane Chronicle -

Book II

Rachel Berlynn

CHAPTER ONE

Aylie knelt on the platform in front of Ryder's uncle, trying to keep her lips from quivering. Colin had told her what was going to happen to her during her rite of passage and it was more horrifying than anything she could have imagined. What made it worse, was the fact that Ryder would be forced to perform the cleansing ritual himself. If he refused, his uncle would do it for him, and it was very clear from the cold, hard look in Alexander's eyes that death would be preferable.

She looked around the room at the cloaked Order members as they stood in a large circle around her, chanting their pagan ritual rites. She recognized Judge Kavanagh first, flanked by both of her children—Sophia and Kyle. Her eyes caught his and he looked away, dropping his gaze to the ground guiltily. His behavior at the lunch table earlier was starting to make a little more sense now. His girlfriend Addison was standing to his left, avoiding eye contact with her at all costs. As she continued to scan the room, Aylie noticed Police Chief Blair and even Coach Cole. Ryder's housekeeper and Butler stood in the back of the room, as if guarding the door against intruders. If she hadn't been in such a precarious position she might have laughed at the irony of it all. The least likely of Silvervane's citizens all coming together to bind themselves in allegiance to Edryd's Order.

Her heart stopped when she recognized the person closest to the platform on the far left. She hadn't noticed him at first because she'd been too busy taking everything in when she'd first arrived. Her eyes settled on him now in horrified disbelief. He returned her gaze, unflinching in his betrayal. Lucas Bryant stood only a few feet from her, dressed in the same black cloak as the other members of the Order. He showed no remorse as he watched her preparing to face her potential demise. Her eyes stung with tears that could not be shed, as Ryder took the knife from his uncle and knelt down on the ground in front of her.

Are you ready? He asked soundlessly.

He was asking her the same question Ruah had repeated over and over in her dreams. The irony wasn't lost on her, even in this perilous moment. Aylie closed her eyes, hoping that the lion was somehow with her now as she put her life in Ryder's shaking hands.

I'm so sorry, he said to her wordlessly, just before he drew the cold, silver blade across her throat. She survived the first cut, as he skillfully sliced the skin at her throat just enough to draw blood but not enough to bleed her to death. The trail left by the blade was stinging as he slowly pulled her cloak away from her shoulder, exposing her collarbone and the top of her left breast. He sliced a star-shaped pattern over her heart, just as his uncle had forced him to. This cut was much more intricate and hurt far worse than the first. It was all she could do not to scream out in pain. She wanted to run from the room, but she didn't know what Ryder's uncle would do. With grim determination, she remained where she was, kneeling motionlessly on the wooden platform as small streams of blood dripped down the front of her cloak.

She studied Ryder's face to keep her mind off of the searing pain, as he took her hands in his to perform the last part of the ritual. His expression was completely blank, as if he had no remorse for the pain he was inflicting on her. Only his emotional connection to her betrayed his true feelings and the anguish hiding just beneath the surface. He hated himself for what he was doing and he wanted to kill his uncle for lying to him and putting her life in danger. He wanted to comfort her, but he had to finish this or things would get much worse.

He'd saved her palms for last, and she wasn't worried about them since she'd survived the other two, riskier incisions. She gritted her teeth as the agonizing pain from the other two cuts threatened to make her faint. Blood was dripping down her neck and her chest as Ryder drew the knife across her palms, one at a time. When he'd finished, he clasped both of her hands in his, looking into her eyes reassuringly. Alexander draped the ornamental cloth over their joined hands, chanting something that sounded like Latin.

Aylie didn't know the exact words they were saying, but she knew the ritual was meant to join her and Ryder together in a bond that could only be broken by death. Collin had explained the purpose of the ritual to her before the ceremony, but she'd forgotten most of what he'd said until now. The blood-bond made them responsible for each other and accountable for one another's actions. If she defected, she would bring a curse on Ryder, even if he chose to remain loyal to the Order and vice versa. It was basically their version of a marriage covenant with a much stricter pre-nuptial contract signed in their own blood.

Alexander removed the strip of cloth and forced them both to stand, resting their joined hands over the silver basin so that the blood from their palms might mingle and fill the bottom of it. She'd lost so much blood already that she began to feel lightheaded and her vision blurred. Ryder tried to help her from the platform. With a stab of pain, she fainted in his arms before her feet even touched the ground.

Made in the USA
Columbia, SC
09 September 2020

18663851R00140